Emron, the Unknown Hero

Ejaz Khan

ISBN:978-91-86173-02-9
From series Fantasy/Adventure/Fairytale

:

Dedicated to the youth of the world.

HERO OF THE PAST

Human history is full of heroes.
Some did lesser deeds and became local heroes, while others achieved marvellous, impossible goals, accomplishing such great tasks that they are still remembered and revered, even after so many aeons have passed. But we should always remember that not all of these great beings are remembered and recognised for what they accomplished during their lifetimes. It is not impossible that some of names, places of birth and even their great achievements have long-since faded from our memories. Everyone knows and remembers the labours of Hercules, and we place him amongst some of the greatest of the heroes of mankind. But very few people know about another hero called Emron, who existed long before Hercules, and who did equally greater things, if not greater than Hercules!
Many of Emron's labours have been lost in the dusts of time. Our hero didn't belong to the hierarchy of gods, but had a humble origin. With great difficulty we have been successful to trace few of these trials.
This is his story.

1

A long time ago, there lived a child in a distant country. His parents gave him the name Emron, which in the local language meant "the lucky one." Emron's father was a wealthy trader who travelled to faraway countries with his servants, slaves and other traders. Sometimes his trips were shorter, but it often took years before he could come back to his family.

Emron was an only child who was equally spoiled by a beautiful mother and loving father. Emron was only ten when he heard the news that his father's caravan was approaching the town. Like many other children, he was filled with happiness and rushed to meet his father outside the town. All children screamed with joy as they saw their fathers and relatives returning from a long journey. There were scenes of kissing, embracing, and even tears of happiness. Emron keenly looked around searching for his father. Suddenly, he got sight of his uncle. His face was lit up as he rushed to meet him. Emron embraced his uncle and inquired about his father. He got no answer, but could feel the patting hand of his uncle, which was shaking. Emron looked up to see the face of his uncle. He wanted to know about his strange silence. His uncle's eyes were betraying tears, he opened his mouth to say something, but couldn't utter anything; instead he just kissed Emron's cheeks and gave him a long hug.

His uncle didn't say a word and Emron dared not ask any questions, but his fearful eyes and alarmed face kept reflecting his fears. He hoped and wished that his uncle would ultimately come with some explanation as to why his father wasn't with them. But all his hopes were dashed when his uncle accompanied him to his parent's large house. There he broke the terrible news that his father was no more in the world.

His mother gave a long heart-piercing shriek and fainted of grief, but Emron stood emotionless. His uncle tried to comfort him, but he was far away from any pain or grief. He refused to believe that his father, of all the members of the caravan, had died after being sick for only a few days. His father was young and strong, how could he possibly die in that manner?

Uncle is lying, he thought. For what reason he couldn't say.

He jealously counted and watched the camels of his father, the merchandise they were carrying, and how much they were sold for. He kept secretly watching each step of his uncle, but to his great disappointment, nothing unusual could be seen in his behaviour. His uncle had sold all of the goods and honestly given the money to his mother. Emron went asking the other people who had accompanied his father in his last journey and listened to their account of the tragic story. They all felt sorry for him, but confirmed the story of his uncle.

Once confirmed that his father was dead, and all gone, his heart got filled with anger, instead of grief. "No, I will not cry," he shouted. "You never loved me, otherwise how could you leave me?" he vainly shouted at his deceased father.

Emron stopped talking to the relatives and other people who came for condolences and to offer him their sympathies. His mother tried to tell him that his behaviour was not only impolite but also insulting. They all were well wishers and wanted to share their grief, but Emron was not convinced to ease his attitude.

"I won't be disrespectful, as long as they leave me alone," he offered as a compromise. Everyone stopped saying anything about his late father. He could only see the pity in their eyes, and he hated them for it.

*   *   *

One year later, his mother married another man. Enron disliked his stepfather, if for no other reason than simply because this man was not his father.

"I'm not asking you to love your stepfather, but you should give him a chance," Emron was asked by his mother, but he felt incapable to do so. He loved his mother and did not want to do anything to hurt her, and so he started spending most of his time outside the home.

His stepfather was a high official and a clever but greedy man. Most probably he had married his mother not only for her beauty, but also for her money. He didn't care if Emron spent most of his time outside, roaming about with other kids.

"Maybe you should send him to live with his uncle and his family," his stepfather suggested one day. His mother became terribly upset and cried. She absolutely didn't want him to live anywhere else. The stepfather retreated by saying that he had only had good intentions for the boy but that he feared that Emron had no future, especially if he learned no trade. "He should learn other skills if he's not interested to learn mine."

"Surely he'll follow the footsteps of his father and forefathers and become a trader!" he was told by his wife. These words reminded him of the fact that all the money and property he was dreaming of belonged to Emron. He wasn't very happy with the idea and started worrying about the future. He thought and thought if there was any way he could deprive Emron of his legacy, but there was no way. Emron was to become a man at the age of fourteen, and he would have a right to demand full control of his late father's wealth.

His stepfather burned day and night by the worry of losing the wealth at hand. He tried to plan to embezzle it, but dared not, so he tried to convince his wife to invest the money in trade.

She plainly rejected the idea for two reasons. First, she was not the owner, just the trustee, and could not make any such decision on her own. Second, if she was to invest, who could be better people to take care of the business than the family of her late husband? The stepfather couldn't counter these arguments but never gave up his planning and hoping for the right time and opportunity. This golden opportunity came and he gladly grabbed it with both hands.

What really had happened no one could tell, except that Emron and a few of his friends were out on a picnic one day. All of them were extremely young, careless, and inexperienced; they had brought toxic drinks along and drank without any restraint or supervision. Some of them got drunk, others simply passed out. The whole incident would have been easily forgotten had there not been a tragic incident involved.

Mysteriously, one of the young boys was missing. Everywhere the search was made but without any result. A few days earlier, the missing young boy was seen having a fight with Emron. This happening was mentioned only as a reference rather than an accusation, so there were no whispers or gossip as Emron's stepfather had hoped. Time went by and the missing boy didn't come back, which gave the stepfather an idea; he started going around convincing people that his stepson was innocent and had nothing to do with the young boy's disappearance.

He was working secretly to make the things worse. The more he tried to defend Emron, the more people became suspicious. Now there were rumours, and it didn't take long until everybody started believing that Emron was the one to blame for the disappearance. Soon, there was a story in circulation describing the full details of the event. It was thought that Emron had killed the boy and hidden the body somewhere. The family of the boy started getting more and more aggressive and many times they threatened to take revenge if the boy didn't very soon return safely.

*   *   *

The stepfather was handling the whole affair in a skilfull and cunning manner. On one hand he showed his concern for Emron's safety and vowed to protect him from all troubles in any circumstances, but at the same time stressing at his difficult position. He was an important official with power and influence, but in this peculiar circumstance, he was unable to exercise much of that influence in the favour of his stepson. Emron's mother was worried but refused to believe that her son had anything to do with the young boy's disappearance.

"If anyone tries to harm my son, the whole family shall fight like a tiger!" she said as she waved away the threats. "I feel for the family of the boy and wish his safe return, but they should look for the boy instead of blaming others." Then, things went from bad to worse.

*   *   *

Emron was informed by his stepfather that soldiers were ordered to arrest him. The best piece of advice that Emron could get was to run away before he was arrested, jailed, and ultimately to be executed by some heartless executioner. Emron was hardly 13 and didn't want to die that young. He was terrified and decided to flee from his home.

"That's the most sensible thing you can do," he was told by his stepfather.

Emron left home and decided to be away as long as the mystery of the missing boy was not solved. He joined a caravan that was heading west to Egypt. They would have never agreed to let him join had they known his real age. But since he had grown fast and looked strong and mature, they believed him when he told his age few years older.

"Why do you want to go to Egypt"? The leader of the caravan asked him.

"I don't know exactly but I've heard it's a better place to live," Emron replied. The leader didn't agree with him, but didn't enter into a discussion about the subject.

"Maybe you've heard rightly, or maybe someone has

fooled you. But you can judge for yourself once we're there" said the bearded middle age man politely. Emron told him that he was out of money. The leader just smiled. "You're our guest and don't have to worry about money" he was told.

The caravan moved with a slow pace covering only a small distance each day. At dusk they would halt, eat and rest. Two or three of them guarded the camp for a few hours, then awaking the others to do their duty, before they would go to sleep.

They kept moving forward without a hurry. They had a long way to go, and it was the responsibility of the leader to take them to their destination with as much comfort and safety as possible. It seemed that time was the least factor in their calculations, even though they all wanted to reach to their destination without any unnecessary delay. Their daily journey was long and tiresome, lasting from dawn to dusk. They sometimes made some other occasional stops, for different reasons. Emron had now been with the caravan for many weeks. They were all traders, who were carrying their merchandise to Egypt and hoped to sell their goods with good margins, intending to buy the Egyptian goods and crafts with a good bargain to carry back home. He could easily understand their logic, since it was his family business, and was well aware of the mechanism. Most of these merchants were young, handsome, and kind. At nightly stays they would eat with good appetites and stay awake for a long time, talking and laughing. They were polite, fearless, and well-disciplined young people. Emron became very impressed by them and wished that he himself could be like them.

He watched the way they talked, the way they moved, and the way they handled the tasks given to them and swore that he himself would turn into a man of dignity. Before their caravan moved into a barren place, the leader made a sign for a halt. A few young men rode on the backs of their horses and went to check if all was well and safe. After a few hours they returned, signalling that there were no apparent dangers lurking there. The food and water provisions were carefully checked. After going through all the precautions, the leader signalled to move again.

Emron saw a complete transformation in the attitudes of these young merchants. They grew more serious and less talkative. Instead, they looked around vigilantly and drew their swords at the least sound or movement in the bush. He could see that despite the fact that they were young; nevertheless, they were responsible and trustworthy companions. Even at the campfires the mood was more tense and jumpy. They were always guarded and alert, day and night. "You should never be off guard, while travelling, especially not in the wilderness," said the middle-aged leader one day.

But the precautions and preparations came to no avail. It was sometime before dawn when Emron was awakened by a loud noise. There were shouts, screams and loud swearing. He got up on his feet in panic and wanted to run away from there, but could not move. It was still dark but he could see the fearful eyes of some of his companions. They were fighting fiercely. It didn't take long for him to understand that they had been ambushed.

The attackers seemed to be many and had the advantage of surprise. So the young men of the caravan were caught in a hopeless situation. They knew that they didn't stand a chance, but that didn't prevent them from dying like brave people! Emron was, despite his appearance, just a child, and as such he became scared to death. He had neither a weapon, nor did he know the skill to use it, so he made a quick decision. In the confusion of battle, he crawled and hid himself in a bush. His heart beat faster and he wept silently, seeing all these young, brave men falling one after another, fighting courageously, and dying with dignity.

If he had been impressed with them before, he became even more so now, seeing them having their last dignified stand. But there he lay in the bush with a horrified and terror-stricken heart, unable to give any assistance to his companions in their desperate struggle for life. He knew that he was not a coward, but was untrained and thereby without any chance to withstand those brutes. One by one, all his companions of the caravan fell and died, leaving the attackers with the victory. He saw how this band of young men waved their bloody swords in the air and made triumphant cries.

Emron could not watch the scene without feeling the compulsive need to shout, scream, and cry at the top of his lungs. But he knew well that by doing so he would disclose himself and consequently die like the others. He didn't want to die. So he closed his eyes, put his hand on his mouth, and cried without making a sound.

The robbers went around, checking if there were some who were still alive. They found no one. They picked up three of their dead companions and carried their bodies on horses, along with other goods and animals belonging to the members of the caravan. One could notice that they cared not for the deaths of their own comrades, as they went, talking loudly, laughing, and singing. Their three dead friends were taken along, as if they too were part of their booty.

Long after the robbers were gone, Emron finally dared to come out of his hiding place. He looked at the slain men, and was aggrieved. He sat nearby and kept looking and remembering those remarkable people, who till some time ago were alive, with ambitions and dreams. Maybe some of them even had wives and children. It brought the hidden pain and suppressed feelings regarding his deceased father. The horrible scene and thoughts about his father gave him so much grief that his heart was filled with great anguish. The crushing turbulence of his anxiety was so great that he thought that he was dying.

He didn't die; instead, he cried and cried bitterly. His whole body shook, tears kept streaming forth, and he rushed to and fro, without knowing what to do about his grief. He had difficulty breathing; it felt like there was not enough air to fill his lungs. Every now and then, he desperately tried to gasp and got more and more panicked by the conviction that he was about to die.

After being in that condition for a while, he calmed down a little. He was still weeping, but he was no longer hysterical. He resolved in his heart to become a strong, brave man, who would live with honour and die with dignity like those young men who lay dead in front of his very eyes, drenched in their own blood. He had promised himself that if provided with the opportunity, he would learn to use weaponry with great skill.

*   *   *

The robbers had taken everything, so Emron was without food, water and any sense of direction. He had two choices: he could follow the direction in which the caravan was moving, and thus come to some village, or he could turn to the side where the robbers had gone. He chose the latter choice, as it looked more promising to bring him back to some human habitations, so he followed the tracks of them.

He kept walking all day until he saw a camp at a distance. It was dark now, so he could move without the risk of getting discovered by the band. He hid himself a little away from the camp and waited for them to sleep. He was relieved to notice that they were either too sure of themselves and saw no need of any precautions or were simply disorganised. After eating their dinner, they all went to sleep. Emron could hear their snoring and knew it was now all clear to move. Carefully, without making any sound he went near to the camels and took a bottle of water and stealthily came back. He was very hungry, but decided to wait in patience for the right moment, if there was to be any. "Better to die of hunger than to die by the sword," he thought. He woke up before dawn, and was astonished to notice that the robbers had slept nearby. They woke up after the sun had risen. There were some shoutings and swearing; they seemed to be in no hurry. They took their time with their breakfast before they moved ahead.

There were fifteen of them that he could count, all riding on strong, swift horses. He could not see the bodies of their

9

dead companions. They must have buried them or gotten rid of them in some other way. Emron kept hiding and waited until they disappeared from his sight. He went to the place where the robbers had their camp and looked for something to eat. He found bones with half eaten meat, and filled his belly. The knowledge that the robbers were forced to move with the speed of the caravan made Emron relax. He could eat without hurrying; the robbers would not disappear from his sight.

For two more days he followed the robbers, always keeping at a safe distance and avoiding any suspicion. He spent the night in perfect hiding places, and came out only to search for food, when they had long gone. After two nights and three days, Emron felt dead tired, but he was forced to follow them if he was to survive. He had used the water very carefully, just sipping the bottle from time to time to quench the thirst, but now the water was running out and he needed a new supply. To approach the band, however, would require a great risk, which he was reluctant to take.

When he was completely out of water, he decided to take the chance after all, as it was impossible to fight his thirst any longer. Even then he didn't abandon his carefulness, and waited to act after they had gone deep in sleep. It was now night but robbers didn't stop to rest. Their march continued, leaving Emron thirsty and astonished. In the dark it was difficult to watch from a distance so he was forced to move closer.

He was so close that he could hear their voices. They were talking loud and swore from time to time. It seemed they had no intention of making a camp for the night. Emron was more worried about water and food for the next day than tiredness or sleep. All of a sudden the voices of these men grew louder and more excited. The next moment they were shouting with joy and few of them were even singing in harsh, un-harmonic tones. Those loud voices were responded by faint voices from afar. Emron could easily understand that these people had come home. That explained everything, why instead of resting, they had kept pushing forward.

*   *   *

The band of robbers received the welcome of victors. Men, women, and children had oil lamps in their hands and greeted these men. They sang songs for them, laughing, smiling, and touching the animals that they had brought with them. They all moved in a procession, with a few elderly walking in front, followed by the robbers and the animals carrying the merchandise, and all the rest coming behind, singing, clapping, shouting and laughing. They walked a few hundred feet, entering their village. Emron waited a long time, wondering whether or not it was wise to follow them. His intuition warned him but he was too thirsty and hungry to refrain. At one place the procession came to halt. It was a broad market-space, with only a few buildings. They tied the animals in the open and went into a building.

The welcome party was to go on all night, where they drank, sang and danced to the music. Emron could easily go and fetch a bottle of water and something to eat and come out of that place without being detected, as no one was there to watch. The people of that village were unaware of the fact that somebody had entered into their territory and was stealing their food and water. Emron decided to spend the night at some distance from these beings.

He must have been extremely tired, because when he woke up it was midday. He panicked by the fear of being caught by these people, but relaxed by thinking that the robbers and the other people must have been tired and sleepy by exhaustion after last night's celebrations. He looked around to assess what type of place this was.

The small village looked simple and unattractive. The scattered mud houses showed a rather depressing view. With a deep sigh he glanced at the village, which stood aloof in the middle of barren landscape. For miles and miles there was nothing but thorny bushes springing forth here and there. He stood there trying to assess the situation and understand the surroundings, but felt more confused than before.

*   *   *

His head was full of worries. He felt pressed to find some quick solutions to his dilemma as to what to do next. Time was short and he had to decide if he was to stay in that desolate place or to head further looking for some other village in the area. A lot of questions were bothering him, making him nervous and at a loss.

He quickly realised that trying to find some other nearby village wasn't a good idea. Not only was it without any certainty that there even existed any such village and even if there were such places around, that didn't mean that they were inhabited by better people than the ones he was so close to. What was he supposed to do next? He couldn't live undetected for long, since there were no hiding places. He could go back a few miles into the wasteland, but how was he to survive there? The more he thought about his situation the more nervous he became. He was in a big trouble, far bigger than he had anticipated before.

"So my decision to follow these robbers' was wrong," he sadly confessed, but it wasn't the time for regrets. He had to act quickly, and find a way to come out of this hopeless situation. The only solution he could think of was to outwit them, but how was he to achieve that goal? He didn't know.

"I have to find a safe hiding place," he thought, realising the emergency he faced.

He went around the village and came to the other side, which was the opposite of the side they had come from last night. The village was quite far from where he had found a place to hide. He took the food, drank the water that he had with him and rested. He could not afford to show himself to the villagers, who were not friendly - as he had witnessed a few days earlier. He continued thinking of all the possible ways to come out of his odd and desperate situation.

The next day he had made up his mind. Without any water and food, he was running out of options. So the only way left for him was to make an entry into the village. It seemed a crazy idea, because those people were to be suspicious if he couldn't answer them satisfactorily. He knew nothing about his surroundings, so he decided to make his entry from the side of the village that he and the robbers had come from, and later on he was happy that he did so.

He looked dirty; he was starving and suffering from dehydration. He collapsed in the middle of the village. No one rushed to his aid as he had anticipated. The villagers were watching him with surprise and a sort of disbelief. No stranger had set his foot in their village before, let alone a youth. They could see that wilderness had taken its toll, and that he was not in the best condition. They came to his side but kept staring at him, as if indecisive.

"Would you go on staring till the devil passes away?" cried one elderly woman in anger, pushing aside the spectators. She looked deeply at Emron, as if to decide whether she liked the sight of him or not. She asked a few of the young boys to carry him inside one of the houses. She tended him by giving him water to drink. He was allowed to rest after he got food and drink.

Nobody disturbed him all evening and he slept comfortably. His sleep was not sound like it used to be. He kept waking up several times haunted by fear, anxiety, and worries. He didn't know what was to happen to him; the only thing he could be sure of was that if he were to die, then it would be with a full belly.

The next day, many of the villagers gathered to listen to his story. They were all curious, amazed, and astonished. How could the youth survive the wilderness without food and water? And most importantly, how had he ended up in their village? Emron looked around and gave a very tired smile. His face became pale and his heart sank when he recognized a few of the robbers. He almost fainted again.

"It seems the boy is not strong enough yet to answer

your questions," said the same woman who had brought him home. "Let him rest for few more hours."

Emron couldn't say if it was a request, an order, or just a proposition. Without arguing they left, giving him a little more time to prepare his story. When they came back, Emron gave them the story that they were so interested to hear.

He told the people that he was a bad person and did a lot of wrong things and was now on the run. He had decided to go far away in order not to fall into the hands of his adversaries or the law. He had hoped for another chance, which he believed was impossible to get in his hometown. He had entered the wilderness without any realisation how difficult and dangerous it was.

"How long have you been in the wilderness?" one of his listeners asked coldly. Emron told them that he couldn't say for sure, but that he could have been there between ten to fifteen days.

"How did you survive without water?" he was asked. He had some water and food with him, he answered, which he used carefully. But from the last two days he was completely without, and would have surely died, had he not found their village.

They kept asking questions, but didn't look very convinced. They didn't hide the fact that they were not fond of strangers. "How old are you?" one young woman asked.

"I'm thirteen," Emron replied.

"Look, he is just a kid!" another woman exclaimed.

Emron could see that his young age was softening at least the women a bit.

"You said that you're a bad person, how bad are you?" one of the young robbers asked.

"I'm bad, very bad," Emron started. "I lie, I disobey my mother, I steal..." a big round of laughter was heard. They all were laughing non-stop.

"Leave the boy alone," said the elderly woman, getting serious. "Don't you know he can turn bad?" They laughed again, remembering that Emron had told that he was a bad boy, while in truth he just talked of innocent things and the elderly lady was making fun of that.

Emron could feel that he was out of danger. These people would not kill him because he had convinced them that he was just a foolish child, one from whom they had no threat. They asked him about his plans, where he intended to move on, and how he was to proceed. He told them that he was without money, without a family and without any particular destination.

"Didn't you say you have a mother?" someone asked.

"Yes," Emron confessed. "But she lives in a far away country and most probably doesn't want me."

The villagers had hoped that he would stay for a few days, get some help, and move on, but now they had a problem.

Most of the male members were less sympathetic towards him, while the women believed that the boy needed a place to live, and that they absolutely should give him a shelter.

After a heated discussion, they decided to allow him to stay in their village, but that this stay was to be temporary and conditional. They were to meet and decide about the fate of Emron exactly one year later, and the condition was that someone was to take responsibility for him.

Suddenly, everyone became silent as if no one was ready for the task.

"Yes," said one old man. "If no one is ready to be responsible, then we push him back to the desert after three days."

"Why?" protested one young robber. "Isn't it better and more merciful to kill him?" This serious suggestion made Emron shiver. He didn't sound very sarcastic.

"I take responsibility for him," said one of the robbers. "But I want to make it clear that it has nothing to do with pity. I believe that he's a big, strong boy and could be a good investment."

"What do you think, mother?" he asked the woman who

had brought him inside the house.

"I don't know!" She answered quite seriously and kept quiet before adding, "What else can I say; the little devil is so bad." They all joined her in the laughter. They continued their meeting, talking with each other, and discussing lesser things, completely forgetting the presence of Emron.

*   *   *

Zariba was a very dominating woman, having fixed ideas about everything. No one could ignore her opinion or challenge her decisions. She had a sharp, cutting tongue which at times was more threatening than wounds inflicted by a double-edged sword. But at the same time, she was the most good-hearted person in the whole village. She was always helpful, caring, and ever ready to sacrifice for others. People respected and feared her at the same time. Zariba had been the mother of ten children; a few had died at birth, and a few others had died of starvation when they were very young. Only four of her sons had grown into manhood. These young men perished as well, one after another except only one, as a sacrifice to their profession, robbery. So he, the only remaining son was Aseem, the young robber who was Emron's guarantor.

*   *   *

Aseem was a quiet, serious, and not a very social person. He spent most of his time roaming around with his bow and arrows. He would come home with birds and animals that he had hunted, which his mother would cook for them. There were periods when younger members of the band went hunting food, while at other times they would disappear for weeks, only to come back loaded down. In the beginning, they all ignored Emron, just barely tolerating him.

He was daily reminded by their stating that he did not belong with them. In his heart, he hated to be with them as well, but needed some time before he could go his own way. He had noticed that these people were extremely good at handling their weapons, and if there was any place in the world that he could learn to use the weapons like the sword and bow, it was here in this village.

After trying to make friends, Emron finally gave up the idea as no one was interested in him. Instead of chasing the other young boys in hopes of their friendship, he started ignoring everybody, as if they didn't exist either. Zariba would push him outside, but he would shortly return back.

"Why don't you go out and make friends?" she would wonder. Emron never told her that he felt unwelcome and unwanted, an outsider. Sometimes she would flare up, "What am I to do with this stubborn donkey!"

One day, Zariba was cooking food. She wasn't in the best mood. Both Aseem and Emron were home. When Emron kept sitting instead of going out and play with the other children as he was told by Zariba thrice, she became furious, started swearing, and ran after him with a burning piece of wood in her hand. Emron was unafraid and unmoved. She was about to start beating him when Aseem intervened.

"Leave the boy alone," he said in anger, holding Zariba's hand in his powerful grip. "Don't you see that he's lonely? Nobody wants him."

Zariba became soft by hearing that he was an outcast. She didn't shout at him after that day, and a big change came in Aseem's attitude: He became friendlier. He started taking him out on the hunt and taught him the art of archery and how to hunt, explaining that hunting was something that required not only knowledge but even a great deal of patience.

One had to be aware of the patterns of different animals, their habits, and their peculiar movements. "You should think like the prey." Whether Aseem was a good teacher or Emron was talented pupil, no one could tell, but one thing was sure. Within a few months, Emron could be counted as one of the best archers in the village. His arrows could shoot down any flying bird or fleeing animal.

He learned the use of sword and other weapons with such ease that everyone was astounded. He was a natural talent. He was strong, quick, intelligent, and had great potential. No one was more proud than Aseem, because it was he who had first seen Emron's hidden potential and recognised an asset in him. Everyone taught him all that they could, but the boy had the thirst for more. After having consultations with others, Aseem decided to send Emron to one of his cousins who lived in a nearby town and was an expert on all types of weaponry.

*   *   *

Emron was away for only a year, but when he came back, he looked taller, healthier, and stronger. Aseem arranged competitions to determine the skills that Emron had developed during that time. He became extremely pleased by Emron's marvellous performance. He had polished his ways, movements and skills. No one could stand before him more than a few minutes in the use of any weapon. He held a heavy sword in his hands as if it was weightless. Aseem had been the best archer they had ever known, but was now forced to leave the crown to Emron, and that he did with a broad smile and a kiss on Emron's cheeks. "Today I have two sons!" said Zariba loudly and proudly.

Emron had come to the village full of hatred for the robbers who had ambushed and mercilessly killed all of his companions. He had come there because he knew no other place to go. He had used his cunning to become part of them, to get a roof, to get care, food, and most of all to learn the use of weapons. But the more time that he spent with these people, the less hateful he became. They were not cruel and heartless people as he had earlier assumed.   Yet they were robbers and outlaws, living outside the vicinity of law and order; their ancestral profession provided them a living. They killed people after they had ambushed the caravans. But wasn't that the natural consequence of an armed struggle, to kill or to be killed? They believed robbery was the wrong term for what they did.

In their opinion, it was unfair to call them robbers, because they did not rob but fought for their right to the resources. Wasn't the all-human struggle about acquiring resources by any possible means? Some used cunning to get them, whilst they used force, the thing they were best at. The people of the village were neither better nor worse than the other people he had met. Emron did not agree with their logic, but knew he could not reform them and decided that it was time for him to move on.

Zariba and Aseem were taken aback when Emron declared his intention to leave the village. "Why?" Zariba asked. "Are you not happy with us?" "Don't we provide you with all your needs?" she went on.

"Mother!" Aseem said angrily. "Give him a chance."

Emron went forward and embraced her. "Of course you have been so extremely kind, you have given me love and care more than my own mother could have ever given me. But it's time for me to move on." After speaking to her, he turned to Aseem and spoke. "There were times I did not like you. I thought you were a cruel and heartless person, but now I know you better. You have been a friend, a brother I never had, and most of all you have been my teacher. You're the best teacher I could ever dream of. All I know now is thanks to you. I'll always remember you and shall pray for your soul. Don't misunderstand me, but I have to go."

"Why do you have to go?" Aseem asked. "You could become our useful hand in the forthcoming battles, you could be our most trusted and skilled asset."

"Yes I could, but I wouldn't simply because what you do is wrong," Emron pointed politely, and could see the colour of anger flashing on Aseem's face. He kept silent and just looked deep in Emron's eyes with sarcasm, wondering what had happened to the bad, bad boy.

*　*　*

Zariba was worried for him. How was he to survive the harsh world with those strange thoughts? Without knowledge of any trade or art he could not provide living for himself or his future family. He was being offered an opportunity to join her son's band, which he so ungratefully had rejected. He tried to convince her that she needed not to worry, because he was single with no responsibilities, with no family to worry about, and most of all he didn't have much material needs. Aseem did not speak afterwards and pretended not to care that Emron was to leave.

Saying goodbye to Zariba and Aseem turned out to be a more difficult task than he had thought. She turned her face when he asked her leave.

"I promise to come and visit you sometimes," Emron said.

"Don't you think I'll be here forever!" she said as if she didn't believe that they would ever meet again.

"Take care, Aseem, and try not to be mad at me," he said, but got no response. He looked towards him and saw him lying on the bed, covering his face with his strong arms. He did not see, but could swear that the tough Aseem was shedding tears. He felt like going there and hugging him, but knew that it would just embarrass Aseem, which he did not want to do.

Zariba gave him his favourite horse and told him that it was a gift. The horse belonged to Aseem, but occasionally Emron was allowed to ride the strong beast. He was surprised but accepted the gift with thanks.

While riding away from there, he felt very sad and sentimental. Without looking back, he waved his hand, feeling that Zariba was still standing there, watching him leave for good. But he knew she was a strong woman who could bear his exit. If she had survived the loss of nine children, then she could survive a loss of him too. He had not felt as sad when he had left his own mother, family and hometown. In just four years' time, he had woven so many bonds with these people who had been strangers to him.

He moved from place to place, not knowing where to go and what to do. He stopped and watched people working, trying to put himself in their shoes to see if it could be an appropriate work for him. Soon, he realised that there wasn't any profession which attracted his heart. The realisation came as surprise but he shrugged off all worries with a smile on the face. Surely there was a suitable profession for him as well, he thought.

2

One day, he saw some soldiers riding on their horses; their clean dark red uniforms looked good on them. They looked happy and content; invoking respect and awe from the people that they passed by. It seemed an easy and attractive job for him. He approached the ruler of that town and told him that he sought work. He was asked his trade.

"Nothing," he answered. The ruler looked at his large, strong body and inquired if he had been a soldier.

"No," he answered.

"Then, I don't have work for you," said the ruler who watched Emron turn to go. "Stop!" the ruler commanded. He gave the youth a second thought. "I'll give you a chance," he told Emron, giving some instructions to his chief guard in a low voice.

The chief guard called for another guard and instructed him to take the young man to the recruiting officer. The guard asked Emron to follow him and took him to the soldiers' quarters, where he was left with a fat officer. The officer was busy eating, and looked annoyed when the guard interrupted his lunch. The tall guard whispered the instructions to the officer who told Emron that he was to wait.

*   *   *

It took some time before the arrogant officer was finished with his meal. A skinny young soldier came to inform him that Emron could now go in and talk to the officer.

"I'm told that you are the young recruit that his highness has so graciously admitted in his royal services. It's my duty to train you," said the officer who looked spitefully at him. "I'm further told that you are good for nothing. Don't worry, I'll make a good soldier out of you!" the officer said with a cruel smile on his face.

The officer gave him a long lecture on the importance of discipline, subordination, and proper training. How vital it was for a soldier to be physically fit, active, and alert. Emron could not suppress his smile hearing him speak of the things, which the man obviously ignored himself. The officer got angry at seeing Emron's smile, but translated it to the careless and casual attitude of the recruit. He was told that before he was to call himself a soldier, he had to go through a long, hard training.

Emron's training lasted for a month, in which he was given lessons on how to wear the uniform, how to walk tall, how to hold the sword, and what to do if he was to inspire the respect of the citizens. Emron did whatever he was told without questioning anything. Loyalty, loyalty, and loyalty towards the ruler were the key words that he was taught. How this loyalty was to be of any help to the ruler or to the poor soldier he was unable to see; he laughed at the foolish training methods.

*   *   *

At the end of the training he was given a clean, dark red uniform and a sword, and was declared a soldier of the royal army. He was not given a horse yet, since he was still very young and inexperienced soldier who needed few years practical service before he could be entrusted in the elite horse riding division. He didn't mind. He had the horse of his own, and he didn't mind if he was just a foot soldier as long as he got paid. Most of the soldiers were like him very young, inexperienced, and uneducated, but all were tall and strong. The fat officer hated to walk, and spent most of the day on the back of his horse, shouting, giving orders, and reminding them that they all were incompetents who needed a cut in their salaries. Only that fear could motivate them to work harder and more efficiently. Whenever the soldiers saw him they started rushing around to show that they were working hard.

*　　*　　*

One day, this officer came riding out on the back of the horse and halted before the young soldiers, who immediately flocked together to listen to his speech that they did every day. He reminded the soldiers of the things that were important, gave the instructions for the day, and was about to come, when his eyes caught sight of Emron's horse, which was grazing with other horses. He liked the horse and inquired about it. When he came to know that it belonged to Emron, the fat man came directly to him and looked angrily to him. How dared he takes his private horse to the royal property? That was a violation of the regulations, which were clearly told to them. The officer went on and came finally to the conclusion. It was a breach of regulations and agreements, so Emron was to be punished. The officer had decided to confiscate his horse.

"No, you would not dare," said Emron without losing his head. He had not known the rule, because no one had ever told him.

"What did you say!" the officer shouted in indignation. His round face was red with rage, and his right hand reached for his sword. Emron stood there unmoved, without showing any signs of fear. The officer repeated his decision, so Emron made it clear that he was not going to allow it. Seeing the determined look of the young soldier, the officer knew that he was in a difficult situation.

"You know that you're being insubordinate, and can lose your life for that!" the officer shouted. He wanted to threaten, to scare the soldier, so that he would retreat from his firm position.

"Maybe so, but you're not going to get my horse that easily,"said Emron in a calm voice.

The officer signalled to two of his mounted soldiers, who came forward to arrest the stubborn soldier. Emron didn't resist, going silently with them. They locked him up in a cell where he remained for the whole day without any food or water. In the evening, a soldier was sent to check if Emron had softened somewhat. But Emron told him that he would not change his mind.

The next day, he was brought to the ruler and charged with the serious crime of insubordination. The officer in question was there to explain the actual happening and plead him guilty. After listening to everything that his senior officer said, Emron was given a chance to defend himself. He said that the story was almost as the officer had narrated, with one important detail missing: he was not aware of the rules and regulations regarding the personal and private belongings. So he was not guilty of any breach.

"But still you are guilty of insubordination. You refused to obey an order," said the ruler.

"What orders? I was never given any orders. Just informed of some stupid decision, which of course I refused to accept," was Emron's straightforward answer. His blunt, fearless, and disrespectful behaviour was so abrupt and unexpected that everybody looked at him in amazement, and waited to see how severely he was to be punished for that.

The ruler looked angry. He raised his hand for silence and spoke, telling Emron that his insolent behaviour was not tolerable, and that if he were not young and foolish, sure he would have been sentenced to death. "But I show you mercy and send you to jail for three years." Emron smiled at this sentence, looked in the eyes of the ruler and said,
"I don't think so."

There were sounds of exclamations and murmuring concerns about his sanity.

The royal guards rushed to kill him, but the ruler stopped them. "What do you mean by that?" he asked in a rage. "Which of my words did you doubt?"

"I don't know if your ears are ready for the truth, or if your eyes can show you anything other than the dreams they are used to, but if you're interested, I can try."

The counsellors advised that there was no point in allowing a mad person to utter his confused thoughts. Either he was to be instantly executed or thrown into a cell, without any further permission to speak. But the ruler rejected their pleas with great irritation, and signed Emron to speak his mind.

Emron explained what he meant by the words he had used. The ruler's soldiers were untrained, ill equipped, and undisciplined, and subsequently were a greater danger than any enemy that the ruler faced. The soldiers were badly paid, inexperienced, and lacked morale. Without a competent army, he could not believe the ruler had three years to survive.

"Oh, really? We shall see what type of brave soldier you are," said the ruler sarcastically. "Tomorrow you shall be given a chance to die with dignity and honour."

*   *   *

In the royal grounds of his army headquarters were gathered the ruler and his functionaries, ministers, and other important people. Thousands of soldiers stood in rows, wearing their dark red uniforms. Even the general public was allowed to come and see a different type of execution.

In the middle of that crowd of spectators stood Emron, not knowing what was about to happen to him. His heart pounded faster, and he was sweating in that warm morning, but he was definitely not afraid.

One of the ruler's aides explained the background, which was the reason for the unique events of that day. It was the first time a prisoner was to be executed with a fair chance to defend himself. The public laughed, and so did the soldiers and the ruler. The commander-in-chief had decided to do the noble work himself, in order to show his loyalty to the ruler and to boost the morale of his soldiers. They all cheered. Emron was given a sword and he took it, weighed it in his hands, made some clumsy cuts in the air and waited, while everybody laughed.

The commander came to the ground, walking arrogantly with two officers walking beside him carrying his sword on a tray. The public cheered. The commander responded by waving his hand at them. When they came near to Emron, he signed the officers to halt. He picked up the sword and raised it high, displaying it triumphantly for everyone to see. He was not in a hurry. He came closer to Emron, looked deep into his eyes, and hissed with contempt, "Get ready to die, you fool."

"But sir, I've no intent to kill you," Emron said in a cool, calm voice.

The commander started attacking, but Emron moved so fast that he could not touch him.

Everyone watched with an intense interest and concentration. They observed the commander chasing the young man in a more and more determined manner. He was getting sweaty, tired, and almost desperate. This running around had taken his breath away. The more time that elapsed, the more impatient the public was growing. In the beginning, they watched the unfolding drama in disbelief and now they were amazed to look at the comic scenes.

The commander paused to catch his breath while Emron teased him, asking if he was too tired to continue the sport. In fury he rushed to attack on Emron, who quickly moved aside and stretched his foot forward. The commander fell on his face. There was a short silence, but then people laughed.

The commander was too tired to continue his chasing, but could not stop, because that would have humiliated him. Emron must have understood his situation. He stopped moving and asked in a good mood, Shall we fight now? If so, I must attack this time."

Emron jumped like a hawk and the commander stood there without his sword, which was laying a few yards away. Emron picked the sword and gave back to the bewildered commander. Three times Emron attacked and all three times the commander could not hold his sword firmly and dropped it. Everybody was hooting, laughing, and making fun of the commander. The words of praise were heard about the young, brave person who had humiliated the commander.

"Send a hundred of your soldiers. I'll prove to you that I'm right!" Emron shouted at the pavilion, where the ruler sat fearful and pale. If his commander could not stand before a young, inexperienced soldier, what could he expect from his army?

The ruler requested a private audience and asked Emron if he could take care of the training of his soldiers. Emron excused himself by asserting that he was too young and inexperienced to be entrusted with such a heavy responsibility.

However, he could recommend someone else who was more skilled experienced and suitable for the job. He gave the name and address of Aseem's cousin. "If you pay him well and he agrees to take the oath of loyalty, you would rule safe and long," he advised the ruler before leaving. Emron was paid well for his insight.

*   *   *

Emron had enough of serving as a soldier. He knew that serving kings and rulers was not an easy task and required the giving up of his personal liberties, which he was not yet ready to do. On the other hand, he didn't want to be a part of any rebellion that was growing in the area as a result of his disclosure of the state of affairs in the army. The place was too dangerous for him to live anymore. One beautiful morning he took his horse and rode away to a new destination.

3

He was riding one afternoon when he saw a few people at a distance, and rode towards them. When he came closer, he noticed that a fierce fight was going on. Quickly he realised that five young men were engaged fighting with one middle-aged man, who was drenched in his own blood.

The man fought bravely but was badly bleeding and had little chance of standing any longer. Emron shouted in a strong loud voice to distract the attackers. They looked at him casually, and turned back to the man, as if to finish their almost accomplished task of killing him. Emron decided to help their victim. He did not know who that man was and what the fighting was about. But he could tell with certainty that the lonely man had been taken by surprise.

He attacked one man with his sword and injured him, and then without losing any time he turned his horse back to attack again and hit the other man. The men stared at him in confusion and anger. They left the dying man alone and started fighting him instead.

Emron jumped down from his horse, came near and inflicted injuries on them. These injuries were deep, though not life threatening. Realising that they had no chance against their swift counterpart, they stopped the fight and fled. Emron could see anger and surprise in their eyes as they were disappearing from his sight.

Emron attended the middle-aged man, who was seriously injured. He quickly bandaged the man to stop the bleeding. The man was dying but still conscious; with great difficulty he pointed to one direction and tried to say something, but could not utter a sound.

Emron put him on his horse and rushed in the direction that he had pointed to. A few hundred yards away he saw a stone house and knocked on the door.

A woman opened it and asked what he wanted. When she saw the wounded man, she started screaming, calling different names in a hysterical manner. Soon there were four or five people gathered from within the house. There were young women and men who took hold of the man and carried him inside, leaving Emron outside. He waited a few minutes and then decided to go his way. He had just turned his horse when he heard the sound of running feet. Someone shouted for him to stop. A young man stood before him. "I'm sorry that you were left alone outside. Please, come inside. A girl standing near the door shall lead you."   Inside the house, he was asked to sit and wait. A young slave brought a drink for him and he asked the slave if the man was still alive. "Yes," he was told briefly, without any further details. After some time, he saw the young man who had invited him to the house, rushing along with another man. He was right to presume that he was a doctor. Emron was curious about the wounded man's condition and hoped for him to survive.

He was sitting there, thinking, when the lady of the house came in the room. She was a tall and elegant lady, with dark brown eyes. She excused herself for not attending him earlier and thanked him for bringing her husband back to her house. She had a lot of questions, and he told her the little he knew. She became even more thankful once she knew that Emron had tried to save her husband's life. She told him that they all had done whatever they could; now the doctor was there to provide the patient the best possible care and treatment.

"Let's hope for the best," said Emron, giving her his best wishes. "Yes we will, and hopefully the goddess shall be kind to him." She looked worried and tired. "If you wish, I can send someone to give you company," she offered before going out of the room.

"I think I should be moving on," Emron said and got up.

"Absolutely not," answered the lady. "How can we

deprive Hakim of meeting and thanking his saviour?"

Shortly afterwards, the same slave came and showed him to his room, which was a little bit away a from the main house. Most probably it was a guest house, consisting of three rooms, which were all linked with a veranda. He was to live there and be their guest for some time. "You can rest now if you please; after a few hours the dinner would be served," he was told by the slave.

The master of the house remained unconscious for four days, listlessly wavering between life and death. One moment they seemed to have lost him to the clutches of death, while the second moment he appeared to be fighting and struggling, succeeding in clinging to the beautiful, kind and merciful hand of life.
The doctor could not say which was to claim Hakim ultimately: life or death. Too tough to die that easily, but too weak to hold on to life for a long time was the doctor's final verdict, which of course was translated into a positive sign. That meant that his chances of surviving were increasing for every day that he lived, because the care and treatment were making him stronger by every hour.

The family's prayers were answered. On the fifth day, Hakim opened his eyes and gave the first strong sign of life. He wanted to speak but the doctor suggested him to speak less, and save energies for the healing process instead. "Don't be overjoyous yet," the old doctor warned the family. He gave important instructions to the lady of the house before he left. Hakim was to rest all the time with an attendant beside him, and nobody was to encourage him to speak. If this condition remained stable for the coming week, they would have a reason to celebrate. He left with a promise to come back the next day.

Hakim made a remarkable recovery. Within a few days he was able to get up from his bed and make small distance walks. These movements were painful, laborious, and energy consuming, but he did it with all the might he had, as his will to live was very strong. Despite the doctor's instructions to speak only a little, he asked about Emron and became happy to know that the young man was still there. He called him to his bedside and told him that it was thanks to him that he lived. He was grateful for his timely arrival and intervention that day. Emron told that he was happy to be able to assist someone in need. When asked who his attackers were, Hakim said that they were enemies who tried to kill him when they found him alone.

"They were five, while you were unassisted. I did not have much hope until you came along," Hakim confessed. "But when I saw you fighting, I liked what I saw," he continued smiling. He asked Emron who he was, where was he heading to, what he did for his living and many more questions. When Hakim came to know all the details about the young man, he offered him work and a place to live.

Emron made it clear that he didn't know a trade. Hakim told that if he didn't know any, he could learn one. He could work on a plantation where he was to tend to fruit trees.

*　　*　　*

He went to inspect the plantation and was impressed by its wonderful gardens. There were trees of all possible fruits spread for miles. He happily took the job, which he could join immediately. Hakim's eldest son Jabaar, who was in his early twenties, was to teach him the work. Jabaar was the young man who was sent to fetch the doctor.

Hakim had had many children, but only three were still alive: Jabaar, Nigma, and Saleh. Nigma was fifteen, while the youngest son Saleh was only eleven. Emron was offered to go on living in Hakim´s house in the guest quarters, but he preferred to live in a little cottage near the plantation. He was allowed to join the family at dinner every evening.

All day long he worked on the plantation with free people and slaves. Jabaar was a good tempered and soft speaking young man. He was seldom angry and almost never shouted at anyone. He explained to Emron each and everything in detail and showed patience for his slow progress. "You have to learn to treat these trees and their fruits with love, affection, and respect," Jabaar would try to teach him. But the words were too much for Emron, who could only laugh.

*   *   *

Emron could never be taught that the plants and trees were a form of life that needed love and care to nourish and give better and sweeter fruits. He was quick, careless, and too hard handed for the job. He wanted to quit his job, confessing that he was too brutal to be entrusted with such a tender and delicate work, but both Jabaar and Hakim insisted that he could do the job, if only he had the will to do it. To his own astonishment he started functioning better eventually.

For hours he would tend the branches and fruits of trees. He learned how to take care of the trees when they blossomed. When it was time to harvest them, he could pluck the fruits without hurting any of the branches of the trees. He could talk to the tree without considering it absurd. These trees and orchards had a great effect on his soul and body. He felt happier and in harmony with nature. He had learned that force was not to be used only in a hard manner, but could be applied in a soft, gentle manner as well. Working with nature had brought him closer to it. He studied with interest and care how everything was bound within life's circle. The cyclic growth and decay due to the seasonal changes forced him to sit and ponder upon life. He became more and more profoundly affected from his silent companions.

*   *   *

Though he spent only a few hours with Hakim and his family every day, he felt as a part of the family. They all would sit and have dinner, and go on talking about this or that subject. In the presence of Hakim it was not difficult to find the subject of discussion. He was a well travelled and well versed person, with many interests. They all enjoyed his tales, which were full of interesting characters and happenings.

Nigma was a very shy girl. Whenever Emron looked at her, she would give a big pleasant smile, before turning her gaze away. He liked her. She was a beautiful young girl. Saleh, her younger brother on the contrary was an energetic little devil. Never sitting still, he hated to keep quiet for long time, and most of all he enjoyed teasing the others. He was a stubborn boy who never gave up if an idea hit his head. After hearing that Emron was a good archer, he kept begging him to teach him as well. At last, Emron had to give up.

"It's okay with me if your father allows you," he said. That was no problem. He could handle his father easily, so he got the approval the very next day.

Emron started giving Saleh lessons, telling him the basic rules, how to measure the distance with his eyes, how to apply only needed force and other important details. He knew that Saleh was just a child, who lacked the necessary concentration and force to handle a bow. Jabaar was not a good student either. Emron tried to teach him the use of the sword, but his touch was too soft, too gentle. "Show your sword some respect, hold her like an iron man!" Emron would tease him and they both would laugh.

One day after dinner he was left alone with Hakim, who after talking about unimportant things came to a point. He said that he was getting old and Nigma had come of age and that he wanted to marry her away. He had noticed that she was fond of Emron, as she was not hiding her feelings from others. But that knowledge was not enough to conclude anything, so he wanted to know what Emron thought of her. Emron felt embarrassed at the direct and abrupt question and didn't know how to answer back.

He kept silent for a while, searching for the proper words. Then, without looking directly at Hakim, he started saying that he liked her as well and considered it an honour to become a part of his wonderful family. But unfortunately he was too young to commit himself to a family life.

"Maybe after a few years, if she is still unmarried, and your offer still stands," was his answer. Hakim didn't take his refusal very hard, and appreciated the youth's honest answer.

*   *   *

For a few days, Emron avoided looking at Nigma, who looked miserable. He felt sorry too, but simply wasn't ready for a marriage. He was already feeling the urge to move on. A few weeks later he informed Hakim of his decision to leave his job and move on.

"I hope it has nothing to do with our discussion the other day?" Hakim inquired. It was not so, he was told. The reasons were more of the inner nature. There was nothing anybody could do to stop him, so he was permitted to leave. Hakim gave him a purse of money telling him that that was his salary.

"What salary?" Emron felt embarrassed and refused to take the bag. "I've been living with you, enjoying your food, hospitality, and love. What more do I need?"

"We feel the same way; nevertheless, you have worked for two years with us, and therefore deserve this money," said Hakim, giving Emron a fatherly hug and reminded him about the agreement between them, according to which Hakim could pay whatever he felt reasonable at the end of Emron's employment.. He then stepped aside to the other members of his family, who also wanted to say goodbye to him and to extend their best wishes. All of the family and slaves were sad to see him leave, but the unhappiest seemed to be Nigma.

*   *   *

Emron kept moving from place to place. A few months here and a few months there, he moved constantly without feeling the need to settle. No place had enough attraction to hold him for a long time. He tried not to think of the past, for it hurt his heart. He avoided thinking of the future, because he was not a dreamer, and wanted to remain in the present. The force he had within was just enough to handle it. He confessed to himself that he was lonely, but couldn't change it, as he was aware of his difficulty in liking and making friends with strangers.

He noticed that he carried some strange contradictions within himself. He loved the bonds of a good family and yet kept breaking them, the moment he became aware of them. He enjoyed the calm and peaceful life, but was still attracted to the unpredictable, turbulent side of it. He loved his friends and companions, but always ended up lonely. What was driving him to this end? What was he looking for? What kept him moving from place to place? Soon he was to get the answer, or at least thought that he was.

*   *   *

Emron became astonished to meet a little old man with a long beard in the middle of a dessert. The old man, holding his wooden staff, was coming from the opposite direction. How long had the old man in that dessert, he asked. After a very long time, he got a short answer. What was he doing there in such a dangerous place, asked Emron again, a little worried for the man. "There are many wild beasts here, and there is a danger for outlaws."

"Isn't the whole world a very dangerous place to live in?" the old stranger said. Emron agreed and gave up his discussion. And what was he himself doing there, the old man asked?

"Just passing through," he told the old man, smiling. "But I'm well equipped and well armed."

"Oh, is that so? And what our young friend is running from?" the old man asked.

He didn't answer and just smiled. There wasn't any point talking to him, the best thing was to leave him alone and go his way. The old man sat on the dry barren ground and invited him, "I'm hungry. Do you want to join me?"

"What do you have?" Emron asked curiously. The old man showed him a few bones and some dry meat. He agreed to share a snack with the old man on the condition that he was to be Emron's guest at the dinner. The old man agreed. The bones were too dry and the meat too salty, but he pretended to enjoy it. Betraying otherwise would be unkind and rude.

After their meal they talked for a while, asking each other questions. The old man told Emron that he was a doctor, who came to desert from time to time looking for herbs and medicinal plants. He told Emron that he had consumed all the food he had taken with him, and now depended on him for further consumption of food and water. Emron laughed, reminding the old doctor that all he had offered was one dinner, and nothing else.

The old man shrugged his shoulders in disappointment. It was very hot, so they decided to rest in some shadow and take a nap. In the evening Emron went hunting on his horse.

"Isn't it better to go by foot?" the old man asked.

"It's not that I don't trust you with my horse, but it is better to be careful than to die out here!" Emron laughed. The old man just smiled.

Many hours passed, but Emron did not return. The old man had prepared a fire and was waiting impatiently. At dusk he saw Emron approaching and greeted him loudly. "Come, I'm starving" said the old man. But Emron looked little down.

He had not brought anything, no bird, and no animal. He was embarrassed. It was the first time he had failed to find prey.

"You must have some food with you?" the old man asked hopefully.

"No," he said and avoided the old man's disappointed eyes. He could offer his dinner guest water but no food and they would have to sleep hungry. He was thinking of compensating the old fellow the next day, by hunting him some large animal or some big fowl, but the whole next day, he searched and searched but found no prey.

A few times he got sight of animals or birds, but before he could aim at any of them they were gone. He felt despair at coming back empty handed. But this time the old man did not protest, on the contrary he tried to comfort him. "Better luck next time," he said patting Emron's back.

They remained hungry all day and felt their stomach crying for food. Emron couldn't understand what was going on. He had always trusted his skills to hunt and knew how to use the available tools. But it appeared as if the whole dessert had emptied itself from all life.

"I know how to hunt lizards, if it's all right with you?" offered the old man.

"No thanks." Emron rejected the offer with disgust. "Maybe I should go try again," he said. The old man suggested that it would be better if they hunted together.

"How would you hunt?" Emron questioned without waiting for an answer. "Perhaps with this staff?" he pointed and laughed. It wasn't a funny joke for the old man, who kept silent as if he was hurt. Emron said he was sorry for the joke and had no intention of hurting his feelings. The old man accepted his apology and watched him ride off in search of prey.

*   *   *

Emron was so devastated, so humiliated by his failure to find any prey that he wished that he had never come that way. He could easily bear the hunger, but to go and face the old man with his piercing eyes was a more difficult task. He was young and strong, but he had started feeling his hunger dominating his thoughts, causing him to worry about the weak old man who depended on him for his survival. The realisation of the emergency made him worried. They had water for a few more days - if they drank carefully - but what next? He went deep in his thoughts when the smell of meat entered his nostrils. In a great hurry he rode and arrived quickly at the place, where he had left the old man. The old man stood there roasting a large animal on fire and singing.

Emron couldn't believe his eyes. The last thing he could expect from the old man was that he would find an animal, hunt it and provide them with food. "How did you find the deer?"

"He found me," the old man answered happily.

"How did you hunt this animal? With what?" Emron put many questions.

"With this." The old man pointed to his wooden staff. Emron could see fresh blood on the staff and knew that the man was telling the truth. The old man kept singing loudly, working happily, smilingly with the roasting of the animal, from time to time looking at Emron as if demanding appreciation. Emron felt defeated: a failure and very depressed. He was happy with the thought of getting a meal, but couldn't forget that it was all thanks to the man whom he had deemed weak, old, and incapable to survive the tough desert atmosphere. "Maybe, luck and coincidence are more important than one's efforts" he humbly confessed, and immediately felt better. "You're an amazing, incredible person," Emron gave him compliments.

"You think so?" asked the old man happily.

"I'm absolutely sure," said Emron amusedly.

*   *   *

The old doctor intended to stay for a few more days in the desert and search for the plants and herbs. He asked if Emron felt like staying there too. What would he be doing there, he thought and wanted to say no, but decided to stay anyway.

"Maybe I'll learn something new."

Suddenly he remembered that they didn't have enough water, but the doctor was not very worried. "I'm like a camel,

I can live without water for a long time," he joked. Emron told him that he was not, and wished to go out of the desert.

"Relax, young man! I promise you that you shall not die of thirst," the old man said They had food for many more days but the lack of water made him worry about both themselves and the horse.

"Don't you think that you take things too seriously and worry too much?" the doctor asked in irritation.

It rained heavily during the night, and they were forced to find shelter. When Emron started cursing the rain, the doctor laughed emphatically without saying anything to him. "There is a good reason for everything, don't you agree young man?" Emron didn't answer; he hated to be wet and was not in a good mood.

"Go around and see if there is any rain water for the horse," the old man asked Emron the next morning, and he was very surprised to find a pond full of rainwater. His horse drank the water and looked happy and content. It was the first time he could realise how blissful the last night's rain had been. When he came back the doctor had gone in search of his plants. By the time he came back, he was carrying a few bottles of water with him. From where had he gotten these bottles asked Emron. The doctor said that he had traded them from a passing caravan. "Traded with what?" asked Emron, confused. "One of their members was dying, so I gave them medicine that shall cure him, so in return I received some water."

Emron was silent, he did not buy that story, but there was little he could argue about. He stayed for two days with the doctor, and became more and more suspicious of him. However early he got up, he would find him gone, and whenever he returned he had something strange with him, sometimes it was fresh bread; sometimes it was camel milk. He always got those things from some passing stranger. If the doctor was to be believed, there was more traffic in the desert than there was in the towns.

It didn't take long for Emron to understand that his

companion was not an ordinary being. This discovery made him scared and he wanted to ride away. He waited until he was sure that old man was fast asleep. He stood up, held his horse and was about to ride on it, when he heard the old man shout.

"Run off, young man, run! With all the might that you have! To all the corners of the earth!" The old man was talking loudly and sarcastically. Emron was frozen.

"Why stop, you! Run! Run!"

"Who are you? What do you want of me?" Emron shouted in anger.

"Why should I want anything from a fugitive? You can keep running, but can't run from yourself."

Emron tied his horse back to the tree and returned to the mysterious old man with unsteady steps and sat down beside him. "Yes, you're right, I'm on the run! And that I have been doing for the last seven years. But believe me, I am not running from any guilt or bad conscious. I escaped from something I never did. I ran away from a crime I never committed. I run..." He couldn't continue, his voice trembled, and he kept silent.

"I know," the old man said, patting him on the back, and the big strong Emron busted into tears. There was no shame in letting those suppressed feelings out, so the old doctor told him.

The old man told him that he was a wizard and could tell the stories of people's lives just by looking at them. He confessed that he was responsible for all of the strange happenings. He deliberately wanted to raise doubts and fears in Emron. Even his inability to find a prey was not a coincidence. "I wanted to deprive you from the crown of your learning. You were too confident and too arrogant, and would never have confronted the problems of the other side."

"Arrogant! Me!" Emron exclaimed, looking amused.

"Deep down, you are big-headed, even if you remain unaware of it," the wizard looked serious.

Emron kept smiling in disbelief and made the old man confess that he might have been wrong in his judgement and just had done that for fun's sake.

*   *   *

The old man was ready to teach him new things and introduce him to another type of forces, but he did not want to have a pupil who was burdened by inner conflicts. "Go and face your problems like a man, instead of running around your whole life. And come back when you are through," said the old man.

Emron agreed to think about the matter and asked, "how can I contact you if I need to?"

"You'll know when you are ready for that! Now try to get some sleep."

The old man was gone in the morning. Emron knew that he would never come back, so he didn't wait for the old man to return so he could say farewell. Emron was now moving in a new direction; he had changed his destination and was more than a little worried.

4

Entering into his hometown, Emron felt strange. Everything looked the same, just as he had left it seven years ago, and still nothing was the same. This time he was not looking through the eyes of a child, but that of a full grown adult who had seen many places. He had some nostalgic feelings, but he overcame them.

Riding his horse in a slow pace, he came to the house of his mother, his birthplace. Emron looked at it for a long time and thousands of memories came rushing back to him. With a sad smile on his face, he came down from the horse and knocked at the door.

A little girl opened the door. Emron was little confused and inquired to whom the house belonged to. She told that the house belonged to her mother and gave him a name. He understood that she must have been his stepsister and wanted to embrace her, but the child was afraid and ran inside.

"Who is it?" he heard his mother's voice. When she came and looked at him, her eyes widened, her mouth was open, but she was unable to utter a sound. For a while she stood frozen. Then she made a terrible, loud sound and rushed to him. She was embracing, caressing, kissing, and crying, all at one time. Why had he left her? Why? She kept asking him beating softly on his back.

*   *   *

All the neighbours and young children were gathered and they all knew that Emron was back. Many children came to greet him that had not yet even been born when he had run away, but still they had heard of him. Leaving all those enthusiastic people outside, he went into the house. His mother was happy to see him, and so was he. He had never gotten along well with his mother, but always knew that she was a loving and kind woman. She was a weak personality who gave in easily and it was that which made him furious.

"Where is your husband? Is he not home yet?" Emron inquired. She kept silent. Maybe she disliked the way he asked. He had never called the man his father.

"Come, Sara, go fetch something for your brother to drink."

"I didn't know I had such a beautiful little sister," Emron smiled and gave Sara a big hug and a kiss on the cheek.

Emron told his mother the story of his life, the reasons that forced him to escape, and the reason why he was back. She was the only person who had believed his innocence. But now he was back to prove it to the rest of the world as well. There was no need to do so, his mother told him. She told him that she was aware of the fact that it was her husband who was the main cause of his runaway. She avoided looking into Emron's eyes as she spoke.

"Sometimes one is deprived of one's faculties and is without any insight or a clear vision of the things obvious to others. How could I be that blind not to see what the man was after?" His mother talked in a sad, regretful manner.

He was told that the missing boy had returned safely few weeks after Emron had run away from home. The boy had been abducted by some slave traders and stayed in their custody until he got a chance to escape from his captors and came home. The boy's safe return brought a great relief to his family, who celebrated the occasion with festivities. But it also brought them face-to-face with their shame and regret regarding the aggressive and threatening behaviour towards the innocent child that they thought had forced him to run away from the safety of his home. The boy's family regretted their rude, insolent and accusing behaviour and begged for forgiveness.

They had sadly discovered that the person behind all the

rumours was her husband who had acted treacherously and forced Emron to go on the run. Immediately after the return of the missing boy, she had divorced her husband because she could no longer love him. Now she was married for the third time, to some distant relative of his father and had Sara from that wedlock.

Emron stayed for a few weeks with his mother, sister, and mother's husband, who seemed to be a pleasant and warm person, and then decided to leave. His mother protested, wishing Emron to stay, to take over the charge of his money and property. "Give it all to Sara when she comes of age," he suggested. He was happy to see her in good health and married to a man who cared and respected her. All of his old friends and relatives tried to persuade him to stay, but he was determined. While riding away he looked at his town and knew he was seeing it for the last time.

*   *   *

He wanted to find the old wizard, but didn't know where to begin to look for him. All directions lay open, except the one leading to Egypt. Three times he had tried to head towards that country, and all three times one or the other reason had prevented him from doing that. So he decided to take the opposite direction. He came to a country where people were tall and fair. Goods were in abundance and the prices very fair. There were big markets, where merchants streamed in from all directions. Things of all kinds were available, and Emron was impressed!

When he gave his compliments to a local, saying that they were great craftsmen and produced such wonderful things, he laughed and told him that it all was due to his misunderstanding. Nothing he saw in the country was produced there. They had just happened to be at the right spot; at a crossroads where merchants from near and far came into contact with each other to buy and sell their goods.

The country was booming and flourishing, without the

need to strive. He smiled thinking about something that the wizard had told him. "Sometimes you strive and strive and even break your backbone, but get nowhere, while others can reach the skies without moving a finger."

One thing he knew for sure. He was not the person who could get anything free from life, but he did not mind that as he loved the challenges! He met traders and merchants from different countries and asked them questions regarding their lands. He was very curious to know how people lived in different parts of the world. He met a few merchants, who intended to go to India. "Why go there, while you can get Indian goods here?" Emron inquired.

It wasn't just because of the goods he was told. "India is beautiful; it is huge, with rich variety and diversity. It offers everything one can think of!" the merchants told him excitedly. They knew that it was a far away land with very many hurdles and difficulties. But they were ready for the dangers, because they were worth taking for the sake of India, a magical land.

They were looking for any caravans leaving for India. Emron showed his interest to follow them if they were to find such a caravan.

"What would you do there?" he was asked.

"Just like that," he answered shrugging his shoulders.

They felt their duty to inform him of the dangers involved. "We must warn you, it's not an easy task."

"I'll take my chances," he replied in a careless tone.

*   *   *

A week later Emron received the news that the merchants had found a caravan of Indian merchants returning home. There were few young people among them; the rest of them were middle aged, but they were strong and well-figured men.

They insisted on meeting Emron and his friends before they gave their consent for them to join them in the caravan. They apologized for their insistence, but replayed that it was necessary. They had to be sure that their new members were strong and healthy and could bear the difficulties on the way. They were used to traveling slow and safe. They had friends along the way who provided them with food, water and protection. These advantages did not make their journey any less hazardous. There were deserts to be crossed and there were high mountains blocking every possible route. Fortunately, there were some passes, but to cross them was a breathtaking process.

They described the ditches, rivers, diseases, and all the other terrible things they had to face. Most of all there were the unfriendly warrior tribes,who could, for no reason at all, turn violent and hostile. One of the merchants changed his mind about the journey, but Emron and another three were ready to join the caravan and proceed.

"One last warning," the leader of the caravan said, remembering something. "Your return back from India will not be our responsibility!" Of course, there were caravans that would be going in that direction, but it could be months or even years before the next caravan leaves. For a while, reluctance could be seen on their faces, but finally they decided to join the caravan.

*   *   *

The caravan was supposed to leave the next day, when suddenly, Emron fell sick. He had a high fever but felt strong enough to take the journey. The leader refused to take him with them. He strictly forbade others from even visiting him. He could not risk any delays. They were already late, and any further delay could jeopardise their whole plan.

Early snowfalls in the mountains could block the passes, forcing them to wait until spring, which they could not afford to do. So there was no option but to drop him. Emron and his newly made friends protested, but it did not help. Emron was left behind, feeling sad and angry.

"Why did I have to get sick that exact moment?" he

argued with himself, "would it have been better if he was to become sick in some long-forgotten place?" The question arose in his head and made him feel a little calmer.

Two days later, he was well again as if he never had been sick. He felt an urge to rush after the caravan. They were only on two days distance and he could easily catch up with them, but refrained. He could not bear it if he was to be rejected once again.

He was walking in his thoughts when he crossed an old little man, who reminded him of the old wizard. What a remarkable resemblance, he thought, and turned in curiosity to look back. He was stunned to see that it was the wizard himself. The man who walked with his wooden staff and had his back toward him, but he knew with surety that, that could be no one else.

"Listen dear friend!" he shouted, but the old man did not stop or turn back.

Emron ran after him and put his hand on the old man's shoulder. The wizard turned and showed his excitement and surprise to find him there. "Oh, what a coincidence!" he cried. Emron smiled back, knowing that the old fox had planned every little detail. "Don't pretend that you were not behind my sickness!"

The wizard neither confirmed nor denied his accusation.

"Why did you stop me from going to India?" Emron asked seriously.

"You mean joining the caravan?" the wizard asked. "And by the way, what did you intend to accomplish in India?"

"Just like that," Emron gave the same answer he had given to the merchants.

"Oh, I see, it's a pattern, because I can see you're not on the run any more," said the old wizard and smiled. "Don't call me 'Doc'. My name is Khafil." They took a long walk, ignoring the hustle and bustle of the people around them.

"Try to see things in their right perspective," said Khafil seriously. "Sometimes things that seem trivial could really be of enormous value, while at other times things that seem impossible to handle may really have a simple solution."

*   *   *

"What do you want to learn?" the wizard asked.

All that you can teach me, from herbs and plants and their qualities to the use of magic." The wizard laughed as if Emron had said something very funny.

"In return, you must teach me how to become an expert of archery, the use of a sword, and the use of any other weapons you know."

Emron told him that was not possible. The wizard was too old to learn all those things, and it required years of training and hard work.

"Oh, I see!" the wizard said, "You're not meant to be a wizard just as I'm not meant to be a warrior. But we can help each other along the way."

Emron was a bit embarrassed. He couldn't see how he could be of any practical use to the wizard, but the old man promised to let Emron know when he could be of service. The old man could not teach Emron to become a wizard, but they could try some mental exercises. By doing so, Emron could learn the basic and elementary things.

Emron's face lit up.

The wizard was seriously thinking; "Now, where shall we start?"

*   *   *

The wizard started explaining to Emron that the world they lived in and moved through was much more complicated and more difficult than most people thought. It was enormous, diverse, and beyond anyone's comprehension.

There were forces all around them that were always in action. When these diverse forces met and cooperated, new energies were born and new worlds began to come forth, but these forms were destroyed when they collided. The wizard did not want to expand much on the subject. There was never a vacuum; when some force withdrew another came to replace it. All forces were either negative or positive; there wasn't anything that was neutral.

On our planet Earth, there are many worlds, each one of them is the result of the interaction between different forces. Some worlds are so microscopic that our naked eyes cannot not catch and register them, others are so subtle and of materials unknown to our senses that we fail to recognize them. We cooperate with some of these worlds and sometimes even exploit them." The key to the all magic lay in the diversity of the worlds. These worlds were made of different energies and substances; therefore, they had completely different strategies for survival, patterns of development, and tools available to achieve their disparate goals.

This magic was not an illusion or a trick. It was a science. It was a knowledge to break the barriers between those worlds, retrieve their tools, bring them to the worlds that they were not meant for, and use them wisely. The wizard asked if Emron followed him, to which he confessed that he didn't.

"I think I better stick to my trusted sword," Emron joked, and they both laughed.

*   *   *

Khafil tried again, this time using easy wording. "Take the example of the movement," he explained.

"The animal world is big, but has not so much need for mobility, so they have developed strong legs according to the need of the animal. Nevertheless, they are using the force of their own bodies to accomplish their given tasks. On the other hand, you are using the force inherent in animals and can travel with much faster speed than you would be doing without a horse. I use the force of movement, which is far superior to our world and can move to any place of the earth in no time. This tool I have borrowed from some other world, where it's just a common happening. But in our world, it's magic."

Emron could finally understand what Khafil was trying to explain. The wizard went on. He told the warrior that the divisions between worlds were not as obvious and clear cut as it sounded. Sometimes the worlds were interwoven into each other without any apparent distinction. As a wizard, he could see the differences and the dividing lines. There were streams of active energies of different colours, rhythmic impulses and vibrations. The varying energies constituted different qualities, potencies and speeds. The beings of different worlds were attached and synchronized with one of these energies and functioned according to its qualities. A wizard could change his rate of vibration and readjust to a given energy type, and thus could achieve the results which were impossible for other human beings. But even Khafil was unable to understand all types of energies, or to use them in their full capacity. He confessed his imperfection, but was happy to know all that he knew.

"Look at this horse of yours, can you go and talk to him?" the wizard asked Emron. "No, of course not," he said.

"But I can, if I want to, using the frequency these animals function by synchronising my rate of vibration and sound rhythm to theirs'."

Emron was amazed and waited for Khafil to go and speak to the horse, but he did not. The wizard told him that he could communicate with birds, plants, trees and beings of many other worlds and thus could gain vast knowledge and information. That's how he could know the medicinal value of the herbs and plants. All he needed was to ask what they were good for, or to ask of their qualities and attributes. Emron's interest piqued and he listened with more care and concentration.

"The ability to move in and out of the worlds may sound very exciting. But believe me, it's not without responsibility and taking great risks," said the wizard. It required secrecy and caution. If this knowledge were to fall into uninitiated hands, then it could bring harm to all of the worlds and their development.

The laws of nature were necessary barriers for the growth of the beings in different worlds. But these laws were not the same everywhere. It could be very dangerous, or even disastrous for two reasons. First, because most bodies were not refined enough to adjust to the higher rate of vibration, they faced a danger of breaking down. Secondly, because these complicated energies were both negative and positive, the wizard had to have a complete knowledge of these energy types.

"The knowledge of these energies is the most difficult task. One must recognize the attractive and repulsive energies before approaching them in a safe and productive way."

Emron listened with great interest, but he was discouraged by the overwhelming knowledge that he must have in order to master the strange worlds of magic. He felt more at home with the mundane world and its forces. "I must confess that I have neither the ability nor the interest required to learn this wonderful science you have been explaining," said Emron.

"So I have succeeded in scaring you away!" Khafil said laughingly. "Although you do not wish to learn magic for yourself, I can take you to the world of the Genii for a brief visit," he added.

"Oh, would you?" asked Emron excitedly. Yes, was the answer, but Emron could not take his horse with him, so Khafil had to arrange some place where they could leave the horse. The wizard took the horse and went in one direction, telling Emron to go and have a good night's rest, promising to meet him the next morning. Emron was very excited about visiting another world. He had great difficulty falling asleep. His mind kept imagining how the world of Genii looked like. However hard he tried, he could not go beyond his own human world.

*   *   *

When Khafil came in the morning, Emron was ready to follow him.

How far away was this world that they were going to go to? Which direction did it lay? How long would they need to travel? Emron kept asking such questions while they walked.

"I can tell that you have been not listening to what I have been telling you," the wizard smiled, without answering any of his questions. "Now it's time to observe."

They kept walking for a few hours, leaving human dwelling places far behind. "We can rest here for a while," the wizard said, pointing to a big tree.

Emron wasn't very tired, but he did as he was asked, and sat down, leaning his back on the trunk of the tree. He saw how Khafil was sitting with his eyes closed, taking deep breaths and telling him about the wonderful feelings the relaxation gave. Emron closed his eyes and also took some deep breaths and experienced a freeing, soothing, and harmonic feeling. "You're right! The air feels much fresher and cooler; I can even smell the sea," Emron said, enjoying the great feeling.

"Very much so, but I believe we've rested enough and must move on," he heard the voice of Khafil and opened his eyes, only to be struck with astonishment. They were sitting on a rock, facing the sea. So the sound of the waves, the smell of the sea, and feel of the wet fresh air was not a product of his imagination. Everything was real. In amazement, he turned his gaze and looked at the wizard with wondering eyes.

"Where are we? How did we come here?"

"I've done enough explaining. Now you should try not to ask so many questions. Just watch and observe. You can ask questions later," the wizard told him.

"Okay," Emron said, agreeing with him. "But one last question, are we in another world?"

"Yes!" he was told. He opened his mouth to ask further questions, but looking at the face of Khafil made him close it again without a question. The wizard was not in any hurry and sat enjoying the cold breeze on the otherwise hot day.

"What a difference," said Emron, remembering the hot, sweaty day they just had left somewhere behind. He sat watching the sea, and felt waves of power and energy entering his body. He could smell fish and other seafood and felt hungry.

"Just relax, keep smelling and breath deeply," he was told by Khafil. "Remember, we are intruders in this world and not everyone is going to be very friendly if they notice our presence," the wizard cautioned him.

He told Emron that he himself was a frequent visitor to the world and knew what to do and what not to do. But Emron needed some extra vigilance and carefulness. He was to pay full attention to Khafil and his words in order to not fall into any trouble. "Don't speak to anyone and don't follow the movements of others," said Khafil. "Stay close to me," were his final words.

Emron was made nervous by all of these instructions. He got closer to the Khafil, who laughed.
"We're only on the threshold right now! My instructions are for the world of the Genii!"

*   *   *

The wizard opened his cloth bag and took out a little bottle from it. He also took out some strange mudlike earth. First, he rubbed this mud on Emron's face and hands, then threw some dry earth at him and smiled. "You're now hidden from the eyes of the Genii!" He kept looking at Emron for a while; till he became sure that he was properly prepared.

"Now be very careful, don't you collide with some Genie!" the wizard said seriously. He asked Emron to take a deep breath and prepare himself for his encounter with another world. He did as he was told, while Khafil uncorked the bottle.

A very strong scent came out of the bottle and entered his nostrils. The smell was so strong that he could not tell if it was pleasant or terrible. He just could say it was sharp like a knife-edge when it made its way into his nose. He felt dizzy and nauseated and a flood of tears coming out of his eyes and water came out of his nose.

"What the devil was that!?" Emron exclaimed, once the shock was over.

"That?" Khafil laughed. "That was the borrowed and temporary sight that you have to use sometimes."

Had he known its effect, he surely would have refrained. But he had involuntarily inhaled it and now waited impatiently for the next step.

"It's time." he heard the whisper of Khafil. "Don't forget what I've told you earlier. Be careful and don't speak until I tell you!"

Emron started walking beside Khafil, who signalled him to walk one step behind. He was excited and looked forward to the experience in anticipation. He looked back to see that the ripples of the sea were the same and so was the sky, but the shades were different. The sky was no longer light blue, and the seawater was not dark blue. The sky was purple and sea was of light green colour. It must have been the effect of the damn smell, he thought, still feeling a little dizzy. He noticed that he had, due to his lack of concentration, lagged behind, and so hurriedly got closer to the wizard.

*   *   *

"Look there!" He heard Khafil's whispering voice and looked around, puzzled and bewildered. He could swear that the voice he heard had come from within his own head.

He looked straight ahead and saw the silhouette of a greyish sky touching buildings at a distance. He wasn't sure what he saw. It could very well have been some sort of buildings, but could equally be some clouds or toys made from some fantasy. They were now quite close to them but he was still uncertain.

The whole atmosphere was cloudy and misty, but he could still see those thin, tall buildings. His eyes were unable to penetrate through the flimsy walls of those houses. He could see that they were made of some strange, subtle material. He saw creatures which reminded of human beings, but who certainly were not. These creatures were also tall and well built. But their bodies appeared to be made of a strange, smoky material. With awe he watched these beings moving around with their cloudy bodies, talking, laughing, and completely unaware of his presence. The buildings had no doors or windows but that didn't prevent them from entering into them. The creatures kept going in and out of the buildings without any effort or difficulty. Every here and there, high flames could be seen coming out of rocky grounds. The place had caused Emron to lose all sense of time; he couldn't even say if it was dawn or dusk.

These beings were carelessly going in and out of fires without getting burned. Emron was awed but not scared. He halted to locate the wizard, whom he had almost forgotten about. Suddenly he felt the presence of somebody quite close to him and wanted to move aside, but it was too late. One of the Genii went right through him, giving his body a great shock. He felt as if his whole body was trembling uncontrollably; he was numb and drained of all energy. Even in this state of physical shock he could see the horrified, distorted face of the Genie, who stood a few feet away, trying to figure out what had happened. He must have gotten some unpleasant feelings too.

"Didn't I warn you?" Emron heard the wizard's serious voice and then his laughter. "Be careful or you shall not survive the next shock," said the wizard, speaking from some inner dimension. They went walking through this habitation for some time, with the only difference that Emron was extra vigilant, and avoided any further collisions.

"Keep walking behind me," he heard Khafil's voice say.

He saw the sun rising from behind the hills and knew

that a glorious morning was in making. They had left the Genii town behind somewhere, and could not find any traces of that flimsy town. The golden rays of the sun were replacing the smoky, foggy scenes he was experiencing just a few moments ago. Were they still in Genii world or back in their own? Emron dared not to ask, because he had not received the ´speak signal´ from the wizard.

The scene was beautiful, with chain of giant rocky hills all around.

"You may speak now," he finally heard the voice of the wizard. Emron heard the voice in a normal, natural way, as it came on the wavelength and entered into his eardrums.

"Are we outside the Genii world?" he asked, still cautious.

"No," was the wizard's short answer.

"Isn't it still dangerous for me to speak then?" asked Emron.

He wouldn't be asked to do so if it was, he was assured. When Emron still kept silent, the wizard laughed saying, "It must be the horrible shock of the collision with one of the Genii. A weak bodied person would have died of that, but you're a strong young man. You can set your mind at ease. We don't have a great risk for such things happening out here," said Khafil.

Emron then had the courage to ask his endless questions. "Why were the houses so high? What were they made of? Why were those houses not proportionally broad? What were those flames and why didn't they burn those beings?"

Khafil smiled, amused. "I knew it! I knew it! I had waited for your never ending questions. I should have given you some basic information before coming here. I don't know why, but I took for granted that you were aware of these basics!"

He started telling Emron that the Genii world was much older than their own human world.

"Unlike us, they are made of fiery elements, and that

explains their smoky appearances. They live and enjoy the same physical world as us, but use completely different materials to build their dwelling places, use entirely separate wave lengths than us, and see differently with their keen eyes. These beings are sensitive to energies, materials, and frequencies unknown to human beings. They are large bodied and like to live at great heights, which is why they've built great, sky touching buildings. They don't need to use much breadth because they utilise a dimension that is unknown to mankind. Even though these houses have no doors and windows, no one can enter unnoticed if he lacks the permission to do so. These houses are tuned to the vibrations of their inhabitants, and will not allow entrance to outsiders."

The wizard had chosen the perfect time to visit that place, because Emron would not have been able to see it otherwise. Fires were used in the nights to light their towns, but that was only for aesthetic reasons; they were fully capable of seeing in the dark. How those fires could go on burning with such high flames could not be explained to him, for the simple reason that he would not understand. The Genii didn't do any physical work, but had strong physical and mental capacities. They could accomplish things in a normal human manner, but only for their leisure or entertainment. No one could match their speed when they were out on an errand. The wizard himself used to apply that very technique, though with far less precision.

The wizard went on explaining about the Genii world. They had other demands and needs and used different energy resources for their survival. They lived much longer and healthier lives than us, but were not necessarily superior to the humans, though they appeared to be so in many respects. For these fiery beings, fire and flames were as mud and clay. They were the absolute masters of the element, and could also control and exploit other elements without difficulty. Being the most ancient dominating force on the earth, they found it difficult and humiliating to allow space for far less intelligent and inferior human beings. But to compete with these persistent, fast growing, and ambitious kinds proved to be a far too difficult task than they had ever faced before. They tried to ignore it, but it didn't help. They offered a hand of friendship, help, and knowledge, but felt exploited. So they declared war on humanity, but could not achieve any greater success than winning small battles. They realised that the war could not be won. The human beings were not as weak and helpless as they had appeared. The power of the Genii could weaken and destroy the individual members of the human world but were unable to touch their collective will and spirit.

They eventually had given up the fight, though skirmish on individual level could not be avoided, which kept on taking place from time to time, resulting in tragic happenings in both worlds. The Genii were mixed, like mankind, consisting of both good and bad elements. However, one could say that if the majority of the human beings were simple, sound, and good-natured, the opposite could be said of the Genii world.

What gave the human beings an edge over Genii was that difference existing between their natures. The entire struggle turned into a battle between good and bad, attracting the help of good extra-planetary forces. The wizard preferred not to expand on the subject, as it required an in-depth knowledge of subjects that Emron completely lacked.

The wizard told him that they were about to visit one of his Genii friends.

"But he will not be able to see me," said Emron. That little treatment he was given could not help in the presence of highly developed Genii, was Emron told. Their piercing eyes could unravel any disguise. That particular Genie didn't like to be in congested places and lived in a big cave.

*   *   *

A young man was waiting for them and welcomed them with a smile. He offered Emron a handshake, which he reluctantly accepted. Khafil explained about Emron's's colliding with a Genie, so he smiled kindly, assuring that in his physical body he was tuned in to Emron's vibrations, and thus there was no risk for any unpleasant and dangerous shock.

He had food and drinks ready for them. They were hungry and the food was delicious. They ate with a good appetite and afterwards thanked their host, who accepted their compliments with a big smile.

The Genie had a very long name, and was so difficult that Emron could not pronounce it, making them all laugh.

"Call him Fob, that is as near to the sound of his name as you can come to," suggested Khafil. Fob knew of their coming, but didn't know their purpose. Well aware of the fact that their journey entailed great risk, he was curious to know why a wizard deliberately took them.

The wizard wasted no time in explaining that he sought the freedom of movement for his young friend.

"What's the need?" he was questioned by the Genie.

"So that he can search for the shield of invisibility," Khafil replied.

"And why does this human need that?" Fob inquired again.

"To fight a common enemy," said the wizard.

The Genie asked no further questions, but kept thinking. Finally he spoke. "You know, I don't question your wisdom, but I must say that the chances of your success in the search are bleak. Your request is surely going to be rejected!"

"Maybe so" said Khafil, "but I am sure that you will try your best."

"My trying is not enough, and you know well that no request has ever been granted to any human being without the return of an equal favour," Fob said, shaking his head. "What is your friend good at?" he asked.

The wizard told him briefly about his friend, but Fob did not look impressed. He promised to put forward the wizard's request, but he made it clear that he could not do so while they stayed with him. He had little hope of any positive response.

They stayed for a couple of days and enjoyed his hospitality. He showed them around and Emron was impressed with the most beautiful things that he saw there. Wonderful gems and stones of incredible sizes and beauties, colourful unique flowers and soil glittering like stardust. The world of the Genii was spread over the whole planet and beyond, he was told. But it could not be unfolded to him more than it already had been.

"I'll inform you about the decision," Fob told them, when they were finally leaving his world.

*   *   *

Khafil took him to the sea, where they both took a long bath. The water was warm and pleasant. Khafil was like a fish in the water. He kept diving, disappearing for minutes, making Emron wonder and worry, only to come back holding shells with beautiful pearls in them. "Can we take them to our world?" he asked. "I would not dare to risk angering my Genii friends. Not that these are considered valuable for them, but because we are believed to be greedy." The long swim made them tired. They lay on the stony beach to relax and gather back their lost energies.

"I believe that we have been here long enough now, we should better be moving," said Khafil.

Emron agreed and got on his feet. Without any surprise he noticed that they were back in the same place that they had left a few days earlier. The big tree was protecting them from strong warm rays of the sun, which was burning the ground around them.

"Welcome back to your own world," said Khafil.

Emron felt happy and sighed with relief. "What was that freedom of movement thing about?" he asked the wizard, who explained that since Emron was not a wizard, he could never learn to use the technique of rapid travel, and thus needed some alternative means and the tools to be able to do so. That freedom that they had requested was a temporary arrangement which, if granted, could make him as fast traveller as the wizard himself was.

Why did he need that, when Khafil could do the job, unaided? Emron asked. That was for two reasons, he was told. First, because he had other important tasks to do but mainly because no wizard could help any being more than few times. Emron told the wizard that it was okay with him. He didn't want any freedom of movement, because he was without need or wish to utilise it. "Who knows, maybe one beautiful day you might need it, so it will be good to have it," said Khafil.

*   *   *

They came back to the town and arranged some place to stay. While Emron went to visit the market place, the wizard disappeared somewhere to collect Emron's horse. Khafil returned after some time, handed back his horse and left, promising to contact Emron as soon as he got some news from Fob.

"How long am I to stay here?" Emron asked.

"As long as you want to; who am I to tell?" The wizard shrugged his shoulders. "I'll find you, wherever you are."

Emron became relaxed knowing that he was not in thrall, bound to that country indefinitely sitting, waiting, and not doing anything. But he decided to stay there for the time being.

To kill time in that busy town was not so difficult. He spent most of his days in the marketplace, watching, talking and observing people, or merely looking and appreciating the lovely, beautiful crafts of different lands. Weeks passed, without hearing anything from Khafil. Perhaps things didn't function so fast in the other world either. He was not in a hurry himself, only a little bit agitated and bored. He decided to wait for a few more days and then move on further East. But he changed his mind when he came to know that those areas were suffering from unrest. People around him were busy doing their business and had little interest in the lives and happenings of the others.

The foreign merchants appeared to be worried, but there was not much news from the troubled East. "What's really happening over there?" some trader asked.

"I heard that there is some battle going on," answered the other one.

"Can this unrest spread here?" asked the same trader responded worriedly.

"No one can say for sure, but I really hope that we will be spared," said another fearfully.

One day Emron stood talking to some merchants when suddenly panic broke out in the market place. The traders started collecting their goods and rushed hither and thither. No one had the time and nerve to explain what was happening there. All the local traders looked surprised and terror stricken and the foreign merchants looked even more scared and threatened, completely unaware of what was going on.

"And you stand there doing nothing," one merchant shouted at Emron with a great surprise. He just smiled thinking what strange people they all were. If they were in danger, what good did all that panic and running around serve? He argued, feeling almost pity for those around him.

All of a sudden, he jumped and took hold of one local trader. "What's up"? But the local trader seemed not to be in the mood to answer.

He tried to free himself, but failed. "Please, let me go, " he begged.

"Not before you tell me what is going on," Emron answered with determination. The man quickly started telling that a big army was approaching from the East, and could be there shortly.

"Why panic?" He asked. "Surely you have an army of

your own that can try to face and defeat those invaders?" Emron said calmly. The man looked at him with widened eyes and looked surprised.

"Nobody knows better than us that none of our soldiers have ever taken part in any battle. By now they all must have ridden to some far away, safe place"

"Is there any one of you, who can take a stand and die like a man?" Emron asked with sarcasm. The man tried again to come out of his grip, Emron let him go and watched with disgust as the man collected his goods, nervously throwing everything in a cart. He went to the foreign merchants' side and told them what he knew. They all looked pale and spontaneously rushed to take care of their merchandise.

"Don't be fools!" Emron cried. "By running away from death, you are only bringing it closer!" It didn't take long for him to convince those merchants that the only way to survive was to have a quick strategy.

"Take your weapons and follow me."

There were about thirty of them fit and strong enough to make a last stand. They were standing on foot and sitting on the back of horses, blocking the way of fleeing traders and their families. Emron was trying to raise their morale, stressing the virtue of bravery. He assured those people that if they were trying to flee from death, they would never be able to do that. The invaders would catch up with them, killing them along with their families, and robbing them of everything they had worked for through generations. He saw the doubt arising from their eyes and knew that it was the right moment to make the last blow.

"If you're cowards it's okay for us, but have the decency of showing love and care for your loved ones. If you made a stand here and now, you may give a chance to the women, children and elderly, a fair chance to escape and live. If you still decide to go, then leave and die with regret and shame. But if you decide to stay behind, you may still die, but it would be with honour and dignity!"

Saying these final words, he moved out of people's way

and so did the other foreign merchants. Emron waited and after seeing them move forward, he turned back and started moving towards the other direction. He turned to look for the last time at the doomed caravan, and rejoiced when he saw that most of the able men, both young and old, were turning back to join them.

Emron asked if there was anyone who could give him some information as to how many those invaders were. "Maybe a few hundred, or maybe a few thousands," was the only guess.

"How far were they? What means of transportation did they use? How good were they in the use of weapons?" There was no one who could provide him with answers. So he decided to make a blind strategy.

Quickly he divided his companions into two groups, mixing locals and foreigners. They all were to hide and wait for the invaders. The group staying in the town would challenge and engage the invaders, and then a second group led by Emron, who would ambush from the rear. A few spies were sent to collect as much information as possible.

"How far do you think they are from us?" wondered one local, who was shaky and doubted if his decision to stay was right. One of the men sent forward came back with the news that the invaders were only a day's distance and hadn't moved as fast as they had feared earlier. There were at least two thousand of them if not more, but they were more brutal than they were organised. Some of them kept dropping out from the invading force. Maybe they had gotten enough valuables and saw no point in continuing the march forward, or perhaps they were tired of all fighting and wanted to return to their families.

Emron could guess that there wasn't enough time to lay traps, and that his fight was to be more difficult than he had anticipated. He was relieved to know that their enemy was not an organised marching army, but only an undisciplined band of people. They were fearless and good in weaponry use, but what worried him most was their superior numbers.

There was no way that his force of no more than few hundred men could stand and win, especially when he knew nothing of their morale, bravery, and skills. But there was no time for any regrets or revisions. They had to face the day even if it looked hopeless.

He kept a smile on his face, hiding all of his worries. He was their leader, their captain, and so had to keep his head cool. They learned that the invaders were now at a few hours' distance and waited with patience. They waited with mixed feelings of fear, nervousness, and anxiety but there was even a little hope. They had the will to live the day and survive, a wish to overcome the strong enemy. This waiting came to an end and the decisive moment was on their heads.

Eventually they could see the riders on their swift horses approaching towards the town like a storm. There was a loud noise of screams and shouts of the invaders, of hoofs, of the leaping horses, and dust arose.

Emron and his men were terrified but resolute. They were looking straight into the eyes of death and were ready to embrace it. The invaders came into town and found it empty. They laughed as if it was an expected scene. They didn't seem to be in hurry to pursue the fleeing people of that town. They came down from their horses and started looking for food and drink. The signal was given and the defenders charged. One group attacked from one side, the other from the rear. The invaders were taken completely by surprise. Many of their men felt lost, but they recovered from the initial surprise and realising that the attacking force was only a tiny one gave them new strength.

Emron was attacking, killing, wounding his enemies, and then he gave the sudden order to retreat, only to attack afresh from some other side. The morale of his men grew higher and higher. They were proud of their hopeless struggle. They had killed many invaders, but there were simply too many of them, and to defeat them seemed like an impossible task. The battle went on, becoming more and more fierce. The invaders looked surprised by the powerful resistance, but were confident to win in the end.

They fought all day and were dead tired. But no side was ready to give up. The invaders realised that it was dangerous for them to fight after dusk, so they retreated. Emron's companions made a triumphant cry, but he was worried and exhausted. His men searched for their wounded companions and took care of them. Seventy of their friends were dead or missing.

"We have succeeded in making them flee," said one of them excitedly. No one reacted to that statement, they all knew it was not a victory, the only thing they had gotten was a night's respite, or maybe not even that. The enemy could come with a fresh attack during the night. So they had to be careful, not to stay in the open where they were more vulnerable.

They decided to have watches while others tried to sleep and recover some strength. None of them wanted to think about the next day, when a more severe attack was expected.

They were not wrong. The rising dust and distant noise was a surety that death was approaching them with the speed and strength of a storm. They were tired and weak, but ready, and this time without the advantage of surprise. The bands of invaders halted a few hundred yards away from the main town, waiting for the sign to engage.

They challenged Emron and his men to come out and fight. It seemed they wanted to avoid fighting in the narrow grounds, and wished to have the battle in the open, where they could easily encircle and crush the little but organised and resilient force. There weren't any fixed rules of engagement, so Emron decided not to accept the challenge.

"No!" He let the invaders know that they were the defenders and they were to choose when and where to give them resistance. They could feel that the enemy, despite a great advantage of being manifold more, was reluctant. "They don't want to fight on the ground where many of their dead friends lay," Emron told his men.

For the time being, there was a deadlock, until the leader

of the invaders shouted. "If you want to die near your home, will help you accomplish that!"

The commander of the invaders gave the signal to advance. The screaming, yelling invaders, with drawn swords and spears in their hands, rushed in their direction. The invaders came to the big market place ground, where laid many of their friends, looking nervously around to locate their enemy, not finding them made them jumpy.

They did not have to wait long.

Emron and his men were to fight them differently this time. Suddenly a rain of arrows started falling on them. Those arrows hit many of them and their horses. Some fell down and died, the others started yelling and swearing in anger. They were confused and panicked, not knowing where the enemy hid. It seemed like they were all around them.

They realised the hopelessness of the situation and fled, again leaving behind a number of dead and injured. This time they didn't retreat too far away. They camped just outside the town, giving a clear message that they were not going to leave them alone. Emron and his men were happy to repel the attack once more, but they had no reason to rejoice. They had inflicted a heavy loss to the invaders without losing a single man of their own, but the question was how long they could resist? They were out of arrows and were forced to go out and face the invaders in a traditional manner. If their enemy attacked once more that would be the end of their story.

*   *   *

The enemy was more careful this time. There came no fresh attacks that day, or during the night time either. The enemy was busy planning a new strategy to get rid of them. They all knew that time was on the side of the invaders, so they could afford to take it easy, leaving Emron's force in a constant state of alert and nervousness. This waiting for a new attack was more nerve-shattering than the attack itself could be.

Emron was awakened by one of the watchmen. The

enemy was encircling them. He had seen the troop's movement on the other side of the town. It was some time before dawn, a perfect time for the enemy to surprise them. All of his men were hurriedly awakened and instructed to prepare for the final encounter. One group remained where they were, while the other group advanced to the other side of the town to meet the invaders.

They could hear the sounds of the horses' hooves. It was quite a big number, they could easily guess. If there were to be a simultaneous attack from both sides, it would quickly be over, Emron thought, but he waited courageously.

"Look!" shouted one of his men. They could feel a great excitement in his voice. "That's no enemy, they are our soldiers coming to help us!" the man shouted. Their faces lit up with hope and joy. Emron sent one man to give the good news to the rest of them, and waited for their soldiers' arrival.

*   *   *

After they all had safely entered the town, Emron greeted them warmly; well aware that there was no time to waste. He briefly talked to their commander and explained the situation and they counselled with each other as to what was the best they could do in the given situation.

The commander suggested that it was best to wait for the assault, while Emron was of a different opinion. The enemy was unaware of the change that had occurred and still believed them to be very few in numbers, and expected them not capable of any offence or other daring step. So the best tactic was to surprise the enemy once more.

The commander was not very convinced, but agreed to aid and fight by their side. They decided to have a very low profile and wait for nightfall.

They could hear the voices from the enemy camp till very late in the night. They talked loudly, laughed, and swore as usual. When the noise in the enemy camp died down, they knew that the enemy had gone asleep except the watchdogs.

The commander and his soldiers quietly left from the direction they had earlier come from. They were to take a long route and come to the enemy's rear and signal their arrival.

Late at night Emron got the signal. He and his men were ready to act. They made a sudden thrust and rushed to the enemy. There were shouts and screaming from the watchmen, awaking, warning others. But Emron and his men were on their heads like a thunderstorm. They could feel panic and chaos there. It was dark, they had difficulty finding their weapons and separating friend from foe. Many of the enemies, instead of standing and fighting started fleeing to the rear. But they did not know that there was no escape. There was not much of a fight; they had defeated their mighty enemy, who was on the run having Emron and his men and soldiers on the heels, chasing them.

The darkness of the night hid the faces of their enemies, but they could imagine the horror on their faces. The fleeing enemy had left with half of its force destroyed, and were not to venture that way again.

*   *   *

The commander, soldiers, and citizens took Emron and placed him on a pedestal. They were singing, dancing, laughing, and making triumphant sounds. The praise for Emron would simply go on and on.

"You're to be our king!" shouted one young local.

"Yeah!" cried the crowd. No one cared that he was not even a citizen.

"Wait a minute!" Emron tried to calm them down. "Don't say or do anything that you shall regret later," he said. "I'm a stranger, a foreigner, who is only here for a short while, like my friends." Emron pointed to the merchants, his brave companions. "Sooner or later we shall go our way. What you need is a local to become your king," Emron continued. He agreed that they had to replace the king, who had fled with his soldiers long before they had gotten news of the enemy. But such matters required cool thinking and sound council rather than any emotional decision.

The commander agreed with him. He himself was not a candidate, well remembering his equal guilt and regret of abandoning the people to a cruel and heartless enemy. "What made the you change your mind and come back?" Emron asked the commander.

"We had left a few soldiers behind to report the further happenings, and learned how you people were to stay and fight. Our hearts became filled with shame that our land was defended by those who didn't even belong to us". They were victorious but their hard work and efforts were still required to bury their dead friends, and to clean the town.

The message of their victory was sent to the people who had fled. So caravans of people started coming back. There were happy scenes of reunification, but there were some sad faces of those who received the bad news that their loved ones had given their lives to protect the lives of others. Emron was a hero, to whom they wanted to elevate as their young brave king. When he politely declined, they came with precious stones and other riches. He refused their gifts, telling them that he did not have any need for those things. The people were confused and surprised. In their long lives they had not come across anyone who rejected both riches and a kingdom. What type of person was their new hero?

5

To the north of the town there flowed a great river. Where the river had its source and where it emptied, no one knew. People were afraid of this river and lived far away from its banks. Most of the time this river was calm, but sometimes the level of water gradually rose and overflowed into nearby areas, destroying everything in its path. One day Emron saw a big procession moving in the river's direction.

There were a lot of people who went singing and chanting. They all were male, both young and old, even children. They looked frightened and unhappy. Emron asked what all was about and was told that the river water was rising, leaving them with no choice but to do what they had to do. And what was that? He asked. They looked in astonishment, but remembered that he was a foreigner. He was told that whenever the river's water reached a dangerous level that was a sign that the mighty river was demanding a sacrifice from them. So traditionally they used to give a young virgin to the river as a bride to appease his anger.

"And where is the bride?" he asked. She was not allowed to be the part of the procession and was to be brought by his father later on, they told him.

"How did they decide whom to sacrifice?" he inquired again, curiously. That was simple, all they had to do was to find the most beautiful and innocent looking girl was the answer.

Emron came with the procession to the riverbank and watched the people who were weeping and crying, begging the river to be kind and merciful to them. This wailing stopped as they came to know that bride was approaching. They watched with grief the young girl and her pale father.

Both of them were walking as if in a trance or perhaps they were drugged. Emron could not see the face of the young girl, but could well imagine how terrorised she must have been at that moment. She was wearing a typical bridal dress and walked unsteadily. A few older people came forward to support her in her last few steps toward the river. Hard winds were blowing, making the river water more powerful and ferocious. The more these people chanted certain words and phrases, the stormier the water became.

"Bring the bride forward! Bring the bride forward!" some elderly people cried in a loud voice. Emron watched the whole scene with horror, as he couldn't believe his eyes. He remained paralysed, as if bewitched.

A young girl was being sacrificed in front of his eyes. A life quenched, a youth drowned and all for what? But there was nothing he could do to stop it. It was their sacred tradition. It was their belief and sacrifice, what right did he have to say anything?

He couldn't watch the last rites and turned to go back, with a saddened heart. "You are a coward again," his conscience taunted, reminding him of the sad memory, when he saw all of his companions slain one by one, and he had kept watching from his hiding place.

"Stop!" Emron turned and shouted at the top of his throat. The young girl was already a few yards into the river, aided by two men. Everyone looked at him with questioning faces.

He rushed into the water and brought the girl out. "No!" he cried again. It was wrong to drown the poor girl. Their tradition was not something to be proud of or to be followed. There was a cry of indignation. People were shocked at his daring and were showing their anger. He was a brave man, their hero, to whom they loved and respected, but challenging their faith, traditions, and beliefs could not be tolerated! They angrily demanded that he should let the girl go so that they could offer the river his new bride.

His interference was considered a bad omen and they

could expect some calamity to befall them. Emron tried to convince them that a human sacrifice was no guarantee that the river would not overflow, but he failed. "Maybe I am unable to make you realise the gravity of your mistake, but there is no way that you can drown this poor girl," he said resolutely.

Many people rushed towards him in anger, but became afraid and withdrew when he drew his sword, announcing that he meant business. Emron could see faces mixed with anger, fear, and anxiety. He took hold of the young girl, who trembled like a leaf in a strong wind, and lead her back to the town, followed by others who were going, discussing this unprecedented, awful happening.

The news had reached the town before they arrived. People started gathering from all directions. Emron felt encircled and threatened by the anger and hostility of the people, who kept staring at him, demanding the girl, so they could proceed with their sacrifice.

"You want to sacrifice?" Emron shouted, not caring about the safety of his own life. "Go jump into the river yourself!" he shouted, trying to make them understand that sacrificing the girl was to be of no good and that the river was not a man who could marry the girl.

But there were a few persons whose hearts were touched by his speech. So he was not alone anymore. The atmosphere was of mutiny, people arguing bitterly, demanding their right to practice their own rituals without the interference of outsiders. The water kept rising.

"Go fetch the commander, we must arrest this stubborn, arrogant young man!" someone cried in fury.

"Bring whomever you want, but no one can touch Emron," answered his friends, showing their determination to stand by his side, even if they disagreed to his judgement, and decision.

When the commander and his soldiers arrived they were faced with a threatening situation. He tried to calm down the two parties, who were equally determined to have their will seen through.

"Let them have the girl. It's a matter of belief. If they believe that they can save themselves by sacrificing her, don't stand in their way. They shall hate you for that."

"Better be hated than to let them kill an innocent, helpless person," Emron told him firmly.

"Arrest this stupid man," shouted someone.

"We'll die but won't allow anybody to come near him!" challenged one foreign merchant.

The commander realised that the situation was getting out of hand. He needed a quick solution if he was to avoid an open confrontation and a bloodbath. He quickly looked around and asked who the father of the girl was. He came near to him and asked, "Being the guardian of this girl, do you agree that she should be sacrificed?" The middle-aged man with a pale face looked at the crowd and seemed scared, but then looked at his daughter and felt terrible pity for her. He cried aloud and said that he did not want his daughter to be the sacrificial offering. A great silence fell over the crowd, as if they couldn't believe their ears.

"If the guardian of this girl disagrees, there is no way you can sacrifice the girl," the commander gave his verdict. He asked everyone to leave.

The crowd dispersed in disappointment and anger. They were angry with Emron and his friends; they were angry with the girl's father and even at the commander who had taken the side of the foreigners.

Emron sent the girl and her father to their home. A few of his friends were to guard and protect them there, while he himself went to the riverside. The water level was still rising.

"What shall happen if the water overflows? Our town is a lowland, we will not have any chance to run away," said one of his worried friends.

"Instead of worrying, go and prepare an evacuation."

"A what?" asked another man surprised.

"Yes, I mean what I said," told Emron. "Transport women, children and elderly to the nearest hills." "But do you know how much time that requires?" The same man asked.

"Yes." He was not only aware, but had seen with his own eyes how fast they could move in case of emergency.

Emron sent them all away, but remained at the riverbank and watched the flow and level of water, which reminded him of the gravity of the situation. It could be a matter of days or hours, before the mighty river would rush out to claim all that actually did not belong to it.

The only remaining people in the town were a number of soldiers and other young men waiting in readiness for any signal from Emron to rush out on their fresh horses to the safety of the hills. They dared not to go near the angry river, because they did not want to be the victims of someone else's sin. "If I were Emron, I would not dare to be that close to the river. After what he has done, depriving him of his wife," said one local seriously.

They waited and waited; at last they saw a horseman riding towards them with full speed,from the direction of the river and started preparing themselves to flee. The horseman signed for them to wait. "I have great news!" he shouted.

The water level had not only stopped increasing during the last ten hours, but had even started falling. Even the flow of water had diminished. The danger was not over yet, but they had reason to hope. It took two more days until the level of the river water stabilised, and they could declare that the danger was over. Families were brought back from the hills and life took its natural course once again. Those people, who were against Emron, were relieved but were still not convinced that he was right in hindering them from making a sacrifice.

*   *   *

The life of the girl was destroyed; no person would ever marry her after having the knowledge that she was the bride of the river. But the father of the girl and many other locals were very happy and impressed with Emron.

Emron was content and pleased with himself and that was more important than anything else. Neither the opposition of certain people scared him, nor the praise and gratitude of others could make him feel elevated. He was what he was, if people loved him for that or hated him; it mattered not at all to him.

*   *   *

The father of Salisa, the girl he had saved, came to Emron and told him that it was his wish or rather the wish of his whole family to invite him to dinner. He humbly asked him to honour them with his visit.

Emron thanked him for the kind invitation and accepted it without much pondering. A few days later, he visited the family and was received with great warmth and respect. Salisa, her two younger sisters, younger brother, and parents welcomed him with big smiles. Salisa´s mother came forward, tried to speak, but was overwhelmed by her sentiments. She raised her hands and blessed him. He could understand what she was trying to convey. After some time everyone became more relaxed and talkative. Salisa was first to break the ice. She was a courageous, bold and confident girl, who didn't hesitate to tell him what she felt when she had confronted her own death.

"I knew there was no point in refusing, denying or fighting my fate. But my submission couldn't subdue my desire to live," she explained to Emron.

That day she had been terrified and had no hope of surviving. She was more surprised to learn that he was trying to save her life, but was sure that the efforts were to be of no use. The fact that she was still alive was nothing but a miracle, and the man who could make that miracle happen was no other than Emron. She thanked him from the bottom of her heart for the life that he had saved, and for the bravery he had shown by resisting the will of such a crowd.

"I owe my life to you," Salisa said with a bow.

The family reminded him of his time at Hakim's and he

felt happy and relaxed. He started visiting them as often as he could. Each time he came, the whole family was joyous. He liked all of them and was very impressed with Salisa, who was very intelligent and witty. Without knowing it himself, Emron had fallen in love with her. He kept coming to her home, always finding excuses. One day he visited her family but could not meet her, because she had gone visiting a relative. He felt strange and left earlier.

"Maybe we´ll move somewhere else," Salisa´s father told him one day.

"Why?" Emron inquired with a surprise.

"You know, no one shall ever marry Salisa if we go on living here." Emron agreed with him. The way that those people functioned, it was impossible for any of them to marry a girl who had been the river's wife. Emron suggested a few places where they could go and live. He knew his friends would help them.

That night came the revelation of how much he had gotten attached to Salisa. Thoughts of losing her made him restless and anguished. He did not want to confess that he was in love, but he had all the symptoms of being lovesick.

For many days he remained at home, not meeting anyone. During this period he realised that he was incomplete and lonely and needed a partner that he loved dearly. The feelings he had for Salisa, and to which he considered feelings of friendship, was nothing else than love for her. It was the right time. Emron decided to go and meet Salisa to confess his love for her, and even ask if she wanted to marry him.

*   *   *

Salisa was surprised by his declaration, and kept quiet for some time. Then, she said in a sad voice that she respected and admired his beautiful qualities, but that she could not marry him.

"Why is that?" Emron asked. Did she want to marry someone else?

She told him that he had saved her life, and she could give up that life for him with a smile on her face. But she couldn't live with the knowledge that he pitied her and made a sacrifice in marrying her.

Emron laughed, "what sacrifice?" he asked. "I'm in love with you. You know I'm not from here and I am not afraid of any river or any other entity. I promise to always hold you dear and love you, and that I'll do regardless of if you marry me or not!"

Salisa looked deep in his eyes and saw truthfulness in them. Her beautiful eyes glittered with happiness after hearing his declaration of love; she shyly bowed her head and agreed to accept his offer.

She was extremely happy to know that Emron loved her too. She felt very lucky to find the love of her dream prince. Salisa´s father wanted her to marry in a traditional manner, with a great feast, but the couple insisted to have a very simple ceremony, where only relatives and close friends were invited to attend.

*   *   *

The news about the marriage was indeed great news for everyone in the town. Everyone kept talking about it. Some were very happy, because it meant that Emron was to become a part of the town, but there were others who were furious. First he had angered and insulted the people by stopping them from practising their beliefs, causing a long-term grudge of the river, which was to punish this act sooner or later. Now he was salting their injuries by marrying her. They felt angered but helpless. It was beyond their power to stop this marriage, but nobody could stop their tongues.

They started spreading rumours that the couple had a relationship long before the incident of sacrifice day and that was the actual reason for Emron's saving her. The river knew all about her and therefore had rejected her as a bride. "She was not even a virgin." The rumours were many, they were low and spiteful, and they kept coming to the couples' ears.

Salisa used to cry but Emron gave her comfort, telling her that the best answer to all accusations and gossips was to ignore them. The more those ill willed people knew about her suffering, the more bold they grew. Emron felt so helpless. He wanted to put an end to all that, but no spear, sword or arrow on the earth could do the job. He so desperately wanted to protect his wife, but failed to be her shield. The poisonous arrows of the vile and spite kept injuring the body and soul of his partner.

By the time Salisa gave birth to a beautiful child, the situation had gotten so bad that Emron was truly concerned. She refused to go out and meet other people, or even to take fresh air. She would hold her baby and cry for hours, and that would surprise Emron who always considered his wife to be bold, confident and courageous. So devastated was Salisa that Emron felt that there was no other option but to leave the place. He took his wife and child and said goodbye to all relatives of Salisa and to his friends, who were not very many. They all were silent and sad, and didn't try to stop them. They knew the situation had become unbearable and that perhaps leaving really was the only solution.

Salisa wept silently, saying goodbye to her siblings, parents, and other relatives. Her heart ached to leave all those whom she had known, lived with, and loved all her life. Salisa's father was a wealthy trader who tried to give them money, but Emron refused to take it. He had decided to go and live with the people he had known better, than to go and live with complete strangers. So he turned west, the direction he had come from.

"Thankless town!" Salisa said in a sad bitter voice. "And how they've rewarded you for your deeds!"

"This town has given me all I could ever dream of," Emron said with a great smile, pointing to her and their few-month old baby. "You are my treasures," he said again, pretending that he was not hurt.

6

Emron and Salisa had quickly adjusted to their new surrounding and were content. The only thing that kept worrying Emron was Salisa´s health. Her beautiful face had a constant pale look, her eyes were ever surrounded with dark circles, and her body was getting thinner and weaker. He took her to many doctors, but they were unable to diagnose her disease, so they could not treat her. He had almost forgotten about the wizard, but now he desperately wanted to see him.

"Maybe he can tell me what's wrong with Salisa and cure her?"

Very shortly afterwards, Salisa was a wreck. Her breast milk dried out, she got tired very quickly and felt like fainting even after the most minor effort. It was not long before she was ordered to take bed rest.

"Is she dying?" Emron wondered with anxiety. What was to become of him and his infant son? He dreaded the idea.

Emron could not bear to see her suffering and decided to call for her family. They all came immediately, leaving everything behind. They were shocked to see her in such a serious condition and wept. There was little hope for her recovery, and the fear of losing her made their hearts bleed. What was wrong with her? What had made her youth wither like that? They were unable to understand. She had been very sensitive from childhood, but to become that sick of sensitivity was an unimaginable thing for them.

Emron was sitting and thinking of Salisa and her mysterious sickness. He felt terribly sad. Even he, a born optimist, had started losing hope of her getting better. "I´ve been searching for you everywhere, and here you are," Emron heard someone say and looked up in a tired, distracted manner. Seeing Khafil standing before him with a big smile, Emron jumped with a renewed hope and energy. "I have news!" Khafil spoke. But Emron did not let him complete his sentence. He told Khafil that there was an emergency and his help was required. He took hold of his hand and ran towards his house.

*   *   *

Khafil looked at Salisa for a long moment and asked Emron if she was his wife. "Yes," he answered. "Please, say what's wrong with her!"

Khafil requested everyone to be out of the room, so he could make the check-ups. He came out of the room after some time and looked very serious. "I believe that your wife is dying," he told Emron.

"What's wrong with her, Doc?" Emron asked in a sad and broken voice.

"I'm not sure yet," was Khafil's answer. And he could not suggest any cure until he did knew what she suffered from. He promised to come back shortly and disappeared. When he did come back, he had a potion which he gave to Salisa in order to stabilize her deteriorating condition. If it did not help, then there was no medicine in the world that could.

Khafil told Salisa's family to stay close and watch her while he went out for a walk with Emron. He congratulated Emron for having a beautiful and strong boy. He could not promise him that he could cure his wife, but was to do all that was in his power. He told Emron that the decision had been made regarding his request.

"What request?" Emron wondered. Khafil looked a little hurt, but ignored his forgetfulness and continued.

"My request for your freedom of movement is granted, but it's conditional."

"Oh, that!" was the brief reaction he could get from Emron, and knew it was not the right moment to discuss anything with him. He changed the subject.

"We can talk about this matter some other time. Right

now we're facing the serious matter of your wife's health. I'll consult some friends and get back to you as soon as possible," said Khafil and left Emron alone to deal with his worries.

* * *

Khafil returned the next day, going straight to Salisa´s bedside and checked her eyes, tongue and heartbeat.
"Continue giving this potion!" he ordered. "Your wife has been attacked," said Khafil very seriously. "There is nothing anybody can do here to save her. This slow poisoning doesn't have an antidote in this part of the world."

"I will go to the ends of the Earth to find that antidote!" Emron spoke quickly, searching for some kind of hope.

Khafil looked equally worried, "Your finding the remedy is not enough. Her condition is very serious. We're already late; we have to do something quickly."

Khafil asked Emron to tell her relatives that they were going far away for a treatment and asked him to get ready for his journey. Emron, his wife, and Khafil left early in the morning and came out of town to a secluded place. Salisa was half unconscious, hardly reacting to any questions. Khafil explained to him in detail everything about the world he was about to venture to. The cautions he was to take, the people he was to look for, and many more instructions.

Khafil made it clear that Emron would have to handle everything on his own. He was only to aid in transportation. "Take this," he said, giving Emron a little cloth bag. "Inside there are some precious stones you can give to the doctor as a fee, and some dry flowers, which you can wither in the wind. I'll know when you're ready to come back. But remember, do it only in some secluded place." He asked Emron to close his eyes and sit next to his wife. He did as he was told last time and took a deep breath, and waited until he smelled a different odour than he was used to and knew they had come to their destination.

He opened his eyes and found that he was sitting with Salisa on a barren piece of land. He did not know which direction to move. Salisa was too weak, and most of the time in an unconscious state, so he had to carry her on his back. He knew that time was short and he had to find a doctor who could cure her. He started running in one direction. It was dry and hot there, and he had difficulty breathing. It felt as if he was breathing and inhaling fire.

Suddenly he saw a flying dragon. His heart leapt into his throat when it started coming in his direction. But the dragon did not attack him; instead it landed safely a few yards away from him. Out of the dragon-like beast's, belly appeared a female who approached him. "Who are you? And where do you want to go?" she inquired.

Emron felt comfort seeing that she was a human and not hostile. He told her that he was looking for a doctor because his wife was dying. She asked him to follow her to the dragon's side. She opened the belly of the animal, helped him place Salisa on a seat, and told him apologetically that she was to transport his wife while he had to walk for few hours. She said that she would be waiting for him there. Without making a sound the dragon lifted herself from the ground, started flying and disappeared out of his sight.

*   *   *

Emron kept walking and running till he came to green fields. He was not sure where the woman was supposed to meet him. He looked around, but there wasn't anyone around. Suddenly he turned and saw a young man standing behind him. He was searching for a woman; he tried to describe to the stranger the woman he had met earlier.

"I'm just a farmer," the young man answered. Emron again explained that he was looking for a woman in a dragon. The mentioning of the word dragon worked like a code. The young man asked him to follow. They walked in the fields of some tall crops, into which they went as if in a labyrinth. After some time he felt as if they were walking in some kind of tunnel. He became surprised to see that he had come to an underground town. There were very many people, men, women, and children there. After quite a long walk he came to the woman he had met earlier.

"Welcome to our country, Atrostia and to our humble quarters, the underground town of Freedia!" The woman said smilingly. "Your wife is in a very serious condition. We can't tell you if she shall overcome the most dangerous venom that she has been exposed to or whether she will die. But we hope that her young body will go on resisting."

"Do your doctors know what she suffers from?" asked Emron.

"Of course they do. In our part of the world, this is the most common weapon used against us. I don't know anything about who is doing this to her."

How did she know that he was not from there, he asked. "In our country there are only two types of people. So it's easy to recognize an outsider. Emron did not understand her but kept quiet. The woman asked him who he was, where he came from, how he could reach their country, how he knew that he could find the cure there, and many other questions. He did not hesitate to tell her about Khafil, and how he helped them. Words like 'magic' and 'wizard' made her look more defensive and alert. Who was that wizard? What did Emron know of him? What did he look like? He could see that he had alarmed her. He tried to calm her down; assuring that the wizard who helped him wasn't someone to be afraid of, but the woman remained nervous. Emron understood that there was something behind her fear of Khafil, so he decided to figure out what that was. It was his turn to ask questions. From the woman's answer he could understand why she was so nervous.

She told him that her lovely Atrostia was wonderful in all aspects. It contained all that one could think of; it had incredible forests, sky-high snow covered mountains, fertile plains, deserts, sandy beaches, and beautiful valleys. A varying climate made it possible to have fruits, vegetables, many other crops all the year around. Their country was full of resources and they never felt any scarcity of anything. The unending abundance had freed them from physical labour, so they enhanced their mental capacities. The minds of the people kept exploring, developing, and discovering new solutions for old problems. They learned how to build high lofty buildings to dwell in. They could transport heavy stones without any problem and could make huge palaces with them. They had discovered artificial lights that replaced daylight in the night. They had even created dragons that could take them wherever they wanted. The people of the country were happy and lived in peace and harmony, but then something terrible happened. The princess of Atrostia married a man that nobody knew. He was a man without any family or any confirmed background. The princess was in love and cared less to know anything about him.

After the death of the king, the young princess became the queen, and that was the beginning of the misery of their country. The queen started giving herself completely to her ambitious, power hungry and ruthless husband. She functioned as if bewitched, losing all of her integrity and mental faculties. That husband of hers was a magician, a sorcerer, who had plans of his own. He combined magic with their scientific secrets, which had been entrusted to the state and soon he had an army of half humans, half machines. They seemed to be on an experimental stage, but were a great threat to all.

The woman kept quiet for a while and regarded him thoughtfully. She could see that he was taken aback by her story.

She continued with her tale. The princess's evil husband Dolec had brainwashed not only his wife, but most of the citizens of Atrostia too, who believed that they were the greatest power in the world, and its resources were to be used only by the elite. The state was the absolute truth and those running the affairs of state were unquestionable. But of course there were rebels who fought the monster Dolec. But with every passing day, they found it more and more difficult to resist his strength. The city of Freedia was the last stronghold of the rebels. They were forced to go underground because it was impossible for them to hide in the open. "They did not expect us to be working underground because that is their speciality," said the woman.

"Do you live in this underground city?" Emron asked.

"No. We don't live here all the time, but spend most of our time here, trying to find ways to fight back," she answered. They kept talking. She was very interested to know about the life in his part of the world, and listened with disbelief about how primitively they lived. "How I wish to be living in those times and places," she said with a sigh.

"Why don't you take the dragon and fly to our part of the world?" Emron asked.

"For one single reason, each dragon is driven by some special stones which are very small. They cannot travel long distances," she answered.

They had been living in isolation for the centuries, and were taught that beyond the great ocean lived monsters and untamed dragons. The world out there was hostile and inhabitable, so people were even afraid to think of that.

"Do you mean no one from your big, great country has ever been to the other parts of the world?" Emron asked.

"I don't know, but I can guess that our kings and the elite knew everything, and found it in their interest to not have any contact with the primitive part of the world." Emron learned very many interesting things from her.

Emron asked the woman, Priva, if he could visit his wife. She told him that it was not very wise to do so. The venom had had such a long time to affect his wife's body that she was practically dead at the time Priva had met her. She was in a coma, from which she could never return. Emron was told to have this possibility in mind. It would be a miracle if she ever recovered.

He insisted to be beside his wife. If she were to die, he wished to be holding her hand, but if she was to live and come out of the coma then he wanted to welcome her back into his life. After some hesitation, Priva agreed to take him to the place Salisa was having her last fight. It was less of her own fight and more of a struggle between life and death.

When Emron looked at her motionless body, it seemed for a while that she was already dead. Her pale face, closed eyes and unmoved body made him weep with empathy. He wished that he could share her suffering or bring back her health. He could give up his own life to save hers. He bowed slowly and kissed her, tears rolling down his cheeks. He felt the saltish water in his mouth and kept staring at Salisa, holding her cold hand. "Please don´t die, Salisa. I will not be able to live without you. Please come back, please," Emron was talking in a whisper, as if she was listening to him.

*   *   *

Salisa remained unconscious for two weeks. Her physical condition was stable and that in itself was a good sign. She was getting a regular treatment of the antidote and other medicines. The colour of her skin and eyes was getting more normal. The young female doctor was now more hopeful of bringing her patient back to life. Emron spent hours sitting beside his wife's bed, hoping and praying. No one could describe his feelings when Salisa made her first movement, indicating that she had begun the slow process of returning from the no-man's land, lying somewhere between life and death. He rushed to inform the doctor, but she was not there at the moment. Salisa kept making small, weak movements, but still was not reacting to the sounds and voices.

The doctor said that it could take days before she would become fully conscious. But already the second day, Salisa got out of her unconscious state. She opened her eyes, looked at Emron and tried to smile. He smiled back and held her hand, without saying anything. He was cautious as told by the doctor. His happiness knew no bounds, but he had to remain calm and collected. He signalled her to keep quiet and went out to give the good news to the doctor, who came running with excitement, made some observations, told Salisa to keep silent and still. "You're a very lucky man," the doctor said with a smile and satisfaction on her face.

*   *   *

Priva was delighted by the news. They were to wait until Salisa was fully recovered but then both of them had to leave immediately, because their stay in Astrosia was full of dangers. Priva and her friends were at war with the state and they didn't want them to be caught in the middle. "You're our guests and your safety is vital to us," said Priva.

Emron asked if he could help them in any way. She smiled, but looked tired and less enthusiastic. She didn't think that Emron could assist them in their impossible task. He wished to see their country but was bluntly refused.

He was then politely told that it was not possible. The knowledge of their presence in Atrostia could be the end of their resistance. "They would close all physical and invisible doors leading to your world; they would ultimately catch you," Priva said, not explaining what was to follow.

However hopeless the situation was, they had only one way to proceed, to fight with all that they had. They had to win or perish. Emron gave up his insistence on visiting and seeing all of those wonders she had talked about. The enemy of his new friends seemed not only mighty in an ordinary sense, but had even supernatural powers at their disposal. He was impressed by the bravery of these beings, which had taken on such an impossible task, which could bring nothing but defeat, death, and destruction.

*   *   *

Before leaving Atrostia, both Emron and Salisa thanked each person who had given them their help, friendship and hospitality. They were always going to remember them. They were especially thankful to Priva and the doctor, without whom Salisa would not have survived. They felt it was difficult to express their gratitude and other feelings. Emron took the small bag out of his pocket and laid the different coloured stones in the palm of his hand.

"These are our humble gifts to you two," Emron said and gave them to Priva. "You and the doctor can divide them as you wish." Priva tried to protest, but couldn't complete her sentence.

"Where did you get these?" she asked.

She looked happy and excited. "These are very rare stones. They have incredible properties and we've been desperately looking for them. How could we ever thank you for bringing us such a wonderful gift!" Priva said, embracing and kissing them both.

The return from Atrostia was less dramatic. They came, with the help of Priva, to a secluded place and said goodbye, since she didn't want to meet the wizard. When she was gone, Emron took the dry petals of flowers from his little bag and dispersed them in the wind. A few minutes later he saw the wizard, who signalled that Salisa was not supposed to see him.

Emron and Salisa sat down, waiting for Khafil. "Close your eyes and try to smell the atmosphere," Emron said to Salisa. She did as she was told. "Oh look, Khafil is here." Salisa heard her husband say and opened her eyes, and saw the smiling little old man. She could hardly notice that they had travelled a distance of thousands of miles. When Emron and Salisa entered their home everyone started dancing with joy. They were all showing their happiness by jumping, shouting, and singing. The only person who kept looking at Salisa with tearful eyes was her father. He had chosen to show his happiness by crying tears of joy. "You were completely lost to us. It's your second return from the land of death," he cried, embracing his child.

7

Salisa´s parents had made up their minds. They did not intend to go back to their home, and wanted to live somewhere near to their daughter's home. Her father was returning alone in order to sell his business and other property and then come back to join his family. Salisa was very happy with their decision and asked them to live with her till they found a suitable house to live in. The only person who had remained untouched and unaffected by the emotional turmoil of the last few weeks was Amroush, Emron and Salisa´s child.

He had hardly been aware that both his parents had been away, and he did not know how close he had been to losing his mother. Khafil came to visit from time to time, but didn't have any serious discussions with Emron, knowing that he was too busy with his private life. He was extra kind to Amroush; he would play with him and make him laugh.

Emron requested Khafil to find out who had poisoned his wife, but Khafil refused. It was not important anyway, they had moved to another town, and had other realities to face, and beside that Salisa was alive and healthy, what more did they want? The plot to take her life had failed. So it was time to go forward and not look back. He asked Emron to tell him about his visit to Atrostia, about its people and other impressions he had. Emron confessed that he had not seen anything of the country, but anyhow told him all he had learned from Priva and others. Khafil listened with great interest and looked worried. He told Emron that he was glad to hear that he and Salisa had had the luck of meeting the right people who could help them, because sending them there was a great risk he had taken. But it was the only way they could try to save the life of Salisa. Emron tried to ask questions about Atrostia, but Khafil suddenly lost the mood to discuss about that country. Instead he took up the matter, which was of importance to him, the request for freedom of movement. He told Emron that the request had been granted, but only conditionally.

"What a quick response!" said Emron sarcastically.

"Things work differently in other worlds, and so does the concept of time," the old man carelessly replied.

To get the freedom of movement, a condition was attached. Emron had to do something of great importance for the Genii in return. It was a special task that would be difficult for him to accomplish. There was a certain big country, where many different tribes lived. This whole area was very thinly populated by human beings, but had a large Genii population. The area was considered important because it was thought to be the cradle of Genii civilisation. The Genii of the whole world and other planets were coming there on pilgrimage all year round. The problem was that the human tribes could not tolerate each other's presence; so perpetual warfare had made the whole area filled with so much negative energy that even the Genii found it unbearable. They were worried about their holy places, their Genii population and other difficulties arising out of the problem.

"How do I fit into the picture?" asked Emron.

"It will be your task to make those tribes friendly with each other, so that the negative forces of the area do not reach explosive levels!" Khafil explained.

"How am I to accomplish that?" asked a surprised Emron.

"I don't know. You have to figure it out yourself," said Khafil.

Emron laughed nervously, and paused thoughtfully before he responded. "I don't see how anyone can stop warriors from spilling the blood of one another, and I don't even need freedom of movement." Khafil reminded him that his statement was untrue. He had recently enjoyed that freedom and consequently had been able to save the life of his wife. Emron confessed that the objection was right; nevertheless, he was unable to take any such mission. He had a family to take care of.

Khafil tried to convince him that it was his duty to accept the challenge, and try to get something, which was not offered, to humans. It was a golden opportunity, which he should absolutely avail himself of. He didn't want to take no for an answer, and gave him some time to think it over. "Think deeply what you can achieve with this freedom," Khafil uttered before going his way.

Emron didn't even want to think of the subject. He had given his definite answer that he was not interested, but somewhere he still suffered from anxiety. Khafil had been kind and helpful. He was responsible for Salisa´s recovery, was it right to refuse him? Was he acting in accordance to his own nature? Emron kept confronting those questions and felt bad.

Salisa could see that he was disturbed. She tried a few times to inquire what was bothering him, but he would evade her questions. "Don't say it's nothing. I can see your mind is straying somewhere far," Salisa spoke, confronting him until he told her what was bothering him. He felt forced to tell her everything.

She listened without asking any questions. After he had told everything, she looked very serious. Emron was expecting some reaction from her, but she kept silent. Emron could see that he had affected his wife. He was sorry to have involved her in his own problems. But what was done was done, and he couldn't change that.

"When shall Khafil come?" Salisa asked.

"He can come whenever it pleases him. He is already informed of my decision ," answered Emron. Salisa sat down with him and held his hand. She told him that she had been thinking seriously about his dilemma. He was split between his responsibilities towards his family and his wish to repay the kindness of the wizard. She agreed that they didn't need any freedom for themselves, but how wonderful it could be to travel with that incredible speed. "Imagine us going and visiting those wonderful people who had helped save my life," she said, caressing the back of his hand. She continued, saying that she considered him a great person with a big heart, and she didn't want to stand in the way between him and his destiny. She would miss him terribly, but would pray and await his safe return. "Now I have my family around and little Amroush to take care of, so you should go if that is what you must do," said Salisa, looking into Emron's eyes.

Emron tried to speak, but she stopped him by telling him that he could go on thinking about the matter until Khafil was to contact him.

*   *   *

When Khafil arrived a few days later, Emron was still not very convinced of taking on this impossible mission.

"You have nothing to lose. If you fail in your quest, there are no consequences. But if you succeed, you would have accomplished something that no one has done before," said Khafil. "I know it's going to be tough explaining to your wife the need for you to go."

Emron said that she already was informed of the matter. He told Khafil that his wife was the most understanding and cooperative partner he could ever wish for.

Khafil looked pleased to know that his wife did not object to the idea. "Look," he tried his strongest argument. "As I have helped you come this far, maybe some other day you will return the favour for someone else who might need it as desperately as you did!" Emron thought for a few seconds and finally agreed to take on the challenge.

"When can you transport me?" he asked.

"No, you're to travel in a normal human manner," was his cold answer. "As I told you before, I have a limit, and I don't want to exhaust all the possibilities just on you." For a moment, Emron had a strong temptation to turn down his request, but he had already given his word and couldn't revoke it. He had a feeling of being trapped, but the moment of decision was gone, forcing him to take the means that were available. "You see, you have already become lazy and addicted to easy and comfortable travel," Khafil said jokingly, he had noticed the irritated face of Emron. Khafil spent more time with Emron, giving him important information and instructions about the long hard journey that awaited him.

*　　*　　*

Emron went on his journey, riding on his trusted horse, which was still strong and powerful. There wasn't anyone he could trust more than Rino. Ever since he had left Zariba and Aseem, Rino had served him with love and affection. He served him without caring for hunger or thirst in peaceful times or on the battlefield. Rino was his silent companion, his dearest friend and his pet to which he didn't need to say or signal anything twice. His alert eyes picked his slightest signal and he obeyed, even it meant certain death.

"Take a younger horse that has more energy," said his father in law, but Emron smiled and told him that he needed not only a horse to ride on but also his trusted companion.

He travelled through the towns, passing through the wastelands and deserts, crossed streams and rivers, climbed up hills and down valleys. He didn't want to lose time. His eyes were fixed on his destination and his heart remained with his wife and child. It took months even to get near the vast country, which bordered the area he was heading to. He was dead tired and so was his horse. Emron decided to rest and gather his energy.

*　　*　　*

Yanobia lay to the north of that tribal territory. It was a powerful country with a vast army and a very strong king. Yanobia and the tribal lords had no direct confrontation right at that moment, but their history was filled with attempts from the Yanobian side to subdue the region. All the attempts to do so had failed. Yanobian kings were unable to understand just how those tribes functioned. They were constantly at each other's throats, inviting foreign intervention, but the moment an outsider army arrived there, they all were like one giant tribe, destroying the invading armies, or forcing them to retreat with devastating loss. If there was anyone in the world who could tell anything about those tribes, it was the Yanobians.

The Yanobians were not very friendly people. They were not fond of foreigners, but the size and the strength of their country made them less suspicious or afraid of outsiders. They were loud, arrogant and boastful people. He soon learned that they were fond of drinking, which made them violent and short tempered. So if he was to avoid trouble, he had to stay away from their Sirbs, places where they could get drunk. One could see the young soldiers moving around, but people didn't seem to be afraid of them, because they never intervened.

"Why don't they try to stop fights?" Emron asked one Yanobian, pointing to the soldiers.

"Because it's none of their business. They are hired only to go to war or to protect the elite." So he came to know that the law allowed individuals to solve their problems the way they saw fit. No doubt he was aware of the laws of the jungle, but was surprised that it was valid there.

Emron decided to be extra careful, as he did not want to have any confrontation with anyone. He wanted nothing but to rest and gather information about the tribes. Most of the people avoided talking about the tribes. The few people who did talk about them were hateful and showed spite for the tribal people. The public opinion described these people as cruel, deprived of feelings and other human qualities. They were harsh with their tongues, impatient in their actions and had no tolerance. They were very different from each other, and yet one could see more similarities and differences in their nature and behaviours. They all loved power, their freedom, and independence, but fought fiercely to subdue others in order to gain dominance. "No doubt they're amazing people," he thought with a smile.

Emron was hungry, so he decided to go out and have lunch. He went to a place and sat in a corner and ordered his meal. The place was full of people. Some were eating; others were busy talking to each other. He was discrete in his observation of people in order to not provoke them. He looked out to the side of the street. Two little girls were passing in a playful manner. They were hardly nine or ten years of age. One girl said something and both giggled. Then one ran to pinch the other one, who ran also laughing. But they didn't see a man sitting near the street having his meal and fell on him. Everybody watched the scene and laughed. The girl became embarrassed, got back on her feet and apologised to the man she had disturbed. The tall, strong man was furious; he got up and slapped the little girl. She cried and protested, but the man gave another slap on her face. Emron watched but stayed at his place. The girl started screaming in pain and insult. The man became more furious and was about to hit her third time, when Emron could not control himself any longer and got up from his seat.

Everybody sat and enjoyed the development, laughing at the misery of the little girl. Emron faced the man and told him that to beat a child was not an act of bravery. If he really was a man, he should pick someone his own size.

"What about you?" the man challenged him. Emron told the man that he was not there to fight with him. All he wanted from him was to leave the poor child alone. The man assumed that Emron was a coward and became more aggressive, and pushed him hard. Emron controlled his anger and turned to go back to his seat, when the man came after him and kicked him from behind, and that was the end of his patience. Emron turned to face his attacker, and landed him with a strong straight first punch. He saw three of the man's friends rushing towards him. He calmly waited for them and their attack. He sent all three kissing the floor, and to remain stationary there. The people around didn't find it amusing any more, they had stopped laughing and were now staring at him.

One young man came near and advised him. "Go, run!"

"Why shall I run, I haven't done anything wrong?" Emron said boldly, going back to his seat.

"Soon someone will call the soldiers," the same man warned him. Emron relayed that he was aware of the fact that the soldiers were apathetic. The young man laughed. "You are really stupid if you believe so. That attitude is for locals and not for foreigners like you and me." Emron saw one of the guests approaching the soldiers. "Run! Come, I can give you a ride until you are safe," the young man gave him an offer. Before answering, Emron looked at the little girl who was fleeing the scene.

"I have a horse of my own," answered Emron.

"Then follow me," said the man, who jumped on his horse and waited for Emron to do the same. Before the soldiers could turn towards them, they were gone.

"I'm hungry, I haven't had the chance to eat my meal," Emron told his companion. "Same here," he said with laughter. "Why did you interfere? You have killed their pleasure."

"It's wrong to beat an innocent child," said Emron. "From which world have you come?" the young man seemed amused.

They found an out-of-the-way, calm place and took their meal and talked to each other there. Emron told the man that he had come from afar; he was interested in rare stones, and had heard that they were in abundance in the area bordering Yanobia. The young man became silent and watched him with interest. Then he started asking more questions. Which direction was he talking about, since it was a huge country? What did he know about the people living there? How did he intend to enter that land? Emron pretended that he knew nothing about the tribes and tribesmen and asked if he could tell him a little about that area, and its inhabitants.

"I can tell you only this; that you should never ever set your foot there, that is my friendly advice," said the man.

"I'll keep it in mind. But why should I avoid those areas?" Emron asked innocently. "Because you're stupid and naïve. That area is not good, not even for the locals. People hate each other and outsiders even more," the young man tried to make his point. He had not heard of any rare stones there, but had much to tell about the people. They were not as bad as most believed, but had no liking for people they did not know. This hatred of strangers had developed with time, and was due to fact that so many attempts had been made to subdue or enslave them. So strong were the feelings that the words 'foreign' and 'aggressor' had become synonymous.

"How can you know so much about these people?" Emron asked. The young man told him that it was because he belonged to one of the tribes, and had to come and live in Yanobia for a short period of time. "People of my tribe don't know that. They wouldn't like it, because even the word 'Yanobia' is unpopular over there." Emron asked why that was so. The young man replied that those tribes did not have big populations, which invoked the invasions of powerful Yanobian armies. All the wounds inflicted by them were still fresh and well remembered. The internal fights among the tribes were something different, said the young man.

"It's more like a family struggle to gain control. But since no tribe is strong enough to succeed, the fighting goes on." Emron asked if the young man could help him to find the area. The man looked in disbelief, and shook his head as if he doubted his mental health. He didn't bother to answer. Emron repeated his request. The young man said angrily, "Why don't you listen to what I tell you? You are not from there, so you are not welcome."

"Ok," said Emron, "I can go on my own."

"If you're tired of life, then proceed," said the young man carelessly. After the meal, he took leave of the young man and headed south in the direction of the tribal area. The young man looked in amazement and deep down felt a pity for Emron who was going towards a certain death. He seemed to be unarmed, but that had little importance, because all the weapons on the Earth were unable to protect him in that hostile land. He stood there thinking for a while before riding after him.

He rode fast and came closer to Emron and said, "I'm heading back home and can give you company till we come to the area." But he made clear that that was to be all, leaving no room for any requests or favours. Once they were to reach the tribal area they were to separate and go their own ways. If he still wished to enter into that territory that was to be at his own risk and responsibility. Emron agreed to his conditional company. "You have a beautiful, strong beast," said the young man.

"A lifelong companion," said Emron and smiled.

*   *   *

The young man, Bental, was not very talkative but when he spoke he used hard and cutting words. He was too straightforward and rude to some extent, but that was his style. He was using his power of speech to communicate and cared less how his words sounded. He was well acquainted with the difficult way leading to his home tracts. "I can ride these paths blindfolded," Bental boasted. At one point he halted, as did Emron. He told Emron that they were to approach the border between Yanobia and the tribal territory. Their paths were to separate, as Bental could not take responsibility for him.

"I've found you to be a nice but a stupid person, take my warning and return, while you still have the time," Bental said seriously, but seeing the face of an unafraid, smiling fool, he shrugged his shoulders and moved in one direction without looking back.

It crossed Emron's mind to follow Bental secretly, but he rejected the thought. The mountainous area was not the best place to hide from the hawkish sight of a local. But the question remained. How was he to proceed from that point? He was completely ignorant of the geography of the place, and knew nothing about how those tribes were spread. He waited a few minutes and then decided to continue his journey in the opposite direction of Bental's way. He rode in a very alert, but fearless manner. He kept watching the heights from where he could be attacked. And it didn't take long before he noticed an arrow, which had missed him by a few inches. He rode fast and took cover. His presence in that area was known. He didn't have to search for the tribesmen; they had found him!

He waited for a while and then rode forward in a gallop, reaching a new point where he could find cover. He could see by the looks of the arrows, that it was a single attacker, who would now be looking for a better place to shoot, when he the intruder could make another attempt to escape. He left his horse in the cover and quickly climbed the rocky hills and came to the top. He looked around and soon spotted the man who was ready for the renewed attack, waiting for the opportunity.

A few moments later, Emron was standing behind the tall, strong man. The man, feeling his presence, turned to look back, and before he knew what was happening, Emron had snatched his bow and arrows from him. The man looked very astonished at the quickness of the stranger.

"Why did you want to kill me?" Emron demanded angrily.

"Because you're trespassing in our territory," answered the man, spitting with anger. Emron took the arrows and broke them, gave back the bow to the man and started going downhill without caring to look back at the man. But he paused. Perhaps this man could be of use.

"Maybe you can lead me to the tribal head. I want to have a few words with him," said Emron. Without waiting for his answer, he continued. "I'll wait downhill for you." The surprised man looked at his bow and broken arrows, unable to do anything to stop the stranger. Emron didn't have to wait for long.

The man came down to him and led him to the tribal head, and told him something, pointing to his broken arrows and bow. The tribal leader was not an old man as he had hoped, but a young man, almost of his own age. The leader seemed angry and shouted at the man who had led him there. He took hold of the broken arrows, and came to Emron, and asked,

"Have you done this?"

"Yes, I was the guilty one," answered Emron looking sorry and ashamed.

"You could have killed our man with these arrows," the leader said, "Why didn't you"?

"Because my intention is not to kill, but to have friendship with you," replied Emron.   "Why?" the leader asked, a little amused.

"Because I don't think animosity is something worth striving for, but friendship is."

"Why have you come to our tribal territory?" the young man asked in a hard tone. Emron replied that he did not know much about their land, but had hoped to find some special stones there. He had the intention of asking his permission to be able to do so.

"What made you think that I will grant you the permission?" the young leader taunted, and everybody around laughed. The leader himself felt more at ease and amused.

"You're a funny stranger. Either you're a very dangerous person, or stupid and naïve. I will not kill you before I know which category you fall into," the leader signalled his men to take Emron and lock him up. Better a prisoner than being a dead man, he thought and waited with patience for further happenings to unfold itself.

*   *   *

"You must be very hungry. Eat it," a man said, offering

him a generous piece of bread. "You're a kind man, though I've heard that kindness is a scarcity in these parts of the world," said Emron. The man looked at him and laughed.

"You're a big mouth. We're different from you. We believe more in strong arms than big tongues." He was right, confessed Emron, he was a big mouth, who had been always dreaming of becoming like them, and that was one of the reasons he had come there.

"To become like us, you have to be born here, and learn the arts of warfare from the womb of your mother," the man said and gave him another piece of bread. "Eat!" he said, "who knows if it's your last meal?"

"I'll die happily here," said Emron, unafraid. "To die in the presence of brave people is a privilege, and I'm happy for that." The guard didn't answer, but watched the prisoner with surprise and almost felt pity for him. Emron could tell that he was winning over the man. "I believe that the leader is right. You really are an insane person," the man turned away from him feeling uneasy.

The leader went on some mission along with his fighters, and might have forgotten about the unimportant prisoner back home. But when he came back, Emron had won many hearts. They all pleaded for his life, saying that the man was no harm or threat to them. He was a simpleton, a fool; a good hearted one, who didn't deserve a death penalty. The tribal leader agreed to let him stay for a while.

Emron made them laugh by acting a little clumsy. They considered him a clown, but he did not mind, on the contrary it helped him to form a plan. Whether it was to work or not was still to be seen.

He was providing them with entertainment, holding the sword; he would swing back and forth, pretending to be out of balance by its heavy weight, and they all would laugh. At other times he would grab the bow, and all would run to take cover and laugh.

He told them that he didn't mind hard work, but when they asked him to carry some heavy weight he would pretend to be a weakling. The old, young, women, and children all became fond of Emron, who was considered of average intelligence, but had no physical strength at all. But he did have something that impressed his viewers. He had an incredible positive attitude and persistence. He never got tired of his hopeless efforts of trying to learn.

To play the role of a clown was not an easy task. He had to face the ridicule of people as they laughed and made fun of him. He had to go through humiliation as certain spectators went beyond all bounds to push and degrade him, thinking it was fun.

He kept up the mask and didn't show anger or irritation of their unacceptable behaviour. He was a clown but only in his physical activities, when it came to the mental strength they were aware that he had a sharp tongue. "He's being compensated for a untrained body," someone would say and they all laughed. He would sit and talk with those members of the tribe who were less important. He would give them the kind of respect and importance they had never received before. He listened to their petty problems and gave them council. His popularity increased among the tribesmen, who were not shy to answer his questions about other tribes.

All together, there were seven tribes living in those tracts. The tribe he was staying with was one of the biggest and the most powerful ones. The unending feuds among those tribes were not the most worrying thing for them. Over the centuries, they had become used to the constant fighting. To kill or be killed was an accepted norm. To live was a conditional thing, which required dying. There was a time to live, to love, to hate and ultimately to die, and all that was as natural as were their sorrows and joys. If they were to lose a hundred men in some struggle with the neighbouring tribe, they were to wait for revenge and kill the enemy in double numbers.

What really worried them was the growing power and strength of Yanobia, their eternal adversary. Why didn't they unite themselves against the Yanobians, and crush their dreams to conquer them once and for all? "A permanent peace among the tribes!" they laughed listening to Emron's proposition and terminology. His words were quoted and whoever listened laughed. He was a funny man with funny ideas. They loved to hate each other and could not imagine a day when there was no fear present.

"The sun shall not rise that day," said someone with conviction. He deliberately kept coming with different suggestions, both funny and serious. He wanted them to be mentally ready for the idea of peace. One day he was talking to the head of the tribe, Kidra and praised their expertise of different games. "Are the other tribes equally good in these games?" He asked.

"I can hardly imagine," said Kidra.

"Then you should challenge them. Give them a chance to prove themselves. They shall be humiliated by the defeat," said Emron.

"Giving us a new reason to fight for another century," laughed Kidra. Emron convinced him that it was a great opportunity to prove oneself in a non-war activity.

"How do you behave towards their envoys?" he inquired. Of course, they enjoyed immunity and were never hurt in their long history, Emron was told. "Then send me as an envoy," Emron asked excitedly.

"A foreigner as an envoy of our tribe?" Kidra played with the words, and got amused by the unique idea. "Why not?" he said with a loud laughter. "If they get annoyed and kill you, at least it will not harm our relationship any further," Kidra said in between his prolonged laughter. Emron joined him, pretending that it was a very funny thought.

Emron's reputation had already reached the other tribes, who requested to see his mastery with weapons. He confessed that he could not claim to be a master yet, but whatever he knew was due to his own hard work and the great masters of the tribe. He showed them his skills and made them laugh more than he had ever done since he came to them. He extended the challenge for tribe to meet and compete in the field of games. They all accepted without any hesitation.

"These games and their results should in no way influence the relations of the tribes negatively. You all have to swear to that," said Emron as a final condition. They reluctantly agreed to this as well. He met Bental, who smiled seeing him, but didn't show anyone that he knew Emron. Bental was sitting next to the tribal chief. "Is this young man your brother?" Emron asked the chief.

"No, he's my eldest son," answered the chief. Emron praised the chief and his son.

*   *   *

The day of the games came. They all gathered in big ground, and games started. By the end of the day the host tribe won most of the matches. But as agreed, no unpleasant incident happened. The losers were blaming the loss on the public, who had been supporting their own teams. If they really were good enough they had to arrange the next games in other tribes. He always found a reason to travel to the other tribes; sometimes it was an inquiry about some missing person, sometimes a warning against some certain deed. There were more diplomatic activities than it had been in centuries. The only person who kept mistrusting him was the man who had brought him to the tribe. The man tried a few times to raise the suspicion of the tribe.

"If he is that clumsy, how had he been able to disarm me in such an amazing manner?" The man had argued, making the leader ask the question to Emron.

"That was not difficult," he told everyone. "The man was sleeping, all I had to do was to pick up the arrows and break them." They all laughed and believed it to be true. The only person who could now move around without feeling any danger or threat was Emron, a privilege not even enjoyed by the most powerful tribal leader. All tribesmen knew him and took for granted that he was on some errand. He was pleasant to everyone regardless of if the person in question returned his politeness or treated him harsh or even with disrespect. By often meeting the tribal chiefs, he had learnt a little about them, their likings, frustrations, and their other characteristics. There were for instance a few of them who would never smile, always looking angry, making the air tense around them.

To these tribesmen he tried to be extra pleasant and funny to make them feel relaxed in his company. There were others who were fixated with arms and weapon training, he would request joining them in the training, they would agree and enjoy his painstaking efforts. A few of the tribal chiefs were more reasonable than he expected. One such chief was Bental´s father Robbas, who would agree with Emron that they had enough of quarrels and fights, and needed a permanent solution to their problems, but held no hope for such a possibility. Emron suggested that the tribes could unite under a single king.

"A collective king!" Robbas repeated his words and laughed heartily, very amused by the idea. "Who would be this king? Maybe me!" he asked Emron, who just shrugged his shoulders and said, "I don't know; it was just an idea." He kept coming up with crazy ideas, making them laugh in astonishment. All his ideas were ridiculed and rejected instantly, but he knew that all the seeds that he was sowing were not to be utterly fruitless. Every chief that he talked to secretly pondered on the points he raised. There were a few who even started having dreams of becoming a king of all the tribes. Was not their whole struggle against each other a perpetual striving towards the same goal, and a thirst for supremacy, a wish to dominate?

Emron convinced Robbas to call a meeting of all chiefs to discuss such matters of importance. They were all astonished and alarmed. There was precedence of such meetings in the past, but usually they were in connection with Yanobian attacks. They tried to figure out what Robbas wanted to discuss in that meeting. Reluctantly they agreed to come, except Kidra, who was very serious and suspicious. He immediately called for Emron, and when he arrived, Kidra ordered everyone to leave them alone. He told him that he was certain that Emron or some of his ideas were behind that meeting.

"Tell me what this is all about?" Kidra asked in a hard voice.

"Yes," said Emron, who happened to know what was to be suggested by Robbas in the forthcoming meeting. He told Kidra that Robbas was to suggest a common leadership. "What?" Kidra screamed in anger reaching for his sword. "You snake!"

"Kill me if you feel like, but listen to me first" said Emron fearlessly. The raised hand of Kidra hesitated and then dropped. He wanted to give him a chance to explain himself before he killed him. Robbas was not to give a proposition that they should accept him as a king. He was only to present the concept of a common ruler; it was for others to accept or reject.

Emron told him that he had travelled around in the territory thanks to the help and kindness of Kidra, whom he admired and wished to repay. "It's you I think of when I talk about a common king," Emron looked deep in Kidra's eyes and said with a confident voice, "A young, brave king."

"How are you to make all others agree to this?" Kidra asked, still not trusting him.

"Who do you think is the bravest and master of weapons in the entire territory?" Emron asked.

"I think it's me," said Kidra confidently.

"I agree!" said Emron with a broad smile. "Now listen to my plan, and kill me if you think I'm lying." Emron entrusted him with the plan and Kidra looked happy and pleased.

"You are a genius," Kidra laughed patting Emron's shoulders.

*   *   *

They were all unarmed, as was the tradition at such meetings. A dozen men represented each tribe. They stared at each other without smiles, and took their seats showing spite and aggression in their behaviours. Robbas, his son Bental and ten other strong men represented the host tribe. Emron walked beside Kidra, who had taken him as a team member against the wishes of many others, who thought it was inappropriate for a foreigner to represent their tribe in such an important meeting. But Kidra rejected their objections by arguing that Emron's wisdom was an asset, which he intended to exploit. He absolutely wanted Emron to be at his side when the matter of his future kingship was to be discussed. He depended on Emron's sharp mind and wise council.

When Robbas presented the idea of peace to the attendants of the meeting, many of the tribesmen smiled. They listened patiently without any exchange of rude words. But when Robbas suggested the idea of a common king, it was too much. There was a cry of indignation. Many hands reached for swords, which were luckily not there. They felt fooled and trapped there, and were to leave in anger when Kidra stood up and asked them to sit down.

Kidra said that he found the idea not very appealing, but was interested to know what Robbas had in mind. Robbas smiled and explained that they all belonged to the same big family. Though they were members of different tribes, they were all warriors. So a king of the warriors had to be a young, strong, and intelligent man; Robbas smiled and looked at his son. He then suggested a way to choose their king. The strongest and bravest of them all was to be the king. When the largest tribes of Kidra and Robbas had agreed to that suggestion the pressure became too much on the smaller five tribes. Rejecting the idea was to confess that they were not confident in themselves and that would have been too much for their self-esteem. They reluctantly agreed.

They discussed the terms and conditions of the engagement. No one was to hurt others on purpose during the competitions. What was fair and what was foul was decided. All the tribes could take part with equal participants. They all agreed that the winner was a person who won the most competitions. All tribes made a binding deal, cutting their fingers and dropping a few drops of blood on the ground, which made their agreement irrevocable. They agreed to accept the winner as a king and to obey him without any excuses. Emron could see their faces and notice that they all were scared to death. They had affirmed the deal with blood, but could that be their signature on their own death doom.

"One final question" asked Kidra. "Can all participate"? He asked.

"Who else"? asked Robbas little surprised.

"Our friend Emron, is he also welcome to try his luck"? Kidra asked jokingly. There was a big laughter, which refused to die down.

"Of course, even our friend Emron can take part. No one shall be able to harm him anyhow," said Robbas and the rest agreed and laughed, making the atmosphere somewhat lighter. The questions of what, when and where were to be settled later on.

Kidra was happier than anyone else. He was to go on dreaming of become the first king of... suddenly realising that he had to find a new name for the whole area.

A date for the competition was set; giving frenetic activities to both young and old, all were preparing hard and especially in the fields each thought that they were less than perfect.

Emron was not showing much interest in training exercises, and mostly went around and watched others with interest, learning their special tricks and other specialities, their weaknesses and shortcomings.

No one minded him watching. He was not a threat to anyone anyway, or at least so they believed. The tribesmen, despite their training and preparations, had mixed feelings about that competition. Most of them already regretted their leaders' hasty decision to choose a king. Why did they need a king? What was to happen if someone from another tribe won the competition? Just the very idea made them nervous and anguished.

The only person who remained hopeful and confident was Kidra. He was so sure of his skills with weapons that he could not imagine even the remotest possibility that he might lose in the approaching event. His arrogance had blinded him completely. Emron had stopped assuring him that he was the only possible king of the future. "It's difficult to guess," was his diplomatic answer. They all were good according to him, so the result could not be told in advance. Kidra used to laugh at such little comments, seeing them as jokes. But he was clever enough not to make any public claim either. He wanted to keep a low profile and not provoke the jealousy of his adversaries.

"Let them be surprised, seeing me shine like a sun on their mud-stained faces, " he would think for himself and smile.

*   *   *

The day of decision finally arrived, a day they all had been waiting for in excitement. There were those who were fearful and some were even terrified. The day ahead of them was to change everything that they had ever known. It was a day that would be a turning point, a milestone, giving them all a new beginning for either good or bad. Many faces that day were shining with hope and expected glory, but many faces were worried and gloomy, unsure of what was to come.

There was a parade of warriors riding on their beautiful, strong horses. Tribesmen from all over kept streaming in. They were tall, strong and proud. Everyone could see that the competition was not going to be easy. Even Emron looked a little down, not so sure of himself. He had achieved great success, but could he win over the warriors? He was not so sure.

He tried to calm himself down, aware that his fear had to give way, like it always did. If he was to come out as a victor, he had to defeat his own fear first. The tribesmen gathered in the large grounds, dressed in their own special tribal dresses and waited for the functionaries, who were selected from different tribes too. There were too many participants, so it had been decided to divide them in groups, and only group winners were to qualify for the final encounter. Altogether thirty groups were formed, who were to go through different competitions all day long. The winners of these groups were to rest the second day, while the others would go on with their sports and non-qualifying, competitions. The final encounter was to take place on the third day.

Thirty groups divided the spectators as well, forcing most of them to go and watch important candidates. Luckily Emron had no such eminent person in his group, so he could work through without arising much attention. He was not so good as it appeared, but he was fighting desperately and anyone could see. He would be losing without any hope, but suddenly luck would turn and he would turn the scores and win in a miraculous manner. People were laughing at his desperation and clapped when he won. At evening the names of the group winners were announced, sending waves of surprise to all, they couldn't believe their ears; Emron was the winner of his group.

Not even the people who had been watching him could remember him winning. Beginners' luck, they thought and shrugged their shoulders. They were surprised by Emron's unexpected performance, but nothing more than that. They had known the man for more than a year and knew how lousy he was in everything, and didn't consider him to be any threat. Emron himself pretended to be surprised by his unexpected success, trying to play down the importance. Some tribesmen even came and congratulated him, not hiding their spite. He could see that it was less of a greeting, and more of a threat. If Emron was to lose in the final combat there was not to be a second chance for him, and his days with the tribes were going to be over, as he would be exposed as an imposter. The realisation of the dangerous consequences of his enterprise dawned on him suddenly. He had initiated something that could culminate on his death. He could not afford to lose the game. His motives were to be questioned, as he had been fooling the tribesmen so long about his skills with weapons. He pushed the disturbing thoughts away and tried to concentrate on the final day's challenges. One lives and dies only once! He thought.

*   *   *

The next day he avoided meeting and facing people, preferring to stay inside. No one came to visit him either. People were busy in their different sports, forgetting about the thrill and anguish related to the next day. There was noise, dust, and carefree laughter in the air. Perhaps the only person, who was terribly worried was Emron. The more he thought of his situation the more he grew nervous. He was sweaty, had a fast heartbeat, and felt almost paralysed.

He couldn't remember any day of his life when he was more afraid than that. It was not the fear to die, that was burdening him, nor the fear to lose in the field either. What worried him most was to be revealed to the eyes of tribesmen as a swindler, an impostor and a treacherous person. These were the qualities that they hated most. He could not imagine any way he could be pardoned for such crimes. The only way he could show and convince the tribesmen of his real intentions to win the competition. These thoughts filled his troubled heart with a new resolve. He had no other option but to win.

On the way to the ground he saw Kidra. Their eyes met and he saw a sea of hate in his eyes. He spoke nothing, but had a devilish smile on his face. Emron felt a wave of fear thrilling through his veins. It was the first test of his nerves and he seemed to have failed it. "Remember your promise!" his conscious reminded him of his promise not to be a coward. "Yes, that time you were a kid, unable to fight, but you're a man now who can fight for his life," his consciousness continued pressing him. In the first few competitions, he was afraid and the distraction made him lose. The wakening came like a thunderbolt. His fear was taking its toll, pushing him to the losing side.

He started giving all his attention and energies to the task, and slowly but steadily started recovering his lost points. But two sporting events were still left, and he was in sixth position. In archery he beat everyone easily and advanced to the fourth position. He noticed that the display of his mastery in archery sent the competitors and crowd numb. There was not a single sound or a clap, when time after time he hit the target in a perfect way. He felt piercing, penetrating eyes fixed on him, but avoided looking at others. Finally the competitors were to show their power and skill to handle the sword. The four best of them were to fight for the crown.

Emron could easily advance to the best four; the other three were Kidra, Bental and a middle age man from a minor tribe. Emron had to fight the man, who was powerful and reminded him of his teacher. The man was much tougher than Emron had hoped and defeating him took much energy. He won but looked exhausted. The crowed was all numbed.

Kidra won easily and kept staring at Emron with hatred. Before they started the fight he raised his sword high, demanding thereby the support and applauds of the tribesmen. The tribesmen had no choice but to give him their wholehearted support.

The fight was between a local and a foreigner. A king was in the making, should that be a brother of their own or an enemy, an impostor? No one had to think twice to guess the answer.

Emron felt lonely, tired and afraid for a moment. Kidra approached him, looked deep into his eyes and said, "I´m sorry that the rules don't allow me to behead you during the fight. But I promise that killing you will be my first deed as a king, you treacherous creep." Emron didn't answer that, but looked demoralised.

When the fight started, Kidra was quick to take advantage of Emron's slow reflexes. He attempted to seize the opportunity by attacking more fiercely. Emron seemed unable to withstand those powerful attacks. The tribesmen from other tribes were silent. They stood dismayed at the prospect of seeing Kidra as their king, but did not wish him to lose either.

Emron seemed to be overpowered by Kidra and everyone could feel that the end was quickly approaching. Emron appeared defeated when Kidra made a last decisive attack. Everyone watched in awe, but then suddenly something strange happened. Emron moved to the side in the last second, making Kidra lose his balance and fall. The crowd laughed nervously, turning the confidence of Kidra into anger. Emron seemed to have been waiting for that moment. He started becoming more active and moving in a co-ordinated manner, effectively avoiding further attacks, provoking Kidra into a seething rage.

Seeing the victory slipping out of his hands, Kidra became more and more desperate. The longer they fought, the more confident Emron became. When he was sure that Kidra was exhausted and no longer posed a threat, he stood and said something that made Kidra even angrier, "My dear Kidra, you can do better than that!" Emron went on provoking him. And then came the inevitable moment that they all had been waiting for.

Kidra jumped forward to chop Emron's head off, but he lost his grip on his sword, which landed on the ground a few yards away. "Go fetch it, I'll wait," taunted Emron with a smile. Kidra picked up his heavy sword and started fighting more fiercely, but lost control of his sword a second time. He didn't pick it up the third time. He was too tired and humiliated to continue.

There was not a human sound to be heard. A few tribesmen recovering from the tragedy of the day tried to rush towards Emron, to hurt him, to kill him, but their elders stopped them, remembering that their blood oaths prohibited them from doing so. They turned pale with grief in their hearts and stood speechless with bowed heads. That was the greatest defeat of their lives. All seven-warrior tribes had been tricked and defeated by the cunning of a single individual, a foreigner, and a stranger. They could not hurt the man, and had to accept him as their combined king. But none they hated more than Emron at that very moment.

"Now we've got a king. Emron the snake!" said someone, but no one laughed. They abandoned their victor. Emron was supposed to be crowned in the territory of the second biggest tribe the following day. Bental and Robbas came to him and congratulated him on the victory.

"Better you as a king than that beast," said Robbas, accompanying him to their area where he would spend the night alone. There were no triumphant sounds, no celebrations and no songs that could be heard. The whole territory of the seven tribes despised the inauguration of the newly crowned king.

*   *   *

The next day the tribesmen started returning to the gathering place. They looked broken and defeated; their sad faces betrayed inner turmoil. They all sat with bowed heads and waited for the torturous ceremony of Emron's coronation, where they were to swear the oaths of allegiance and loyalty. How were they to make such an impossible task? The spirits of their ancestors would curse them for what they had done. How could they be so stupid as to fall for such an obvious plot? Their shame paralysed their souls.

For centuries they had fought for their freedom and no one had ever been able to defeat their iron will. They had fought and destroyed the most mighty invading armies. But they were completely taken by surprise and defenceless before a single enemy.

When Emron approached the stage together with

Robbas and his men, they remained sitting with bowed heads. Their faces would have been less gloomy if they were facing a sure death. Robbas reminded them of the importance of that historic day: they were going to be united under the same leadership. The people were to obey the laws of their newborn country, giving allegiance to their new king. Emron had won the competition and therefore was their rightful king. The tribesmen were very uncomfortable with his long introduction and wanted him to complete the ceremony as quickly as possible so they could go home and mourn the loss of their pride in peace. However, they were very concerned about where the new king would place his throne. No tribe wished it to be in their territory.

Emron wanted to say a few words before the coronation ceremony. He looked extremely happy. He spoke well of the land they occupied, praised their great traditions, their hospitality, and above all he admired their bravery, national pride, and their love for freedom and independence. He noticed that many of the tribesmen wept because they knew that they had lost those qualities through their own stupidity.

Emron explained the importance of peace and non-violence among the tribes. His heart bled seeing the sad faces of the people who had been so kind to him. Yes, he said, they all had good reasons to be bitter and angry with him. He had not been completely honest when he had concealed his skills from them. But if he had done wrong by becoming a king, he had done so to bring them peace. It was the first time they could choose peace for themselves. Emron was ready to bargain with them.

"Make a blood oath for permanent peace and I'll give you back your freedom and sovereignty," he offered. The tribesmen did not believe their ears. They looked happy for a moment, but suspicion and mistrust got hold of them again. How could they trust the man who had made fools of them? Emron repeated his offer, but there was silence.

"You can't change anything. If I was to become your king and ordered you to live in peace, there is little you could do about it. It's the last time I'm asking you; are you ready for a treaty of peace or not? If you agree to that I am ready to release you from your oaths and denounce the kingship."

One after another all tribes swore to live in peace with each other and solve their problems in a peaceful manner from that time on. He begged all the chiefs to join him on the stage. He honoured them, and once again praised them in front of the crowd. The crowd erupted with joy. People were shouting and dancing to celebrate the recovery of their sovereignty. Not only were they regaining their freedom but were even being offered peace. They were ready to walk that path. How were they to live a life in security, without the possibility to kill or to be killed, was the headache for the tribal heads.

Kidra and other tribal chiefs were ashamed of their rude behaviour, but Emron just smiled, assuring them that they had nothing to be ashamed of. Were he one of them he would have been equally hurt, angry and bitter, "I don't have any hard feelings for you, you all have been wonderful to me, and I will remember all of you fondly."

All members of seven tribes gathered to say goodbye to Emron. They were singing and dancing in their tribal colours and costumes. For the first time in their history they were singing something other than a war song. They were pledging themselves to him, promising to always remember him with warm feelings. He was not their king, but their hearts were to be reigned by Emron forever.

Emron was touched by their songs and beautiful expressions of gratitude. They brought presents of gold, silver and precious stones. They offered him to take wives from their tribes, but he thanked and said that he was pleased with his beautiful wife.

"Emron, you're most welcome to visit us whenever your heart desires so," said Kidra, still ashamed.

"You're not just a great warrior, but also a great being. You've written your name in our history. As long as our tribes live, you'll be remembered," said Robbas.

Bental just came forward and gave him a hug and bade farewell. "Take our finest horse," offered one tribal chief. "No thanks" said Emron and patted his horse and whispered in its ear, "I'll never trade you with anything in the world." The tribesmen tried to escort him to the border, but he politely declined their offer. He had been surrounded by people for as long as he could remember and wanted to be alone for a while.

*   *   *

Emron had hardly entered Yanobia when he met Khafil. He smiled at him.

"I've heard the news!" Khafil shouted. "I had never doubted that you could make it."

"Have you visited my family, how are they?" Emron asked.

"Everyone is just fine," Khafil told him. They stopped at a local street vendor for a meal. "I love Yanobian food," said Khafil, chewing. They talked about different things. Khafil greeted him on the success of his mission and told him that he had earned the freedom of movement. Emron asked how that would work.

There were so many alternatives when it came to mobility. Khafil used the same method as the Genii. But Emron had to use a simple method because he couldn't learn that complicated and very difficult means of travel.

"I've arranged something that you will like very much," Khafil told him with a smile. "And what is that?" Emron asked eagerly. Khafil avoided the question.

After their meal Khafil asked if he could borrow his horse for a while, which Emron did without any objection. He became a little irritated when he did not return for several hours. Khafil came back at dusk, and said that he was delayed, hoping that Emron had not minded. "Darkness will merely force us to stay for the night at this place, unless you're ready to transport and risk your limit," Emron joked.

Khafil just smiled, and then answered. "I do not have to. You're a resourceful man now." He told Emron that his horse was to become his transportation channel. He could use his horse as a beast with ordinary power, or he could convert him to a speedy creature that could transport him anywhere on the planet within a twinkling of an eye.

"Shall we try?" he asked Emron and without waiting for the answer he jumped and sat on the horse singing, asking Emron to do the same.

"Close your eyes," Khafil said and slowly counted to ten. He did so and opened the eyes. He was in the desolate place, from where they had travelled to Atrostia. "You can go home now; I'll come back after a few days to instruct you how to use your horse from now on."

It was late at night. Emron gently knocked on the door and heard the voice of his wife, who wondered who could knock her door that late. She rushed to open the door, and saw that it was Emron. She was out of herself with joy. She held him tight in a warm embrace and kissed him passionately. "Welcome home!" She cried of happiness. "I'll wake up our son. How happy he is going to be seeing his father!" she tried to rush, but he stopped her. "Let him sleep, I can see him in the morning."

He was extremely happy to have come home to his family. "There is nothing like the sanctuary of home," Emron said holding her in his strong arms and smiled, looking deep into her tearful eyes, they sat and talked all night. She was so curious to know everything at once. There were too many questions she wanted to ask but the most important of them all was if he had succeeded in his mission. She did not have to wait for an answer. The shine in Emron's eyes and a broad smile on his face was an answer in itself. "Oh, Emron I'm so proud of you," she said and caressed him

8

In the morning, he met his son and tried to hold him in his arms, but he was shy and didn't recognize him. Smilingly he introduced himself but the child ran away, Salisa laughed and said that that was the natural result of his extended absence. Amroush was now almost one and a half years old. They were to spend little more time as a family from then on, said Emron. But not a week had passed when Khafil appeared again. He told Emron that it was time to learn how to use his newly earned freedom, and he needed exercise and training. He gave him a secret word which was necessary to convert his horse into a speedy dart that moved faster than the speed of lightening. Choosing a particular destination and then reaching that exact location was serious problems, which required guidance and mental training. But the worst problem was travelling to unknown destinations. Since all travel weren't time consuming he could afford to experiment.

"Can I take my wife with me?" asked Emron.

"Take whomever you want," answered Khafil. Emron was curious to know why they had to close their eyes before making such journeys.

Khafil smiled and answered, "Believe me, it's better that way."

After a few weeks' training Emron was able to use his horse as a swift travelling machine, though it was still imperfect. He felt happy and excited. He made short and long journeys. At times he succeeded in reaching the desired destinations, but at other times he ended up in completely strange and unknown places. But it didn't matter, as it was simple to come back or try again. For every passing day he felt more confident and very soon he could control the new talent skilfully. A few times he even took Salisa and his son on a ride. Salisa felt even more excited than he did. She had not been outside her birth town, and could now visit all the places Emron had been telling her about. She expressed the wish to visit Atrostia, but Emron told her that it was not possible since Khafil had particularly asked him not to go that way. He didn't know the reason, but intended to follow the advice. Eventually, they had travelled almost everywhere. They had been eastward and westward, they had visited the green belts of the south and the snow-covered, freezing north. They were amazed and happy, but the excitement decreased over time. They both liked to be able to travel in this fashion, but realised soon that the comfort of the home was nowhere else.

One day when they came back from a trip, Khafil was standing outside their home. Salisa went inside the house with the child, while Emron and Khafil started walking. "How are you doing"?, asked Khafil. Emron replied that he could now reach his desired destinations without any significant problems.

"And you're careful to choose only desolate places, while making these journeys?" asked Khafil. He received a positive answer from Emron.

"It seems then that you're ready," Khafil said, as if speaking to himself.

"Ready for what?" Emron asked a little alarmed. "Now that you can easily travel, you have to go and search for the shield of invisibility," Khafil told a surprised Emron. "Look, Khafil," Emron started, "I never had any interest in the magical world. I'm thoroughly happy to have you as a friend. First, so much trouble for this magical gift of yours, " he pointed to the horse, "and now some invisible shield. Please! Why don't you understand that I'm simply not interested? If it is that important to look for it, why don't you go and find it yourself?" Emron said in irritation. Khafil looked back at him, as if he could understand his feelings.

Emron went on telling him what he thought of the whole matter, which was now turning into some ridiculous thing. He stressed everything that was more important to him and worth striving for. All that he held dear in life was completely different than what he was being offered or suggested by the wizard.

Khafil listened carefully and patiently, agreeing with him in every detail. Khafil kept silent for a while and then he spoke. He said that he agreed with Emron, but only in principle. Most people of the world would also agree with him, because they lived and followed similar ideals. Everyone lived their own life and strived to protect their own interests. But that was without any doubt a selfish act. To live for oneself was an easy task, but how many were there who could sacrifice their own good for the sake of others? Emron could not see what was he driving at, but agreed that there were few such people.

Khafil went on, explaining that he lived in a world that was threatened by evil forces again and again. It was a constant war between good and evil, sometimes the balance tipping in favour of one or the other. Their world order was threatened afresh by the prince of Atrostia, who had the means and designs to take over the world. The only person who could stop him was Emron. He was the chosen one.

He told Emron that the destiny of the human world lay in his hands. The burden was Emron's, who could bear that responsibility with a smile or walk away with a lifelong regret that he had let the whole world down.

Emron shivered in his bones. He wished he could vanish from the sight of the wizard, but kept listening to him. He tried to convince Khafil that he could not be the chosen one, and could in no way stand and fight the evil prince, who had power of science and magic at his disposal, invincible armies, great wealth, and flying dragons and terrible weapons, which he could not counterbalance. It was not that he was scared, but it was simply beyond his ability. Even if he were to find the shield of invisibility, how could he possibly defeat such a mighty enemy?

Khafil interrupted him, assuring Emron that he understood what he meant. Khafil had told him what he had to, and did not press him to make a decision then. Emron was to think deeply and seriously and make his own choices. If he was to decide not to pursue his destiny, then there was nothing Khafil could do but respect his decision and leave him in peace. But if he chose to heed the call, Khafil was to help and aid him wherever possible. With those words he took his leave and went his way.

*   *   *

Emron went home and Salisa could see that something was wrong. Emron looked so pale and poor. She didn't need to ask what bothered him. He told her all of his discussion with Khafil, without leaving any detail. She listened without showing any surprise. The expression on her face was calm and peaceful as ever. If it was his destiny, then there was little else he could do. If he had been entrusted with the great responsibility of saving the world, then they should rejoice instead of mourning. She was proud to be the wife of such an important man. Emron tried to explain his reluctance, but she could not understand. To spend a year without him was the hardest thing she had ever done, but with the freedom of movement, he could steal a few moments and come back every now and then, or he could take his family with him wherever he went.

Emron was relieved. He was happy to have such a wise wife. He kissed her and admired her wisdom. She just smiled and said, "Go search for your shield wherever you want. But this time your family will be with you wherever you go."

*   *   *

Emron, Salisa and their son were taking trips to different parts of the world. There was no sign of Khafil, who could tell him what he was supposed to look for, and where was he to find it. Perhaps he had given up on Emron and was not to come back.

One day, while their hometown was devastated by the heat, they went to a place that was cool and pleasant. On one side was the sea with its stony beaches; far away one could see glorious mountains. The landscape stretched for miles and was practically covered with grass and small bushes, and there were rocks formations scattered across a plain. It was a perfect place to relax. It was pleasant, but the water was too cold, so they sat on the beach and took their meal. Emron's faithful horse was grazing at a distance. Suddenly, the whole area started shaking. They looked in surprise to find out the reason. The horse was also alarmed and came towards them. At a distance they saw some huge animals rushing in their direction. Emron sensed danger, but found hardly any time to fetch his son, who was playing with the stones near the beach.

He took the horse and Salisa and rushed towards the water, and looked nervously for his son, but he wasn't there. His heart leapt out of his chest. Could it be possible that he had already entered into the sea? Emron and Salisa were driven into the sea by the stampeding animals. The earth shook violently beneath them. Emron and his wife hadn't seen anything like this before, but their hearts were too worried to think about anything else than their son. When the mountainous animals had moved away, they could dare to come out of the sea. They looked around, calling his name in desperate voices. Salisa jumped off the horse and called at the top of her lungs. She ran like a mad dog chasing its own tail. Emron had difficulty breathing.

"Where is my child?" Salisa asked Emron, as if he was responsible for his disappearance. Emron looked at the sea, but dared not speak of his fears. He held her and noticed she was trembling badly. They both were crying, Emron silently and Salisa in a loud uncontrolled manner. Emron had never seen her in such a poor state. "Mama, mama!" they heard the voice of their son and looked at the direction, but couldn't find him anywhere. There wasn't any place he could possibly hide, they searched desperately. Salisa went on calling him in order to make him speak again, so that they could find him.

All of a sudden he was there, sitting near the seawater, playing and looking at them with his big beautiful eyes. They both rushed and embraced him and cried of relief and joy of finding him safe and sound. They both went around and around trying to locate any hiding place, but found no such thing. They went on and on until they gave up. The mystery of their son's disappearance could not be solved. They were curious but had to return home from that place, as it was getting dark.

*   *   *

Many days passed, but their minds could not come to rest. They were extremely happy that their son was unharmed and had come back to them, but still were dying to find some logical explanation for his disappearance.

"I think we have to go back there," said Emron.

"Never again in this lifetime," said Salisa.

"Are we to live with this mystery for the rest of our lives?" insisted Emron with equal determination. Finally they compromised; they were to leave the child with her parents and go to the mysterious area themselves. They went to the place at noon and searched, not leaving any stone unturned, but failed to find any place where their son could have hidden himself that day. In the afternoon they heard the rumbling and shaking of the ground and took refuge in the sea. After the strange animals had gone their way without taking any notice of them, they took their horse back to the beach.

"Perhaps it was meant for them to leave the mystery alone and move on back to their lives," said Emron. He sat on the beach, almost exactly where his son had been sitting that day. He was throwing small stones in the sea water, while Salisa was enjoying the sunset.

"I always love the sunset, but this one is unusually brilliant. Look at the beautiful colours of the sky," said Salisa, and looked back at him, when he didn't answer. She panicked. There wasn't any trace of Emron! She called his name hysterically.

"What has gotten into you? Why are you so tense?"

"Oh my, I can hear you but I can't see you! Tell me where you are and what you are doing. Whatever it is, it's the answer to our mystery." All of a sudden she could see Emron's surprised face. "What were you doing? Why could I not see you?" Salisa asked in excitement.

Emron replied that he wasn't doing anything special. He was simply throwing stones in the water, and had come across a stone that felt a little strange in his hand. He was ready to throw that one as well, but was distracted by the milky white stone. "Where is that stone?" Salisa demanded to know. Emron picked it up and placed it in the palm of her hand. She instantly disappeared. Emron fainted. He woke up to her laughter.

"My darling, you are without a doubt the chosen one. Look! The object of your search has found you. You now have the shield of invisibility!" Emron could hear the happiness in her excited voice.

Back at home they placed the unique and priceless stone on their mantle and watched it for hours. This beautiful stone was oblong and all white, but reflected rays of light in other colours like a diamond. It was not invisible, but disappeared as soon as it came in touch with the flesh, and so did the person who touched it. Salisa and Emron took turns holding it. They both were like children who had found a new game to play. While they were distracted someone knocked at the door. It was Khafil, who apologized for coming so late but had some important things to discuss with him. Emron invited him into the house and said that he was all ears.

Khafil was interested to know if Emron had given a thought to the matters they had discussed earlier. Emron replied that he had made up his mind. He was not interested in any invisibility giving stone or saving the world. Khafil appreciated his straightforward and honest answer and stood up to leave. But instead of going to the door, he turned back, with a surprised look on his face.

"How do you know it's a stone? I never told you that!" Khafil looked confused.

"Oh yes, you did!" said Emron placing the stone in his hand. Khafil looked around in a puzzled manner, then Emron could hear his laughter.

"Now I can see you," he said happily. Khafil was so happy to know that Emron had succeeded in his second quest and that without any effort. "It's another proof that I´m right to claim that you are the chosen one."

Khafil told him that he could not see Emron in the beginning, because he didn't expect him to have the magical power.

"How did you find me then?" asked Emron like a child.

"As I knew that you were present in the room, all I had to do was to change my vibrations to locate you."

The coincidental finding of the stone indicated that his prohibition to come into contact with Atrostia was to be over soon. He knew he should start preparing for his most important and difficult mission. Salisa silently listened to their talk and kept looking at her husband with a smile and a silent support.

"Can Salisa follow me to Atrostia?" Emron asked.

"Absolutely not!" replied the wizard emphatically. "She would be needed to be here while you accomplish your task." They were to discuss the issues some other time. The little old man was not trying to hide that he was happy. "Don't you think he knew before coming here that you had found the stone?" Salisa asked. Emron agreed, but if Khafil liked the game of pretending, it was okay with him.

Khafil came a few times and discussed matters of importance with Emron. "You're to visit Atrostia, and meet those people to whom you had contacted last time during your visit over there, evaluate the situation, and to see what is required to make the resistance stronger," said Khafil and gave him further instructions as what to do and what to avoid in Atrostia. He had to be absolutely cautious, discrete and on guard, both for his own sake and for the safety of others.

"You are not to have any confrontation or to be provoked, because that would give your enemies a clue of your presence and your own future struggle against the evil prince and his mighty army." Khafil made clear the importance of everything he had imparted and discussed.

There was a little problem regarding Emron's horse. He could not take his friend with him to Atrostia, simply because they had no horses at all in that country and it would be a big problem and risk his stay there. Khafil suggested that he could follow Emron to Atrostia, only to bring back the horse.

"Or we could apply the same method as we did previously?" Khafil asked.

"Wouldn't that prevent future possibilities to help others?" Emron asked a bit surprised, reminding the wizard of his mentioning such danger. Khafil looked confused and embarrassed, but then he laughed emphatically.

"I told you a lie to trick you into physical labour, which was required if you were to succeed in your mission."

Emron didn't like his laughter or the answer, but kept silent, as he did not wish to argue about something in the past, but it did force him to conclude that the words of Khafil could not to be trusted at face value. He looked disappointed and crossed and Khafil must have noticed that as he voluntarily explained his position.

"I can see that you don't look happy for my lying to you on that occasion, but believe me there was no other way for me to convince you to take up that journey on the back of a horse as it was required."

"It's not the exposure to hardship that upsets me, but the simple fact that I was tricked into it," Emron said dryly.

Khafil avoided elaboration on the subject and took up the matter of his transportation to and from Atrostia.

*   *   *

As they had agreed, Khafil accompanied him to Atrostia, and

escorted Emron's horse back home. Before they went their separate ways, Khafil mumbled a sacred blessing for Emron's success. Emron had fit the white stone into his dagger, so as not to drop or lose it. He put the dagger closer to him; all he had to do was to hold it in a certain way or to make the stone touch his body to become invisible.

He followed the way he had taken before and came to the fields and walked invisibly through the crop and entered Freedia. He could lose the grip over the dagger, but somehow felt some danger lurking there, and refrained from doing so. He was astonished to find that the number of inhabitants there had dropped drastically. All the faces seemed unfamiliar. When he got closer he noticed that the people he saw moving around were not at all like those he had met earlier. These people were wearing special dresses, as if it was some sort of uniform. Something terrible must have had happened there, because it even smelled differently. There was a smell of helplessness and decay in the stale air.

He walked around in search for the answers and soon found a big hall with iron bars. Behind the iron bars he saw people who were locked up. One of these prisoners was doctor Guliaki, who had saved Salisa´s life. There were no guards outside the large hall, so he took off the ring and tried to draw the attention of Dr. Guliaki. She was surprised to see him there. Emron called her to his side. She did not attempt to hide her displeasure in seeing him. She ignored his request and looked away from him. But when Emron refused to give up, she came near to the iron bars and angrily asked what he wanted.

"Tell me, what's going on?" Emron asked, looking around. "Why should I tell you anything, so that you can betray us again?" she spat bitterly. Emron could not guess what had happened to Freedia and its inhabitants, but he could tell for sure that whatever had befallen that unfortunate place; he was blamed for that miserable state.

He was deeply insulted, but there was no time for such emotionality. "Look, if you believe that I'm responsible for your imprisonment, then you are wrong. I'm shocked to see you in this terrible condition. Please tell me if Priva is also imprisoned, and if so where can I find her?" Emron pleaded.

Dr. Guliaki was angry. What did he think of himself? What did he consider her for? Was she a fool to tell him about her whereabouts? She slightly raised her voice, "Get out of here!"

"Please don't shout, you'll draw the attention of others," Emron pleaded, but she continued shouting. All of a sudden he heard the approaching footsteps and immediately held the dagger and disappeared from Guliaki's sight, but he could see the fear and astonishment in her eyes. She stood there with an open mouth, her words frozen in her throat. Two uniformed guards came. They had some strange type of weapon in their hands.

"What's going on there? Why do you shout?" one of them asked harshly.

"If you do it again we shall lock you up in the ghost house," warned the other in the same hard voice. Since Dr. Guliaki was standing near the iron bars they took it for granted that she was the troublemaker.

When the guards had gone away, Emron appeared again and spoke softly to her, telling her that he was sorry to see her and others in that awful state. He had come to help them. They needed a plan, but for that reason he had to meet Priva. "Can you lead me to her?" Emron asked.

"Yes, I know where she is," she replied.

Emron promised to come back later in the night. At midnight he came back to the prison, and stole some keys from a sleeping guard. He unlocked the door, took her out, locked the door again, and disappeared for a while to put the keys back. She was to become invisible too, and thereby could leave Freedia without being detected. He asked her to hold his hand. "Trust me and don't speak," said Emron, he could feel her sweaty, shaky hand. When they came to a safer place Emron asked her to continue holding his hand until they arrived at a safe place. But she could speak, since there was no danger that anybody could hear them.

"How far away is Priva?" he asked.

"We first need to flee to the safety of my home, which is still not in the knowledge of the authorities. One of my friends should be able to get a message to Priva. If we keep walking for a few hours, we will arrive at a place called Niso where we need to take the Serpent to my home." Emron had previously thought that that Niso was some form of local transportation. But he was wrong; he learned that Niso was the name given to the place where it was located. The mode of transportation itself was called the Serpent. There were not many people near Niso, so they could enter the Serpent unnoticed, which started moving slowly like water on a soft smooth marble surface. Soon it was moving very fast. They kept silent all the way, and came out of the Serpent when it slowed down and finally stopped. When they arrived at their destination, he finally said that they could stop holding hands and walk freely.

Guliaki released his hand, and was shocked to find that Emron was still invisible.

When they reached her home, he finally reappeared. "Are you a magician?" she asked him.

*   *   *

The next day, Guliaki told Emron that she met a friend in the marketplace and sent a message to Priva. If she was not out on some mission, she would be contacting her as soon as possible. Emron requested her to inform him of the developments that had occurred lately. She begged for his forgiveness regarding her inexcusable behaviour at the prison before she preceded the subject by saying, "I must confess that the awful conditions of the prison along with the hopelessness had made me bitter and suspicious."

"I don't blame you for anything," Emron said with a smile.

The doctor gave a sigh of relief and began her story. After Emron left Freedia, enemy soldiers captured it and the people of Freedia became their prisoners. She was not very keen to discuss the story of Freedia after its capture. He could see her bleak face and clouds of horror in her eyes. Just the thought of the days that had gone by was making her shiver. She looked sad, defeated and terrified all at the same time. Emron didn't push for any more details than she felt ready to impart. If the unexpected and sudden fall of Freedia was a shock for her, then seeing her brave friends and companions suffer in the hands of their captors was an even greater shock. Members of the resistance were asked politely to give up information regarding their goals and motives, disclose names of other members of the movement, and reveal their other hiding places. But her friends withstood all the pressures and the other cunning interrogation techniques. Seeing them steadfast in their resolve, their captors deemed them to be hopeless cases and decided to pacify them instead.

"How did they do that?" Emron asked. She kept silent before revealing that a terrible thing was done in a systematic and organised manner. It was a process in which the victim was drugged constantly until he or she lost all of their integrity and control.

"One feels as though one's free will is replaced by hallucinations. If this torture goes on for too long, the victim will never recover, walking among the living dead."

How did you avoid becoming like the others? Emron asked curiously. It must have been a combination of awareness of the drug and its effects, her will to live and most of all, sheer luck. She was happy that she had succeeded in cheating her captors, giving them the impression that she did take the drug like others, and by showing the symptoms that she had been pacified and possessed no longer the will of her own. She was taking her medicines like others in a submissive, apathetic way, only to spit them out when no one was watching her. She concluded that the fall of Freedia could not have happened any other way than a betrayal by the young couple that had visited them shortly before the invasion.

"I thought you were an infiltrator, a spy!"

*   *   *

After sundown, Priva came to visit Guliaki and looked surprised to find Emron there as well. Both Priva and Guliaki embraced, shedding tears of happiness. They had lost all hope of meeting each other again. Dr. Guliaki gave Priva the short story of her imprisonment and how she had escaped from Freedia with the help of Emron.

Priva smiled in a tired, sad manner, when Guliaki told her how badly she had behaved towards Emron, suspecting him to be the person who was behind their unending misery. Priva told that there was nothing to be ashamed of. Even she had been sure that Emron had been sent by the enemy to find their hiding place. But now she knew better.

Priva told her that the enemy had discovered Freedia accidentally and still didn't know that it was just a fraction of a whole movement that was building against their tyranny. They had considered it an isolated enterprise of few individuals to escape from their organised society structure. That was the reason no torture was employed, no investigations were made, and no witch-hunts were initiated. The proof of this was they were sitting and talking about the matter. Had they suspected anything deeper, Priva could not be free and Guliaki would not be able to retain her ancestral home. Once discovered, the inhabitants were to be punished for their attempt to sneak out of the system.

The ones who were captured were drugged until they no longer posed a threat to the state. Since they couldn't use them as effective tools any longer it was best to imprison them. Guliaki was lucky to escape! There was no way she could continue the pretence. Sooner or later she would lose her integrity and sanity if she were to remain in captivity.

The tragic discovery of Freedia by the forces of Dolec was devastating to the resistance movement. They had lost not only an important stronghold, but were also abandoned by many of its members. The groups of rebels working outside Freedia became more careful and scared. They were forced to lay low, freezing all their activities in order to not make the enemy conscious, because if their presence was discovered, none of them would survive. Luckily, the prince and his machinery were under the delusion that they had the support of their people. The little opposition, which was thought to exist, was considered inconsistent, disorganised, and impotent. In other words there was nothing to worry about.

Emron could see a clear difference between the woman he had met before and the one he was facing at the moment. That former woman had been optimistic, energetic and full of enthusiasm. The later Priva was defeated, worn-out and resigned.

She looked like a person in an unending dark tunnel, without any hope to come out. She was unable to provide any information regarding the army of Dolec and its might. Suddenly Priva's eyes flashed, remembering that one of her childhood friends served in Dolec's army as an officer.

"Isn't he the one who is madly in love with you?" asked Guliaki and Priva nodded. "You can invite him over to dinner, and try to get him to talk about the army. Emron can be on your side, as an invisible listener." Priva agreed, but didn't look very enthusiastic.

*　　*　　*

Emron requested to see their town, which he had heard so much about. He couldn't visit the town without catching the eyes of its residents, he was told politely. He neither talked nor looked like a native. So if he insisted on visiting the city he had to be their invisible guest, which he had nothing against. They waited until evening to leave the house. At that time of the day there was less danger of Emron's accidentally crashing into someone. He could enjoy the beauty of their unique town at night, but if he were to see it in its full glory, he would have to revisit that beautiful city in broad daylight.

He was baffled by the beauty and magnitude of the wonderful city which lay before his eyes. The luxurious broad highways with green belts of vegetation on both sides, sky touching buildings, mansions, and palaces, they all looked like masterpieces coming out of a dream world. All the streets and buildings were lit up with some strange white light. There were walking paths of stones that glittered when the light fell on them. It was like walking among the stars. He could see that most of the buildings were only a single storey or two storied. But the heights of the ceilings were remarkable and so were the sizes of the stones that were used in the construction.

Emron could not believe his eyes; it felt like some sort of dream. Though there wasn't any obvious resemblance it still reminded him of the Genii world. This city was more solid, more real, and more magnificent and more inspiring than the smoky city of the Genii; perhaps the only similarity was the magical effect they had on his brain. They went on, walking through its alleys, boulevards, decorated gates, market squares, and other wonders. There were fountains and artificial lakes throughout the city, and streams flowing in the middle of the city with golden bridges. He was bewitched and could not resist the city's charm. Emron walked like a baffled little child, unable to describe his feelings. He had fallen in love with the city of Pooba.

He wanted to stay in this city and be there forever and ever without getting tired of it, the city he felt like lingering on to but had to leave, and was not to revisit for a long time to come. Priva believed it was late and to stay any further in the city could be dangerous. They turned and came back to Guliaki's home.

They were all tired from their long walk, but kept talking all night. They both were proud and their faces glittered of happiness when Emron told them that it was an astounding experience that he had had, and confessed that there were no appropriate words which could describe the beauty and glamour of the city. They had lived their entire lives there, but still couldn't agree more. It was a city without parallel. There were other important things in life than to sit and praise and admire the beauty of a city, reminded Priva, excusing herself and left for her home. Emron slept where he sat and dreamt of the city of Pooba.

He could go on sleeping all day long, but was awakened by Guliaki at midday. She had prepared lunch. "You can eat and sleep again," she told Emron. Though she considered it wise not to sleep at all if he didn't want to upset the body rhythm. They took their meal in silence as they both felt a bit tired, but afterwards Guliaki gave him a hot drink, which was so refreshing that he no longer felt any trace of tiredness in his body. They sat and discussed many different things.

When Priva's friend came to visit her, he was not wearing an army uniform, perhaps remembering how much Priva hated the army service. He was strongly built, of medium height and wore a thick moustache. He laughed in a very peculiar manner, and when he did so his whole body shook in a funny way. He was handsome except for his unusually crooked front teeth. Perhaps he was conscious of that, as he kept putting his hand before his mouth each time he opened it to smile.

Emron, sitting in a corner, didn't like Hetzog, Priva's friend. Emron could tell that the man was heartless, untrustworthy and the repulsive type whose eyes were betraying an inherent cruelness. He could understand why Priva didn't feel attracted to Hetzog. He had an uneasy happiness that betrayed insecurity. He kept looking at Priva trying to figure out what had made her change her attitude towards him. It was the first time he had ever been invited by her to dinner.

They talked while they ate, with Hetzog looking at her from time to time in a secret, admiring way. Priva started asking how it was going for him in the army. He told her that he was happy and satisfied, and expected a promotion in the near future.

They were overburdened with work and had hardly any

free time, but that was just part of his duty. "Why is there so much to do?" Priva asked casually, in order to not alarm him. Hetzog opened his mouth to answer but closed it without making a sound. He pretended to miss the question but Priva was not to let him go that easily. She repeated her question.

Hetzog smiled and told her that the army was growing in numbers, so the officers had to train those new recruits; teaching them the use of weapons and giving them an appreciation of the discipline. Why did Atrostia need an expansion for its army? Priva asked again. As far as she knew, both the internal and external situation of the country was calm and stable, so from where did the need for an explosive growth come?

Emron could see the anxiety in the sweaty face of Hetzog. On one hand, he didn't want to discuss the subject but on the other hand, how was he to come out of that uncomfortable questioning without angering or hurting Priva? After a short silence he abandoned his reluctance to talk.

"I don't know why such precautions are required. I just do what I'm told to; I'm a soldier," Hetzog said.

Priva didn't accept his lame answer and teased him. "I thought you to be more clever and intelligent than that!" She knew his weakness from childhood. Anyone questioning his intelligence was always too much for Hetzog. He looked at her with serious eyes, smiled and confessed.

"Yes you are right. I wasn't telling the truth, because it's a secret. The queen and her government don't want to scare the public, but a danger is growing." Hetzog went on. Somewhere far away from Atrostia, a plot was being prepared to attack their fatherland, to destroy their flourishing civilisation, enslave them, drag them back to some unspeakable savage levels. The wisdom of the queen and her noble husband was demanding quick action to prevent such a happening, so the army was preparing Atrostia for all possible situations and challenges.

Hetzog was speaking with a strong conviction, and in a

fervour. One moment he talked about the great danger posed by some mysterious enemy of incredible power, and the other second he spoke of their duty to destroy that enemy, to deliver the world out from the hands of some cruel, power hungry tyrant from the primitive part of the world. The world needed their selfless efforts, it needed their sacrifices, it demanded liberation, and Atrostia was getting ready to heed the call.

Priva could clearly see the apparent confusion in his speech, but didn't mention them. She told Hetzog that he had made her worried. She wondered how their enemy intended to attack their otherwise isolated country? He smiled, as if he had expected such a question. According to the reports they were getting, the enemy had a plan to attack through the sea. They had built some sort of vessel, which could easily sail to Atrostia with a large army.

Priva looked scared and said that she was terribly frightened. She feared for herself, for Atrostia, but also for his safety.

He looked with an arrogant gaze, and told her not to be afraid. "We are well prepared, so we can destroy the enemy. We have developed weapons that the enemy cannot resist." He told Priva that in the presence of Queen Sirenica and prince Dolec, no Atrostian had ever to fear any enemies.

"If only I could show you our brave soldiers and their skills. You would be so proud, and get rid of all fears and worries," said Hetzog very proudly.

Priva tried to press him for visiting his army headquarters, but he told her that the whole army headquarters was a strictly non-civilian zone, so it was beyond his power to do so.

Priva told him that she had heard about the discovery of some underground city, and inquired what that was all about. Hetzog became surprised and alarmed when she mentioned that city, they had desperately tried to keep it a secret. He pressed her to tell him how she knew about the top secret.

"I have my channels," she tried to joke about it.

But Hetzog would not let it go.

"A brother of my friend was one of the soldiers who had discovered that city, but he refused to elaborate on the matter."

"So wise, dutiful, and trustworthy are our soldiers," he said proudly and smiled. Yes, those soldiers were out on a mission, investigating and surveying in those parts when the discovery was made. No, they had nothing to do with the enemy. They were their own confused and misled citizens, who were taken care of, and were on the way to become harmless once again.

"What were they investigating"? Priva asked. Instead of answering her back, he looked at her with a smile and said, "You never change. You and your unending questions! I can only tell you that that was a part of our defensive work."

Early in the morning he had to return to his job. It was late, so he asked if he could stay at her place. Of course, she said and prepared him a place to sleep. Emron was very sleepy too, but was afraid to fall into a deep sleep. He lightly dozed for the rest of the night. In the morning when Hetzog went out, Emron followed him.

*   *   *

The walled city was well guarded by the guards, who stopped and checked all those who wished to enter. Even Hetzog was to give his name, rank, and code number before he was allowed to make an entrance. Emron quickly followed Hetzog inside before the gate was closed once again. There were vast grounds with pavements, but very few people were seen walking on them. Most of them were entering or coming out of the Serpent. Emron followed Hetzog and entered the belly of the Serpent which quickly transported them to a large building where Hetzog had his office. Two young soldiers were guarding the door of his office. They greeted him with a salute and opened the door.

He went in to change into his army uniform. He ordered

a breakfast, making Emron more aware of his own hunger. One of the soldiers knocked on the door, made an entry and whispered something. Hetzog got up from his seat and followed the soldier out. After a few minutes when he came back and looked at his breakfast, he looked confused. He was unsure if he had taken his breakfast or not, because there was nothing of it left.

Emron followed Hetzog like a shadow all day. He wanted to learn as much as he could about the army of Dolec. The knowledge he got during one single day was as unbelievable as it was crushing. He was horrified, and wished to be out of that place immediately. If he were not witnessing all of those things himself, he wouldn't have deemed them to be true. His heart pounded uncontrollably, and he became aware of the impossibility of the mission he was asked to undertake. He had never come across an army like that in his entire life. They were numerous, well-trained, well-disciplined and swift in action.

Some soldiers had uncovered faces while the rest were wearing armour and head cover made of iron. Burdened by these heavy armour and head covers, this still didn't seem to slow them down at all. They held the weapons he was familiar with: swords, spears, arrows, daggers, etc. They were attacking each other fiercely, but strangely, none of them got hurt.

All the weapons of his world seemed to be like harmless toys in the hands of these big-bodied soldiers. The swords were becoming crooked and dull, the shafts of the arrows were broke easily, and the arrowheads lost their sharpened edges and so was the case with all of the other weapons. They were busy training, making exercises and getting prepared to meet some enemy, which was completely unaware and unprepared for them.

He didn't believe his eyes when he came across thousands of soldiers riding on speedy horses, who were also covered in armour and yet galloped like he had never seen any horse do. He looked at the sky, where dozens of dragons flew, spilling fire from their nostrils and tails. He saw those soldiers firing with strange looking weapons, which turned rocks into dust.

So it was true, the army before his very eyes was invincible. The armies of his world could not stand before those soldiers who were without a doubt irresistible. The only future his world had was a very bleak and dark one. He had seen only a fraction of a gigantic, powerful, and indescribable force, but was already convinced that no one could stop Dolec from achieving his goals. He had seen such a demonstration of power with his own very eyes that he felt panicked and wanted to run away from there.

*   *   *

He returned to Priva and Guliaki but avoided talking about what he had seen and experienced. He advised them to go on with their restraint from an active opposition. It was best to accept the reality of their situation rather than waste their precious lives in a meaningless struggle.

Priva and Guliaki looked at each other and could easily tell that Emron was not in his senses. They gave him something to drink to calm him down. But he kept shivering and uttering nonsense. They gave him another drink and he slept, but not peacefully. All night he turned sides, talking, and screaming, warning about some danger. In the morning when he got up he looked somewhat calmer but his distressed mind was somewhere far away.

"What happened there?" asked Priva, worried.

"I think I had high fever," told Emron. They both rejected his explanation, since they had checked his temperature earlier that night. Emron did not want to alarm or scare them but he had no choice but to tell what he had seen the other day. "They were more like the monsters than men," Emron told them. "And believe me, there is nothing in the world that can stop them from achieving their goals."

"Oh yes there is," said Priva with a smile on her face.

"Who? How?" asked Emron.

"The great sea," said Priva calmly. "Maybe you didn't know that the people of Atrostia hate the great sea, and dare not venture into it. An inborn fear of getting drowned had prevented us from seeking contact with the rest of the world." Priva went on with her theory that as long as the Atrostian were afraid of the seas and its mighty waves, their mighty army, with all its destructive weaponry would be no danger to his world, and the superiority of Dolec's army was no threat to the outside world.

If they were really afraid of the sea then they might have developed some ways to cross that by fire spitting dragons, Emron told them. They rejected the idea because no dragon could cross the sea, and even if they did, could in no way transport the army of millions. They had never heard of fire spitting dragons before so they requested him to explain. Priva told that right after the discovery of the Freedia by soldiers, the use of dragons had been prohibited by the authorities, claiming that they were dangerous to ones' health, causing serious diseases. So that was a plain lie if the army continued to use them! Priva had not surrendered her dragon, but could not use it either for the fear of breaking the law.

Emron told his hosts that he had come to Atrostia with the intention of assisting them in their resistance against the Dolec, but regretfully had realised that all he had learned in life was not sufficient to stop Dolec's forces. He wished that Priva's assessment were right that his world did not face an immediate threat of invasion, but if she was wrong, his world was doomed from the very beginning.

He announced that he was returning to his world to think and to ponder on all he had learned; perhaps the situation wasn't as hopeless as he thought it to be. He begged them to be careful and not do anything in haste. They were to have their ears and eyes open. But that was it, nothing more, and nothing less.

*   *   *

Back at home, Salisa became happy to see him return that quickly. She was curious to know how it went. She was sorry to hear that the authorities had taken Freedia. The unhappy fate of Freedia was not something she had expected to hear from him. But the news that both Priva and Guliaki had made it gave her some comfort. Emron then told her about the city of Pooba, its beauty, glamour, and charm.

It was an amazing story and she listened with great interest, wishing that she could have been there too. He told her each and every detail of his stay in Atrostia, but didn't mention anything about his visit to the army town and what he had seen there. He was ashamed to confess to her that he had been terrified;, but for the overwhelming power he witnessed, a power that could destroy his world completely. It was a force that he could hardly believe existed in the world. He was paralysed before that giant mighty entity and found himself so powerless, tiny, and insignificant. To narrate all those horrifying feelings to a person who looked up to him as she did, was not an easy task. However, he felt at ease when he discussed the matter with Khafil, who listened to him without showing any surprise.

Khafil told Emron that he had never made the claim that taking up the fight against Dolec and his army was going to be an easy task. On the contrary, he agreed that it seemed like an impossible mission, but he believed that Emron was able to defeat the monstrous force and save the world.

"How?" Emron wondered desperately. Khafil shrugged his shoulders. He didn't know; it was Emron's task, not his own. When Emron told him about Priva's theory about the sea he agreed, but stressed that that was just a temporary hindrance. Ultimately, Dolec would find some solution to this handicap, if he hadn't found one already.

Khafil had not seen the armies, but based on Emron's description he could understand that they could not be engaged and destroyed by conventional weapons.

"We must seek the cooperation and counsel of the conflicting ones."

"Who are they?" Emron asked.

"There are others, who have something to fear from Dolec and his mighty army. Remember, he's a sorcerer," said Khafil. He didn't expand much on the subject, but looked a little distressed. "There are some worlds I can contact, like the Genii world, and gather more information about Dolec, but I doubt it can be of any great help." He looked a little pessimistic. "These conflicting ones don't cooperate with each other, they are like repulsive forces; we have to find some way to seek and convince them to help you. If we are to fail or to succeed, only the future will reveal."

Khafil promised to come as soon as he collected some information or had any news. Before leaving he asked if Emron had told anything to Salisa regarding Dolec's army with its terrible power to attack the world. Emron said that he had not yet discussed the matter with her. Khafil advised him not to worry her.

Khafil left and Emron was all alone to think, wonder and worry about the task he was about to undertake, or perhaps had already undertaken. On one hand, the problem was not abstract anymore, concerning some unknown country, but was a real one threatening not only the stability but also the very existence of his own world. He found it impossible to stay at home and hide his inner unrest from his wife, so most of the time he was out hunting and bringing home animals and fowls.

The hunting expeditions brought back the memory of Aseem and Zariba. He wondered how they were doing and had a strong desire to see them again. Emron asked Salisa if she would like to go with him to visit Zariba and Aseem.

*   *   *

The village dogs were the first ones to greet them when they approached. The dogs kept barking all the way to the village running, following the tail of Rino, announcing their arrival. A few people came out from their houses to find out what made the dogs so alarmed and anxious. Zariba was one of them. She had poor eyesight so she didn't recognise Emron from such a long distance. It was Rino she recognised first, and became joyous. She ran towards Emron with open arms. "Look, my Emron is back!" she cried loudly.

Emron jumped off from the horse and met her halfway. They both embraced. Zariba was crying of happiness and said something that he was unable to hear.

"I have waited seven long years for this day," she said, kissing him on the forehead. "I had given up the hope of ever seeing you again," she continued.

Emron smiled and asked, "How could you doubt my coming and visiting you! Didn't I promise you that?"

"How could I trust a devil's promise?" she was quick with her response and laughed. Zariba was so very absorbed with Emron that she hardly took notice of anything else; suddenly she saw Salisa and Amroush and looked at Emron with questioning eyes. Emron was amused to watch her confusion as he introduced his wife and child to her.

Zariba went to Salisa and gave her a warm welcome hug. She tried to hold Amroush but he would not go to her.

"You're a little devil just like your father!" Zariba said to his son and they all laughed. She tried to hug Amroush, but he clung on to his mother. Finally, Zariba gave up and welcomed them all into her home. Everybody followed them into Zariba's house, as was the custom.

"Where is Aseem?" Emron inquired. Zariba told him that he didn't live there any longer; since Emron's departure everything had changed. Aseem had abandoned all of his friends and companions. He spent most of his time either at home or out hunting. She was worried both for him and for their livelihood. If he was not to go and rob the caravans, then what were they to live on? Zariba had argued again and again, but Aseem didn't care.

"We have enough to live on, without going and killing

others," was his ready answer. "One day he got tired of my shouting and left," Zariba told him.

"Has he not come back ever since?" Emron asked, feeling pity for her.

"He does every now and then, she is just trying to become a martyr before you," answered some neighborhood woman instead. They all laughed, making her conscious of others' presence in her house. With a broad smile on her face she shoved those women out, saying they needed some privacy.

Zariba told them that Aseem and his cousin had taken a job in a town and where they happily lived. Aseem had also been married for several years ago, but he had no child.

"I'm happy that you've fulfilled my wish to have a grandchild. You..." she suddenly turned to Salisa, "Do you know how lucky you are to marry my diamond-like son!"

Salisa smiled in agreement. "That's why I have brought you this present," said Salisa and handed over a beautiful diamond necklace she had brought with her. Zariba looked at the necklace almost shocked, her eyes wet. She went forward to her and kissed her on the cheeks, and told her that it was the most beautiful diamond she had ever seen, and was extremely happy but couldn't accept the worthy present. She was too old a lady wearing that, she argued. It better suited Salisa, who was young and beautiful like the diamond itself.

The discussion went on until Emron intervened, saying that there was no way she could refuse to accept their present, putting an end to the whole discussion. Zariba kept looking at the necklace, and praising its beauty and craftsmanship silently. She thanked them both with warm hugs, accepting their gift and promised to hold it dear and safeguard it for the rest of her life.

*   *   *

She was not the same woman that Emron had years back left behind. Time had been not very kind to her; she looked weaker and older. She pretended to be physically fit, trying to move around in a quick pace but her body betrayed her.

"Who is taking care of you?" Emron asked.

"Why should anybody take care of me?" she sounded hurt. "I can very well take care of myself and others," Zariba protested.

Emron smiled and took back his words. "Say hello to Aseem from me. I'll try to visit him another time. Tell him that his decision to take an honest trade has warmed my heart," Emron told her.

"If by saying all these things you mean to take a leave, then you are wrong. There is no way I'll let you go before a month or so," Zariba told him in a determined tone

"If only I could do that!" Emron said with a smile. All of the arguments of Emron were unable to remove Zariba an inch from her determination to hold him and his family hostages as guests. At last a compromise was made and Emron was forced to agree to stay at least for a few days at her place. "You can see for yourself what a stubborn mother I have," Emron said looking at Salisa.

"Nevertheless, she is absolutely right. I wouldn't let my son go that quickly either," answered Salisa defending Zariba and her stand. Zariba's face lit up and she laughed triumphantly as she noticed Emron retreating; a strong alliance was taking shape between these two women.

They lived at Zariba's for almost a week and enjoyed every minute of it. It looked like some festivity was always going on there, in which the whole village was participating with songs, dances, music and a whole lot of food! These activities could go on until late in the night, making everyone too tired to get up early in the morning, but then why did anyone need to rise early in the first place? Zariba had not had enough, she expected and demanded from them to extend the stay even further but Emron politely declined and despite her strong insistence, they left her and the village.

He gave her a bag of gold, saying that she shouldn't refuse it since it required no sacrifice on his part; he was a rich man and was just paying back his old debts.

"You don't know how happy your visit has made me," Zariba said crying and went inside without standing to wave them goodbye.

*   *   *

Back at home they got a midnight visit from Salisa´s father. He looked and sounded nervous. Emron asked him to relax before asking what was bothering him. Were all the family members okay? Had something bad happened? Both Emron and Salisa were very much worried by his untimely visit. No, everything was not all right; he informed them with a shaking voice. He had just gotten the news that his old hometown was troubled again by the East. There were new clouds of worry arising in its sky. He felt worried for the sake of his relatives. Emron comforted him, saying that there was nothing they could do except hope and pray. "You know that we all have been begging them to come and live in this town, which is more peaceful and safer, but they have never listened to us," said Emron. The old man kept staring at the floor.

"I know that the people of my town have been thankless and cruel to you," his father-in-law said without looking at him. "But I can't help wishing that they will find someone like you to help them out, if they were to have trouble."

Emron didn't speak, but smiled sadly. Salisa became angry with her father, and Emron tried to calm her down, telling that it was not wrong to wish something good to others, even if they were thankless. "Maybe I should go rescue your relatives," said Emron. Salisa and her father kept silent, principally agreeing to his offer. Salisa wanted to follow, but Emron wouldn´t take her. Even if the attack was not in the making, it could be dangerous.

"Why do you want to follow?" asked Emron. "To make sure that you just rescue my relatives and not unnecessarily get involved in showy bravery there," said she. Emron told her that he had no such intentions. Salisa came out with him and asked him to be careful and not take any risks.

"Transport them in an ordinary way," she stressed.

*   *   *

He came to the market place when it was still dark, and found it deserted. There were no signs of any destruction caused by a battle, so he could tell that nothing bad had happened. The only thing he could tell was that the inhabitants of the town were busy enjoying their night's sleep. He was confused as to what to do next.

After pondering on the matter he decided to awaken those whom he intended to rescue. He headed to Salisa´s uncle's house and knocked on the door. Someone opened the door. Emron asked for the uncle, who came half asleep and looked astonished to find Emron there. Salisa's uncle invited Emron into the house, and asked if all was well. Emron told him the reason of his coming. The man shook his head and said that the message they sent was a few days old. The situation had stabilised since then. The turmoil in the East was perhaps only a false alarm. There were no further reasons to worry

"Give the family our warm regards, and tell them that we're grateful for their concern, but we aren't moving nowhere."

Emron tried to convince Salisa´s uncle that even if there was no imminent danger of attack, it was wise to move and live somewhere else, where it was safer. The riches of the town in combination with a complete absence of any organised defence would inevitably attract invaders. Her uncle seemed to be of a different opinion. He believed that the town had been thriving for centuries and wouldn't disappear because of such dangers. If there was a danger of such great magnitude he would send his family to them. But for the moment they were to stay. He offered Emron to stay for a couple of days before returning, but he declined, saying that he had to be back to his family.

Emron was curious and wanted to know exactly what

was happening in the East, but found little motivation to do so. Even if he did find out that the enemy was cunning and wanted to take the town by surprise, he would not be able to convince Salisa's relatives to pack and leave. He had done his best and could do no more, so it was time to return home. When he came back, his father-in-law had gone home and Salisa was surprised to see him back that early. He told her about his conversation with her uncle. She looked disturbed but said nothing.

"What do you think, are they safe there?" She asked after a while's silence. Emron said that it was difficult to say. If he was the enemy, he would not announce his coming, especially after the previous bitter experience.

Emron and Salisa couldn't give the news to her father yet. He simply wouldn't believe them. There was no way he could go and come back within hours to his hometown. The realisation of this problem gave them another headache; what was Emron to tell him if her family came to visit? Emron looked a little ashamed that he had not been struck by those thoughts before.

"Since I can't stay at home, maybe I should go fishing," Emron joked. He could go out to hunt, but that would not busy him for a few days, so he decided to take a little longer excursion.

He used his usual method and imagined some beautiful place. He opened his eyes and was struck by the beauty of the scene. The entire area was covered with snow. At a distance he could see the snow-clad mountain tops. He was not dressed for such a climate but strangely didn't feel any cold creeping into his thinly clothed body. He started strolling, looking around and enjoying the lovely scenery. On one side he could see the snow-covered tall trees, and on the other there was a spring, bringing forth water from the earth. He kneeled and touched the water with his hand, and was surprised to notice that it was pleasantly hot. He felt the temptation and gave in to it. He took off his clothes and jumped into the water. He could not describe the feeling of taking bath in hot water and watching the winter atmosphere all around. Coming out of the water, he felt a chill for a while but his body quickly adjusted itself to the temperature.

"Who are you? How did you come here? And what are you doing here?" He saw someone standing and asking him all those questions.

Emron smiled at the stranger, introduced himself and said that he was thrilled by the beauty of the place and felt forced to take a warm bath and now was on his way back.

"How did you come here?" the man asked. Emron didn't speak, but pointed at the horse. The man looked towards the horse, and looked even more surprised. He went a few steps towards the horse, but immediately retreated. He kept looking at Emron and the horse, as if trying to figure something out.

"Are you a human being?" the man asked, as if he was not sure.

"What else?" Emron answered. The man was about to turn when Emron asked what type of place this was and why he looked so surprised seeing him there. The man looked pensive, as if indecisive whether to talk to him any further or not. He came close and said he was ready to answer his questions, if Emron promised to do the same.

"Alright!" Emron said. "You shoot first."

"I can see now that you are human, but why the colours you reflect are different than those reflected by normal humans?" Emron laughed at that question, because it sounded so ridiculous. Getting serious he told the man that he could not follow his question and therefore found it not possible to answer. Suddenly he noticed that he was carrying the magic stone with him, and that realization puzzled him as well.

"You can see me!" he panicked. What had happened? Had the stone lost its magic? He looked aghast. The stranger smiled politely, seeing him getting nervous, knowing that something was terribly wrong with Emron. Yes, he could see Emron, the stranger told him, smiling at his illogical question.

"And what made you believe that you could be invisible?"
Emron refrained from answering or putting any question forward of his own. He wished that the stranger would go his way, leaving him to figure out what had happened to his magic stone, but the stranger seemed to have no intention of leaving. The stranger had a few riddles to solve before he could go his way. What really bothered the stranger most was not his unlike human colouring, but his arrival on the island on a horse.

At last the stranger decided to solve Emron's confusion, and by doing so he expected Emron to help solve his. He told him that though Emron could see him in a human form, he was a member of some other world. There lived no other humans on the island. His presence on the island could have been ignored, had he not been giving off the vibrations he did.

"The colours you reflect and the vibrations you give indicate that you're connected to some other world than your own. May I ask which world that is?" The stranger inquired in a straightforward manner. Emron told him that he was not connected to another world, but had received help from the Genii. A big smile spread on the stranger's face. But the mystery was only partially solved. As to the question why Emron looked shocked and panicky when he realized that he was visible, he showed to the stranger his dagger with stone and said,

"This stone is supposed to make me invisible. But it seems that it has lost its magic." Emron seemed to have recovered from his initial shock. The stranger looked at the stone and turned pale.

"Where did you get this stone?" he asked without wasting any time. Emron told him how he had found the magical stone and that he was not so sure of its magical power any more, if the stranger's claim to see him was true. The stranger sighed and told him that the mystery of his reflective colours was solved. It wasn't he, but the stone that was the reason for all the confusion. The reflective colours and intense vibrations of the stone got so mixed up with his human body that no one could distinguish one from the other. "The invisibility works only with an imposed limitation. You shall always remember that," he warned him.

"And what exactly do you mean by that?" Emron asked.

"It's not for me to elaborate on the subject, but I can tell you that this magical stone would never work in our world." As to the reason why he smiled, he told Emron the things he didn't know about the stone earlier.

According to the stranger, the stone had come from his own world, and was a rare commodity even there. It had other characteristics and qualities that no human could ever understand or utilize.

"I can give you anything in return if you give me this stone," the stranger tried to bargain. Emron rejected his offer, saying that he needed the stone himself. The stranger wouldn't give up. "I can take you to our king, I'm sure from him you can get an offer that you would find hard to reject..."

Emron denied him even that request, but finally agreed to meet the king on one condition; if the stranger agreed to tell him about the world that he belonged to. Reluctantly, the stranger started telling that he belonged to a world that Emron might not heard have much about.

"We are volcanic beings, who live in the depths of the earth. Like Genii we are made of fire, but in many ways we are the opposite of each other." He went on with the description and underlined the differences. He was keen to make it clear that they both were not related to each other, not even distantly. Genii lived on the earth, sharing the same space with others, while volcanic beings lived beneath the earth, and only in specific spots. Genii were more temperamental and ferocious, while volcanic beings, despite their element, could think, plan, and act without any hurry and were usually peaceful. He confessed that those qualities were not always there, but then again, who was perfect in nature? They lived, worked and created what they were supposed to do and preferred to live in isolation. It was forbidden to be in contact with other life forms, including Genii. Was it not for the stone, Emron could never find the volcanic beings and their world.

"You have something that is precious to us, and we can pay any price to get it back," the volcanic being said, and asked if he was satisfied with the answer or needed some more information.

"How can I trust you and your king, what guarantee is there that you'll not try to snatch it from me?" asked Emron, a little suspicious of that being.

"It's very simple," said the volcanic being. "We are not Genii, we don't work deceitfully. We are pure like the uncorrupted flame. We stand for our words. If I wanted to steal the stone, I needed not stand and bargain or beg. All I had to do was to rob you of the stone, without you being able to do anything about that - Look behind you," the volcanic being cut his speech and warned him to watch his back.

Emron felt some danger lurking and turned quickly and found five, six volcanic beings staring at him. Emron turned back to see if the being he had been talking to was still there. Not only he was there, but even held his dagger with the stone in his hand.

"Do you believe me now?" he asked Emron smilingly and gave him back his dagger. "Do we have to go underground to meet the king?" Emron asked.

"No, if you want I can bring him here," said the volcanic being. He quickly disappeared in the mist and came back after a few minutes, accompanied by another being who didn't look different or superior to the one he had been talking to.

King Kimertong surveyed him for a long time before he spoke. He told Emron that he had been informed about a visitor from the human world who had one of the precious stones, once belonging to their world and which was missing for centuries. He asked Emron for permission to hold the stone for a moment. Emron handed over the dagger without any hesitation. He took the dagger and looked at it for a long time, his eyes shining like glittering diamonds. He looked enthralled and happy. Yes, there was no doubt about the fact that that was the missing stone. He told Emron that the stone was priceless; as it was a part of their history, and the only rightful place it could be was in the volcanic world.

"We've many valuable things in our world, we can trade it with as many diamonds as you want." Emron told him that if he had not the pressing need to keep it, he would have given the stone to them without demanding anything in return.

"And what is that emergency?" asked the king.

Emron told him about Atrostia and its prince, about his mighty army, and the threat that he posed to the world of his and others. That was one of the reasons for his getting the freedom of movement from the Genii. The king confessed that he didn't happen to know anything about Atrostia or its prince. He told Emron that they had Volcanii living in different parts of the world; he was to inquire from them, and the other worlds, about the man that he felt the worlds' were threatened by. If that was the only reason for his not giving up the stone, he could count on volcanic world's full support and help in his fight.

*   *   *

The three of them entered some misty grounds and walked for a while until they came to a strange place. It was some sort of a huge cave. It must have been a hollow mountain. He looked up and was amazed to see glittering crystals hanging from the ceiling. The walls of the cave looked as if gold and other precious stones and metals had been used to decorate them, on the other side was a deep ditch. They kept walking on the narrow path, following each other, since there was only enough space for one person to walk. Finally, they came to a place the King Kimertong called Zorti, a dwelling of the Volcanii.

Emron could not see their real shapes, and only could

recognize them if they were to take a human shape. However, the king made these beings' habitations appear before his eyes. The entire place was filled with big globes that were made of precious stones and metals. They glittered and glowed, sending out beams of million colours. There was no apparent source of the light, but everything was visible like in the bright day. There were many such places like Zorti, where lived the other Volcanii.

He was told that even though in substance and essence, the Volcanii were subtle, they preferred to live in solid material places. He learned many things about them during the time he spent there. They didn't live in the volcanoes as he expected, using the crater as a passage to get in or out, and they were not made of lava as he had thought. They described volcanoes as their eternal workshops, and lava was the energy that they worked with to accomplish the work they were supposed to do, which was more related to the inner core of the earth than to its surface. What that statement meant, he was not very interested to know. They explained that volcanoes were always active. The period of super activities when the eruptions took place often happened in connection with the occasional surface work. At the time, the active energy was released to do the needed task of destruction or reformation of the landscape. Emron asked if they too were subject to the cycle of life and death.

Emron received the answer in the form of a question. "Are not all beings of all worlds subjects to the same eternal law?"

"How long do you live?" Emron asked.

"How can you describe what a moment is to an entity which is not conscious of time itself?" They couldn't convert their measurements in human terms that Emron could understand, and therefore were unable to answer his question. The length of the time was not as important as its quality of that sequence.

Emron enjoyed his stay in their major Zorti, and felt comfortable and welcome there. He was the first human to have come there and live with them. Other humans had come from time to time in one or another of their Zorti but that was often in search for minerals, but they could never see or touch them. "We don't want to harm the humans, so even though they come near to us, we remain alert but not hostile."

When Emron wished to leave, the King and his nearest ones wished him all the luck, and gave him many precious stones. The King promised to contact him as soon as he heard anything regarding Dolec. Rino was brought to him before he even asked for him.

"It's obvious Rino is not a simple animal. He vibrates with extremely refined energy," said King Kimertong, patting the horse on its back.

Emron came home and found Salisa very worried. Where had he disappeared to for such a long time?

"What long time, I had been away for just a day or two?" Salisa looked in disbelief and cried. "I don't mind your being away, the only request I have is to be informed that you'll be away for so long!" Salisa told him. It was his turn to be astonished, when he came to know that he had been away from home for more than a month. He explained his visit to the Volcanii, but could swear that it could not have been more than a day or two. Salisa and her family had been worried to death while he had been missing. Her uncle had confirmed his brief visit but could not add any more information. Salisa had suspected him of having gone eastward to check the situation there. Emron asked if there was any news from her hometown or from the area East of that.

She explained that though her hometown had remained safe, there was still unrest, chaos, lawlessness and uncertainty in the East. The law enforcing institutions were systematically attacked and destroyed by some mysterious bands of horsemen who would come from nowhere, kill all the soldiers they encountered and disappear as if they had never existed.

"What do the attackers look like?" Emron asked, looking

worried. Salisa replied that there had been no survivors to say anything about them. Emron could understand the anguish of his wife after she heard such worrying news. What had her relatives decided about moving away from the centre of the troubled area, asked Emron?

They refused to abandon their businesses for some temporary upheaval was Salisa´s answer, "You know how materialistic they are." Emron believed that her relatives' approach towards the problem was very dangerous, but he was equally aware that his opinion was of no particular interest or significance to them. He was worried about the development that was taking place in some far away country. He hoped that the appearance and disappearance of some mysterious bands had nothing to do with Dolec and his mighty army.

The more he tried to push the disturbing thoughts away from his head, the more powerfully they returned. There was no way he could stay untouched. He told Salisa that he felt the compulsion to go and check for himself what was going on to the East of her birthplace.

Emron took his weapons, which showed the gravity of the situation and left on his horse. That town city was exactly as he had anticipated. The people there were wild, rough in talk, and unpleasant even to each other. They were treacherous and cunning, making it almost impossible to rule them. But their rulers had been clever too, always forcing those people into submission by exercising constant pressure. There was always a strong, mysterious enemy lurking in the dark to annihilate them, making the people afraid and ready to accept the authority of the rulers, who would protect their lives and properties in return for their loyalties and obedience.

The enemy's only interest seemed to be to demolish the existing power structures, and didn't show any signs of replacing it with anything new. These apparently inexplicable acts left them in a vacuum, which was now filled with bands of robbers, thieves and other criminals.

These organised and disorganised groups were making life miserable for everyone. Emron was stopped by many such roaming gangs, who were interested to know who he was and if he carried valuables. Seeing him armed and without carrying anything of material value they let him pass without making any trouble. He went on meeting people and asking questions, but nobody could add new information.

He met one young boy who was showing interest in his bow. He started talking to him and asked if he had ever used a bow. The teenager said no. When Emron asked if the boy wanted to give a try, his eyes shone with happiness. Emron showed him how to hold the bow and pull the string and aim. The boy was as clumsy as any other new beginner, but looked content and happy. "Can you show me how to shoot?" asked the young boy. Emron smiled and aimed at a tiny flying bird and shot it down. The young boy jumped of excitement. "You're as good as the iron men."

"Which iron men?" Emron asked casually. The boy looked aghast; perhaps he had mentioned something he didn't want to.

"I was just joking," the boy said retreating from his earlier statement.

Emron could see that the boy was afraid and nervous. He calmed the boy down, assuring him that he had nothing to fear from anyone. The boy looked hesitant, but then decided not to resist. He told Emron that the reason why he didn't want to talk about the strange beings was that each time he had told anyone about them it had caused him pain and distress.

"I've been laughed at, ridiculed and even beaten for talking about it."

Emron told him that he was no such person. The boy said that he had seen a band of people, who rode iron horses and were even themselves covered with iron. If they were made of iron, or just had iron coverings, he couldn't say. He had seen them from the top of a tree, where he sat plucking some fruits. The boy had seen them with bows and other

162

weapons..

"Do you know where they came from or where they were going"? The boy told Emron that he could show him the place where he had seen those beings.

"If you can help me, I'll buy a bow and arrows for you," said Emron, giving him an incentive. The boy happily led him to a place outside the town. He showed him the tree and the place where they stood, and finally pointed to the hills where the iron men had headed afterwards.

Emron thanked the boy and gave him enough money to buy the very best bow and arrows. The boy looked happy and thankful. Long after the boy had disappeared from his sight Emron remained standing there, pale and worried. If he was to believe the description given to him by the boy, there was not a single doubt left that his worst fears had come true and that Dolec had found some way to bridge the separated parts of the world. Their shield of isolation had been broken and he and his world stood now completely unprotected from the forces of Dolec, who could take over his world without any kind of resistance.

*   *   *

Was Dolec planning to attack his part of the world, or was this still an experimental stage? Did he want to capture the power instantly or did he want to break the existing power base to replace it with his own at some later stage?

Emron couldn't solve the mystery. He knew that Dolec had an army of millions. Why did he only send a few soldiers to such an insignificant place? With a worried and disturbed heart he came back home. Salisa smiled to see him return. Her husband was sometimes a strange person who would not return for months when she expected him to be away for a short time, and now when was expecting him to be away for weeks, he was coming back, just after one day's absence. Looking at her husband's worried face she could tell that something was wrong.

Emron avoided the subject by telling her that he did not discover any additional information. He felt unease and anger towards Khafil, as if it was he, who had been responsible for the new emergency. It was the unavailability of Khafil that was causing irritation. He had known the wizard for so long and still didn't know much about the man. He wanted very much to contact him, but didn't know the address. There was nothing more he could do but to patiently wait.

9

One day he was out on some errand. When he came back, Salisa told him that a man had been looking for him. She could not provide any more information; because the person was a complete stranger to her and who had not left any message either except that he was to return later. Emron wondered who that could be. He didn't have to wait long, as the man really came looking for him after few hours. King Kimertong had sent the man.

"How did you find me?" asked Emron.

"I didn't directly," the Volcanii said with a smile. "I only needed to find your horse. There is no other creature like Rino in the whole world." He had a special message for him; the King had received some new information, and wished to see Emron as quickly as possible. Emron asked the Volcanii to go and tell the King that he was on his way.

*   *   *

He could tell that the King was waiting impatiently for him. By looking at his agitated eyes, Emron could tell that the matter was serious. Kimertong wasted no time with formalities; he told Emron that he had the needed information about Atrostia and prince Dolec.

He received new information from those of his own kind, living in that great country, which not only confirmed the facts that he had learned from Emron but even added many more new details. All that information had been the reason for his worry and anger. Dolec was not an ordinary prince, and neither was his army. He was an evil sorcerer, who had combined the forces and energies of different worlds with his country's advanced knowledge of science. He had been taking aid and help from the beings of other worlds and now threatened not only the human world, but even the under earth worlds like the world of Volcanii. "How come?" Emron asked. The King considered the matter for a while and then said, "It's little complicated, but I'll try to explain..."

The information he had received from Emron regarding Dolec and his army was no doubt worrying in itself, but the knowledge that the Atrostian army was handicapped by the sea was soothing and a little inspiring, as it gave the other parts of the world a natural protection and provided it with a period of respite.

Unfortunately, that was not true anymore. Emron agreed with him in his conclusion, but wanted to know how Dolec and his army had been able to overcome that hindrance. King Kimertong kept silent for a while, before he spoke

"We Volcanii belong to an underground world, but are in no way the only ones. There are other beings belonging to other worlds, living side-by-side, performing different duties than us. Subterranean beings belong to such a world. They live deep down in the earth, very near to the nucleus of the planet. These beings can live both deep down or on the surface of the earth. Their work requires constant mobility in all directions. These beings have solid physical bodies, like you humans, and thus need physical paths to travel," the King explained but was interrupted by Emron's question.

"What do these beings have to do with Dolec and his army?"

"Have patience, I'll come to that," said the King and continued to tell Emron that those Subterraneans were forced to build underground paths. So they dug uncountable chains of tunnels, connecting all parts of the world. No one knew about these well guarded and well-concealed tunnels, until Dolec came in contact with some misguided and misled individuals of that world. He convinced them to cooperate with him and in return they were to rule over all the underground worlds. These worlds above the surface on the other hand were to be dominated by Dolec.

These Subterraneans gave him access to materials of incredible power; the materials that he needed to build weapons to subjugate the world. These beings even revealed their secret paths and the tunnels that could provide his armies a safe passage for quick and undetected movements. His army was already using passages under the seabed to cross large distances. "In effect, nothing can hinder them from attacking wherever they like," said the King. The movements of the troops in their tunnel system had taken the Subterranean world by surprise. But there was little they could do about that. They had been betrayed by their own people. The knowledge that those beings were equipped with devastating weapons effectively deterred the Subterraneans from fighting for their transport system. They could not afford the destruction of the paths, which had taken thousands of years to build.

"So if the Subterranean world is taken over by Dolec, we don't know how we can protect ours," said King Kimertong with anguish.

"We must simply help each other," said Emron reactively

Kimertong was not sure if that was to be of any help but he expressed his willingness to fight by his side. "We have such limited power!" King Kimertong lamented.

"We'll find a way to gain allies, fight back, and ultimately we will overcome them," said Emron optimistically.

The King smiled, "You humans are amazing. You are the least powerful world in nature, but the most optimistic and daring," Emron laughed in agreement, and said, "Perhaps that's the key."

*   *   *

Salisa was aware that Emron was distracted, and she was absolutely sure that it had to do with Atrostia, but had no clue as to what was going on. She was keen to know but didn't want to be obtrusive.

"He will talk to me about it when he's ready," she told

herself. It was very hard for Emron to conceal anything from his wife. He eventually decided to confide in her. Salisa listened to him carefully and looked cross when Emron confessed that he had been withholding knowledge of the matters and other important information from her ever since his return from Atrostia. She said nothing and patiently waited for him to continue. He told about his adventures in Atrostia, along with his impressions and judgements. He even told her of his own fearful state of mind. He told her about Priva's and others' opinions, about the terrible weapons he had seen, the iron horses, iron covered soldiers and all the rest. She listened with open mouth trying to find any clue in case he was pulling her leg. But no, he was serious like always. She could feel the colour leave her cheeks.

"It's good that Dolec is confined to Atrostia. What a nightmare it would be if they were to find the access to our world," at last she spoke, though still worried.

"They are not limited to their world any longer," said Emron, and told her about the new developments and the news he had received from the area he had recently visited, and what he had learnt from the King of Volcanii.

"What are we to do? What will happen to our world?" Salisa panicked.

Emron comforted her, it was not all about their private tiny selves, but concerned so many different worlds and their destinies. So they had to think with cool heads, and not be afraid, because fear often paralysed and made the outcome an even bigger disaster. But Salisa was overwhelmed by the fear.

"We could take Amroush and Rino, become invisible and go far away!" Salisa spoke nervously. Emron had not seen her this nervous before. Perhaps that was why Khafil had advised him not to tell her anything. He didn't reject any of her propositions and just tried to comfort her by holding her tight.

Salisa was not herself. She looked anguished and troubled, avoiding eye contact with Emron. She wanted to forget Emron's words, but remained shaky. The prospect of losing everything she held dear was too much. She went to bed early saying that she had a headache. Emron felt sorry for her, but didn't blame her for her anxiety. In the morning she was herself again, smiling and talking cheerfully as usual.

She came forward to Emron, kissed him good morning, and smiled. She told him that she had been thinking seriously and came to the conclusion that the world and its affairs were too much for her to worry about. Her worry didn't help anyone! That would certainly not stop the march of Dolec's army, and neither would it help Emron find a solution to the gigantic problem he faced - to prevail against an invincible enemy. She had decided to be calm and supportive, so that he could concentrate and try to find some possibility to win over the evil. She promised to be stronger, when it concerned her own personal feelings. If he failed to win the battle, there was no shame because he was hopelessly outnumbered. He stood without enough trustworthy companions with the task of facing the army of millions. But if he was to prevail and overcome his mighty opponent, he was to go down in history as an incredible hero, a great master of warfare.

Emron smiled, satisfied, he loved her not only for her beauty. She had been a solid rock for him, a sensitive friend, and an orator who could choose the perfect words at the right time.

*   *   *

Khafil appeared one day out of nowhere and pretended as if he had just been away for a few days. Emron gave him the news that Dolec's soldiers had already found a way to their world. Khafil told that he had been aware of this fact though not mentioning his source of information.

"What have you been doing?" he asked Emron.

"Not much," he gave a short answer. If the old man wanted to play a game, it was all right with him.

Khafil noticed his sudden reluctance to talk, and asked if Emron was irritated by something. Emron told him that he was not very comfortable with his appearances and disappearances. His inaccessibility was frustrating. He disliked the unequal relationship. Why couldn't he contact Khafil if he needed his advice, while Khafil had the privilege to come and go at will? Khafil smiled and agreed that they both had different privileges. Emron was too keen to notice Khafil's privileges, but had chosen not to remember his own. He was told that that was not the right moment to discuss those trivialities, they had a great task ahead and needed to concentrate on that. He asked Emron to tell him everything he knew, and what had happened while Khafil had been away. Emron agreed that that was not the right moment for them to waste time, discussing something of lesser importance.

He told them about the unrest of the areas East of Salisa's former town, his visit to the island, and encounter with the Volcanii.

"That's strange!" Khafil exclaimed. "Highly unusual. They don't usually make contact with humans," he said, surprised. But when Emron told him about colours and beams that the being had been talking about, he smiled as if he could understand the phenomenon better.

After listening to everything, Khafil said that his information was more or less the same except that though Dolec and his Subterranean friends were all solid and physical, they had developed some means through which, if successful, they could control and rule the subtle, invisible worlds as well. This new addition made every single world in nature both inside and outside of the planet vulnerable. It was a unique and unprecedented happening, which made them all equally nervous. Emron asked if Khafil could help him meet the Subterranean leaders.

"I don't think so," said Khafil.

"Why not?" Emron asked.

"First of all, they don't like to have contact with human beings. Secondly, they feel threatened by your world. They shall not differentiate between you and Dolec," said Khafil.

"Very unintelligent approach. I don't confuse them with the Subterraneans who are cooperating with Dolec!"

"You've made your point," said Khafil and promised to investigate the possibility. "What about you? Have you thought of any way to challenge their might?" Khafil asked.

"Yes, I can appear on the back of Rino, make them follow me, only to disappear from their astonished sight!" Emron joked. Khafil didn't think it was funny.

"No, I don't think it's possible to destroy the army even if we find a way to kill a few of them," said Emron getting serious again. Khafil was listening to him intensely. "Can the Genii help?" Emron asked.

"No, it's beyond their power to do so. They themselves are scared half to death. If you fail then we all are without a hope." Khafil said, making Emron smile bitterly.

"How very easy it is to shift all the responsibility onto my shoulders," he pleaded sarcastically. "Is that so because I have freedom of movement and the shield of invisibility?" he asked Khafil with the same sarcasm.

"No." Khafil said in a low voice. "These are just tools at your disposal, and have no other significance in the forthcoming battle." Emron felt a little ashamed of his being too hard on Khafil. If Dolec was evil and had the plans to take over everything, it wasn't Khafil's fault. He immediately apologized for his rudeness.. Khafil patted his shoulders and said that he was not the only one feeling great pressure and distressed.

"But we shouldn't give up. We simply can't afford to." Khafil promised once again that he would try to arrange a meeting between him and the Subterraneans, and departed.

*   *   *

It was complete silence in the country East of Salisa's birthplace. He didn't hear news of any new attacks from there or anywhere else. No new ruler emerged, since no one was strong enough or had a viable force to fill the power vacuum.

The lawlessness persisted and had become a new reality, forcing everyone to be strong or to perish. Many weaker individuals felt forced to move westward, most of them without any money or valuables. In their new hometown they were hardly welcome. They found it difficult to survive, but had no other choice than to go on struggling in those unfortunate conditions.

Emron visited Toriba, Salisa's hometown, when he wanted to sell some gold or valuable stones. He could see the people's misery and provided them with food and shelter. He felt bitter and angry with the heartless people of that town. But it was beyond his power to change the poor conditions or those hearts of stone, which characterized the Toribians.

He was not sure when and where the soldiers of Dolec's army were to appear, but he knew for sure that their plans must have been in progress. He desperately wanted to know if there were some weaknesses in the army that he could exploit, or if he could get some unexpected help from a new ally. But it seemed that there was nothing he could count on, it was all black, without even the slightest ray of hope. There was silence from Khafil, no news from King Kimertong, no message from the Genii. Was he the only one worrying about this? Many times he thought of going to Atrostia to find out what was happening there.

*　　*　　*

One day he was in Toriba on business. He felt a strong impulse to visit the place the young boy had shown him some time before. He went there and was looking around when he heard the strong rumbling of the earth.

He looked to the direction the sound was coming from. He saw in the distance a few horsemen coming with full speed towards him. Emron was alarmed. He jumped on the horse and rode as fast as he could, making it look like he had succeeded in escaping. But then he stopped and looked back. The riders were four in number and sounded angry when they realised that he had succeeded in escaping. He couldn't see their faces that lay hidden behind their iron coverings. But that was the first time he could watch them that closely. The horses they rode were not animals, but some kind of machines made of iron. The riding soldiers were completely covered from head to toe with iron, making it impossible to hurt them with conventional human weapons.

Suddenly he saw the glitter of an eye. He took his bow, placed an arrow in the string, aimed at one soldier and shot. He silently fell from the horse, dead before he hit the ground. In the confusion, Emron had another chance at hitting the other one. He fell in a similar manner.

The other two were terrified and rode away in great haste, leaving their fallen companions behind. Emron followed them and could see them entering a hidden passage. He smiled to himself for his first victory against the enemy he deemed invincible. He had won the first battle and was proud of it, still convinced that he could never win the war.

He came back and looked at the bodies of the soldiers. He couldn't figure out how to open up their armour, and nor did he know what to do with the heavy iron horses, which stood lifeless. The only possible help he could think of was the Volcanii. He rode out to them and requested some help.

King Kimertong sent a few Volcanii to go and see what could be done. They followed Emron and expertly took off the armour and head coverings off of the dead soldiers. Emron asked if they had been well acquainted with such armour before, they replied negatively, but confessed that the task had not been difficult at all, as all types of metals were their speciality. To transport the horses was a problem. None of them knew how the beasts functioned. They could demolish them, but that was not what Emron wanted. So they hid the horses with branches of a tree, and decided to leave the matter alone for the time being. The Volcanii took the armour with them, to investigate them properly. Just by looking at them they could tell that it was masterly work.

Emron came home and told Salisa about his encounter

with the Atrostian soldiers. She looked pale, but proud of him, greeted him on his minor but important morale-boosting success.

"You see, perhaps the enemy is not as indestructible as you have previously thought!" said Salisa with a smile.

Emron looked satisfied with himself, but that was only for a brief moment. His gloom quickly returned and got hold of him. "You know, Salisa," he spoke in a tired, defeated tone. "I feel so lonely, so isolated, and so very powerless in the forthcoming struggle. The fate of so many worlds is at stake and I haven't got a single soul at my disposal, to aid me. I'm not afraid, but tell me how am I to face and destroy such a powerful enemy. I have neither an army nor comparable weapons!"

Emron was not very enthusiastic when Khafil came with the good news that the Subterraneans were ready to meet him without any conditions.. Khafil had expected a complete rejection from them, but on the contrary, they were eager to have the meeting right away, either in their own world or in the human one, and Khafil told Emron that it was his choice.

"I may visit their underground world some other time. You can arrange this meeting here," said Emron half-heartedly. Khafil noticed that he was not in high spirits, but didn't make it an issue.

"Shall I bring the Subterraneans to your home, or do you want to meet them somewhere else?" asked Khafil before leaving. Emron told him that his home would do. "Then just stay home; I will soon be back," he said and left.

A few hours later he was back, accompanied by two very tall and strongly built strangers. They looked straight into his eyes, and nodded without a smile.

"We have been told that you are interested to have a meeting with us. We don't see any good coming out of this, but we wanted to give it a try, so we're here," said one of the Subterraneans without losing any time by offering greetings and introductions. Emron could not be similarly rude in his own home; smilingly he welcomed his guests and offered some food and drink, which they refused.

Emron started speaking about the problem that they all faced, the seriousness of the matter, and the need to find some amicable solution to their shared problem. The guests looked uncomfortable and irritated. At last, one of them interrupted him in the middle of his speech. "We all know the background and the problem, so get to the point," said a Subterranean in a cold manner. Both Khafil and Emron looked at each other, Emron looked very angry at that insulting behaviour, but controlled himself.

"That's the human way to talk. Maybe you are used to some other way, so please don't interrupt me next time, even you find it the wrong way to talk," Emron said seriously, without getting rude. Both guests kept silent and Emron could detect a smile on Khafil's old face.

He continued talking, without making any haste. His guests looked bored, but didn't interrupt him again. "We know that prince Dolec is using your territory and transport network, and thereby have succeeded in having an access to our world. We are told that beings of your kind are providing him with the means and materials to be used in their destructive weapons production. We have no defence against these weapons. In short, your world is playing a most vital role in this threatening situation." Emron went on, but was interrupted again with an angry response.

"We had expected this type of treatment! What a very typical human approach!" said the Subterranean. "We knew that you humans were going to blame us for all your ills. But we shall not listen to it!"

Emron tried to calm him down, explaining that in no way did he intend to offend his guests. All he wanted to do was to underline the facts, which necessitated a plattform to find a solution for their problem. It required a combined effort to analyse their peculiar situation, and discover any possible solution. The Subterraneans calmed down and looked less defensive after that.

Another Subterranean, named Forsa, explained, "We have no shame in confessing that the knowledge of a few powerful Subterraneans working with humans was completely ignored by our authorities who didn't consider it a threat to anyone."

The same could be said of the materials and minerals that were taken out of their territory. The dangerous nature of these materials was unknown to them. So there was no cause for alarm. The problem was recognised when it was already too late, when the human soldiers started using their transportation system, occupying the space at times, and threatening their whole existence.

The Subterranean said that they couldn't survive without their transportation channels, and if they were to be used by humans, there was no hope left for them, making it clear to Emron why they didn't resist Dolec. Initially, they had thought about fighting, but changed their minds when they saw what resistance would mean to them.

"We were taken to Atrostia by our own traitors to witness the most destructive weapons that the Atrostian soldiers had at their disposal. We were horrified to see what those weapons could accomplish," the Subterranean said quietly, perhaps reflecting on his fears regarding the complete destruction of his people, if they had resisted. So they surrendered their authority over their tunnel system, accepting Dolec's right to use them whenever he wished to do so.

Time passed, and the Subterraneans saw that by losing their authority over their own territory, they had given in to a blackmail, which ultimately would lead to a bigger catastrophe. "We feel that our time is running out and very fast. The moment they have enslaved the outer world, we will be next on their list."

Dolec and his Subterranean companions were already breaching the agreement by coming to their cities unannounced, and trying to assimilate and take support from the locals. "By now, one third of his army consists of Subterraneans," said the same person. The iron horses that the soldiers use as a mode of transportation are a modified version of Subterranean vehicle. Since the distances were enormous, no one could cross the tunnels without the help of those speedy vehicles. Emron and Khafil listened with care. When the Subterranean fell silent, Khafil asked if there was any way to stop those soldiers. They said that if there was, they were not aware of it. Emron asked if they knew how the horses worked.

They thought they did know, since they were built on the same principle as their own vehicles, only differing in shape and appearance. Emron told them the reason why he asked, and took them to the place where they had hidden the horses.

The Subterraneans had seen those horses passing through the tunnels, but only now could they look closely at them for the very first time. One of them went around, but found nothing, and then he sat on the back of the horse, with the help of his companion and started touching around the neck of the horse. The horse first moved in a slow pace and then galloped, disappearing from their sight.

When the Subterranean returned, there was a smile on his lips. He halted the iron horse and came down. The horse functioned as he had thought, with small variations. For instance, turning around in a quick manner was a fantastic addition, likewise the slowing down and acceleration processes.

"It is an amazing improvement," he confessed.

"What fuels it?" asked Emron. They failed to understand what he meant. He tried again by saying that everything needed some energy to work, so what did that iron horse need to function?

They smiled when they finally understood the question. The iron horses had special hoofs, which were made of a certain stone. That stone had an enormous capacity to charge energy and could carry the vehicle for thousands of miles. When drained of energy, they could easily be recharged.

"What was that energy?" Emron asked. The only answer he got was that the energy was everywhere and in abundance, but it was their secret energy source and they had no wish to reveal the secret any further.

Emron smiled at their careful attitude. "If there was a mechanism in the iron horse's movement, there must have been another to slow the speed and halt it to a complete stop," said Emron.

They both looked uncomfortable by his questions, but could not refuse him the information. In a very complicated way they explained how the iron vehicles were slowed down and how were they halted completely. After they told Emron all that they were willing to tell, they wished to return home.

Before leaving, they welcomed Emron to come and visit them if he had any question or some important information he wanted to share with them. He requested those beings to take the mechanical horses with them, since he didn't have any use for them. They would just attract everyone's attention once they were discovered. They agreed with him, and took the horses with them.

"There is one request," said Emron.

"What?" they asked.

"Please, keep your eyes open. Note and record how frequently they cross your highways, to which directions they move and how large the bands moving around in the passages are." Emron told them. They promised to do accordingly and left on their swift iron horses. Khafil had some important task to do, so Emron was left alone. If it were normal circumstances, he would stay and have his meal there, but the whole decayed area anguished him so he decided to head home instead.

*   *   *

At home, he discussed the matters with Salisa and told her everything he had learned about the situation, confessing that he was getting more and more pessimistic. She listened carefully and tried to be supportive, but knew well that all her husband needed was some concrete force at his disposal and not just some comforting words. She realised that there wasn't anything she could say or do to boost his morale at that very moment. But at the same time she had a strong wish to drag Emron out of the hopeless, miserable state, in which he was being pulled down to.

Perhaps he needed some distraction in order to get rid of the feelings of loneliness, she thought.

"Why don't you go and visit your tribal friends?" said Salisa, encouraging him. He looked amazed as he was thinking of those brave friends right that minute. Smiling, he bent forward and kissed her.

"You're amazing! Where would I be without you?" he said, holding her little hand. He decided to take her advice to go and visit his tribal friends but before that, he wanted to meet Aseem and his cousin. It was not difficult to find Aseem, who now worked in the same army as he himself had once served. Aseem was extremely happy to see him. "Oh, you have grown into a handsome young man!" he said embracing Emron. He told him that he had heard about his visit to his mother. "You didn't need to buy such expensive gifts for her," he said. Emron just smiled.

"I've brought one for you too," said Emron and gave him the beautiful sword with an embroidered sheath. "It's solid gold, decorated with precious stones," said Emron.

"Is the sword made of gold?" Aseem joked. They both laughed. "Come, let me introduce you to my wife, she is so keen to see you," said Aseem.

"Some other time," said Emron, excusing himself, stressing that he was in a hurry.

They talked about things and exchanged news about people they knew and discussed family members. Aseem said that his cousin was the new commander, and was very thankful for Emron's recommendation. He was proud to have turned the little army into the best fighting force in the whole area. Aseem confessed that despite all their success, they had failed to produce anyone like Emron again. To discover a pupil who could beat the teachers afterwards was not a common happening. Emron smiled at those compliments and looked a bit embarrassed.

"I'm ever thankful to you and others, who have helped me become what I am." He was humble like always.

All of a sudden Emron changed the subject and started asking questions about the ruler. What type of person was he? Could he be made agree to borrow some of his best soldiers to him? Aseem looked at him with a great concern and inquired,

"What's the matter? Are you in some kind of trouble? If so, then all your worries are over." He assured Emron that as his elder brother, Aseem would take care of all his problems from then on. Emron thanked him for his support and for expressing the most beautiful feelings, but what he needed was not any immediate help, but a promise that he could borrow some of the best-trained soldiers.

"You know I'm not in a position to promise anything, but through my cousin we can put forward the request. The way the ruler regards you and my cousin, I don't see any reason why he should decline your request," said Aseem.

"Look, I have to go further in search for other possible help. I'll stop by on my way back, and we'll talk in detail. Don't worry about me, I'm doing just fine," Emron told him before leaving.

"Wouldn't you like to meet my cousin, he would be so happy to meet you after such a long time!"

"I have to rush, perhaps next time! Bring my regards to him," said Emron and left. He headed on towards the tribal area.

His unannounced arrival there was a reason for both happiness and alarm. He was still remembered and revered, but had taught them a great lesson. To never ever trust any foreigner again! They were extremely happy to have Emron back with them, but the way he had broken their barriers by arriving there undetected showed them that their defence mechanism to detect and stop unwanted elements already at the borders had failed completely.

"But here I am a foreigner among you once again," Emron joked. They all laughed, saying that he was no more a foreigner, he was in soul and essence one of them, a great warrior.

The news spread quickly to the other tribes, who came hurriedly to meet him. They sang, they danced and they celebrated refusing to discuss anything serious. After two days of feast and celebrations, they got exhausted. Most of the members returned to their tribes, inviting him to visit them as well, wishing him a very pleasant stay and best of luck. The peace treaty seemed to have succeeded, with occasional happenings involving individuals from different tribes.

"What has brought you to out tracts again?" asked Kidra. "If it's gold, we have plenty of, if it is stones we can load you with them, if it's women…" Emron interrupted him.   "I don't need all these things, I've found plenty myself," he replied, looking at the chiefs. I'm here for one single question. Can I count on your help if I need it against an enemy?"

The chiefs looked at each other, as if to choose, who was to answer. "Emron, as we have told you earlier, you're no other than a part of us. Your friend will find our doors open for him, and we shall chase your enemy to the doors of hell," spoke Kidra with determination.

"Even if the enemy is mighty?" Emron asked.

"Who could be mightier than death? We'll stand and fight even against that, if you ask us," said Kidra, and Emron trusted his every word. All tribal chiefs swore to give him all of their male warriors, to stand and fight by his side. Emron already felt stronger and confident. He thanked them for their wholehearted support and blind trust in him. They didn't even try to ask for the details, they were ready to fight any enemy of his at any given time.

They talked about other great things they had

accomplished ever since he had left. Yearly sports and competitions among tribes were now traditions, and so were intermarriages. They had formed an inter-tribal council, consisting of the elderly tribesmen, who discussed and decided about the disputes and problems arising between tribes. They even had rules and regulations regarding individual crimes and violations of the agreed matters. Emron was proud for bringing peace to them. He was sure that if peace among them survived for a relatively long period of time, that would surely make them forget the bitterness of the past, ensuring its continuity, perhaps forever.

When he came back home, Salisa saw his glowing face and knew that meeting with his friends had had a positive impact on him. He looked relaxed and in good spirits. He told her that he had a wonderful time with his friends.

Aseem and his cousin had convinced the ruler to help Emron. Likewise he had been successful in getting the full support of all seven tribes, who were ready to sacrifice their lives for him. "Have you told them the nature of the enemy? Maybe after hearing about it, they will revoke their offer," said Salisa.

Emron didn't see any such danger when it concerned the tribesmen; because he had lived with and known those people. He had witnessed the fearlessness and strong convictions of those brave honourable people himself. He could count on those friends for whom the words of honour were more important than life itself. But when it came to the soldiers, he was not so sure as he didn't know much about them.

He was fully aware that his situation had not changed, but he was glad of the prospect of having a few people at his disposal in his hour of need. He was conscious that if he was to engage himself in a fight, he needed to prepare his strategy wisely, knowing that he was outnumbered and could not win a traditional war.

"If the tribesmen have decided to fight by my side, they will. It will be my duty not to sacrifice those people's lives unnecessary," Emron said.

"But that does not answer my question," Zariba gently insisted, forcing Emron to confess that he had not told anyone about Dolec and his mighty army yet.

Salisa was happier for his change of mood and enthusiasm than anything else. He told her that he was to relax and take it easy for some time. He had had a very hectic period with so many worries and activities, and knew not what lay ahead. So he wanted to collect some new energy before deciding to take on the impossible mission and fight the incredibly powerful enemy or surrender without a fight, like the other worlds had been doing. He wanted to spend quality time with his family who had been so supportive, dedicated, and sacrificing. If the end of their world were approaching, they would rather enjoy their last moments together.

*   *   *

To shut the world out and concentrate on family was a good idea. For months, he had not given any time to Amroush, who was happy to get his attention. Even his contact with Salisa had been rare and stressful. They all had the feeling that the time they enjoyed before Emron's journey to the tribal area had returned. They talked, laughed, and spent carefree days. That was the life Emron had always wished for himself and for his family.

A whole week flew away like a songbird. Since no one had contacted him, he could prolong the inactive days. But the sense of responsibility began to take hold of him once more. If the Subterraneans had not contacted him, he could reach out to them. He took Rino and went to see the representative of that world, Forsa, who was astonished to see him.

Emron explained that Khafil had helped him in an otherwise impossible task of finding their underground world. Emron could see an obvious change of behaviour this time, because his host was less formal and defensive than the previous time. He welcomed him to the Subterranean world, but made it clear that Emron could not visit their cities or passages.

"And why not?" he asked smilingly.

"We can't risk that your presence among us is known to the enemy," he presented an excuse.

"My presence?" Emron laughed. "The enemy doesn't even know that I exist!"

Forsa was a little embarrassed. He had wished to be polite but now found no other way than to confess that the precaution was necessary, if they were not to announce any cooperation or collaboration with human beings. There were already anti-human feelings, which could even turn against their own leaders if it was known that they were making contact with humans.

After small formalities he got to the point and asked if they had the requested information. Forsa told him that the information they collected was authentic. The soldiers that were using their passages were moving in all possible directions. They were not equipped with the heavier and more destructive weapons yet, and carried with them the traditional human developed weapons. If it was the lack of the need or some logistic problem, they were unable to tell. Those bands of the army units that were involved were between fifty to hundred soldiers. Most of those units were sent to destroy the existing power structures in their part of the world. These units followed fixed patterns and routines. As soon as some unit was completing the task and leaving, another band was sent to attack some other side, only to accomplish the mission and then return, and so on. They had not seen or heard any news of a big scale attack. It seemed Dolec and his army were not pressed by time. They were confident and were not expecting any opposition, at least not from their own primitive part of the world. They had succeeded in so many places and so easily that there were claims that Dolec's army could win the world in a single day.

"Take all this information and judge for yourself if it could be of any practical use," said Forsa.

"Before we decide to fight till death or surrender without giving any resistance, we want to know if you and your world are unconditionally with us," Emron asked.

"We shall give you moral support," said Forsa as a reply. Emron laughed.

"To save our world and yours, we are ready to sacrifice our lives, and you're ready to give us moral support."

Forsa stood speechless. Emron went on. "We demand that you give us all the help you can, whenever and wherever it's required," Emron concluded. "If we take the responsibility of physical combat, as an ally you have to bind yourself to other duties as I have mentioned."

"But it's not possible!" Said Forsa.

"And why not?" Emron asked.

Forsa gave the lame excuse that they could not afford to anger Dolec, who could destroy their whole world.

"If you're afraid to show your colours, it's fine with us. But you have to agree to our conditions if you expect us to take the challenge of facing Dolec and his mighty army," said Emron decisively. He requested that Forsa and others in high places consider his conditions. If they were to agree, he could come and discuss the matter in detail and find out in which manner they could help and assists in order to make the struggle a possibility. But if they decided not to take an active part then they could not expect any help from the humans either, because the rescue of the world depended on cooperation and mutual efforts and not on selfish attitudes.

He felt a bit disheartened by Forsa and the Subterranean world. Instead of returning home he went straight to King Kimertong. He had decided not to waste any more time in guessing and hoping. He gave him the detailed report, and asked the straight question.

"I've told that you're very honest people, so I need a very honest answer. If we humans are to take a stand against Dolec's army, what type of support we can expect from you?" King Kimertong tried to explain the limitations of Volcanii.

"No, you don't get it. I'm not demanding that you accomplish something that your world is incapable to perform. All I ask is how far are you willing to go? Can you and your world become our allies in this struggle?" Emron rephrased his question.

"You can count on me and my world. We shall assist you in all possible ways and still be thankful for your sacrifices. That is a solemn promise of a Volcanii!" said King Kimertong.

Emron gave him a warm handshake, saying that he had been hoping for such an answer from him. At least there was one world he could completely trust and expect support from. How possibly they could assist and help him, he did not know at the time.

*   *   *

There was still one world left. Khafil had warned him not to venture there since it could be dangerous, but how much more dangerous than it already was could it get? The only problem was that he had no contact person in that world. Suddenly Emron thought of the Genii. He spoke the word to the horse, who seemed to be reluctant. He was conscious that it was not the fault of Rino, but still he felt betrayed.

Maybe I should use some other method, Emron thought. He knew if a certain code didn't work, he could always confront the problem from a different angle. This time he tried to reach to the person who had been his contact person to the Genii world. He closed his eyes and opened again finding himself in Genii land. He stood facing the sea enjoying the fresh smell. The sea colour, the colour of the sky and the chain of hills, everything was the same. His earlier code word had worked anyhow.

It was not difficult to find the place he had been earlier along with Khafil. He was surprised to see Khafil standing, waiting for him outside the cave.

"What took you so long?" he said to Emron, as if they had an appointment.

"So you're on a visit too?" he asked. Khafil ignored his remark and they went into the cave. He had brought some fruit and drinks.

"I've been expecting your visit for some time," Khafil said. He told Emron that the cave was his own home and not belonging to a friend as he had earlier told him. He had reasons not to tell him the whole truth before. He was no wizard, but a Genie who had a human form. Emron was both amused and angry. He felt tricked by Khafil, but he could see the similarity between his own act in the tribal area and the act of Khafil, and a smile spread on his lips, easing his tense body. "No hard feelings?" asked Khafil with a smile. "No hard feelings," said Emron with laughter. "I must confess, you're a remarkable impostor!" Emron complimented his mentor. They talked about his real name, appearance, and other trivial things until Emron remembered the purpose of his visit to him.

"Now that I know that I've always been in a direct contact with Genii world, it's necessary to clear up other things as well," said Emron. Regardless of who was in charge of the Genii world, could he count on Khafil as his contact person?

When he got a positive response, he came to the questions he had put to the others. Khafil couldn't give him any right away answers on behalf of his world, but promised to come back to him after discussing with others. Emron insisted that without the active and absolute help of other worlds they all were doomed. He agreed that Dolec threatened many worlds, but disagreed that the danger was equal to them all.

"Don't misunderstand me when I say that our Genii world is least touched by this threat. I'm telling you this because I want to underline that our help is due to our good will and that in no way we are forced into some alliance with other worlds."

Emron smiled, listening to his arguments. He kept silent for a while and then spoke. "Of course your world is going to be equally affected if Dolec is to succeed," he said confidently. "Don't you and us share the same space? Don't our actions make difficulties for you? Doesn't our negativity create a great problem in your world?" Khafil listened with great care.

Emron went on, if their world was unaffected and not a threat, why the need to contact a human? Why was he granted the freedom of movement? Why all the trouble? Emron did not buy his argument that Genii world was giving them some favour by offering them a helping hand. He stressed that Khafil was not the only source from where he got his information. He had other channels by which he could tell that Dolec's scientists were working on instruments that could detect invisible worlds like Khafil's. They were almost done with weapons that could freeze and destroy beings like him.

Khafil looked aghast. Emron was amused to see his reaction. He couldn't elaborate because he knew so little about it, except that Dolec's scientists were working on some vibration measurements, and studies of wavelengths, they were quickly learning how different energies blended and functioned in separation and cohesion. They knew that Genii world was made of flames and could not survive below certain temperatures, so these scientists had almost succeeded in creating such weapons and tools that could give them their required effects.

Emron concluded, "I must make it clear that our survival is not a separate issue, your world is connected to us, and our failure is equally yours. So I plead for your whole-hearted help. Make sure that we are not going to be sacrificial lambs." Emron said his final words and waited for Khafil response, which politely told him that Emron had made his point, and which required some serious pondering. He promised to come back as soon as possible.

"I know things move very slowly in your world, but we have no time to waste," said Emron, before asking for a leave. Khafil smiled noticing the change in Emron's confidence.

To his utter surprise, the Genii world was swift in response to his call, offering him unlimited and unconditional help, making it clear that they considered it an alliance for combined struggle to achieve the mutual benefits and goals. This underlying stress was ego boosting for Emron for the single reason that he wasn't begging any favours from others. The only answer he still awaited was from the Subterraneans, whose sovereignty was threatened the most. Without their help and involvement, he couldn't even think of giving any viable resistence. From their complete silence, he understood that they were too scared to take a risk. But then some unexpected happening forced them to take a quick decision. Dolec had asked for two things from them. First, he wanted them to help him quickly produce a large quantity of iron horses, and second, he wished that the passages be closed to others during the time his armies moved from one point to another.

They could read between the lines. It was a command, not a request. They didn't answer him at once but came to Emron, showing their willingness to ally themselves in his struggle.

"We know that these requests are the first signals that we're about to lose our sovereignty," said the Subterranean.

Emron told him that their decision was wise, and that they were not going to regret it. He told Forsa to wait for the details, as to how they were to cooperate and communicate with each other, what kind of help he was to ask of them and in which manner they could provide him that. He asked how their intelligence was functioning within Atrostia. Forsa told him that the soldiers' activities had enhanced, but there was no full-scale invasion on the way. There was a single obstacle that was still hindering Dolec from fulfilling his dream to conquer the world, and that was the shortage of his iron horses. Many of his Subterranean friends had warned Dolec not to use Subterranean vehicles for transportation of soldiers, as he had earlier planned. The reason they did so, was their mistrust of the Subterraneans world that they had betrayed.

*   *   *

Emron quickly called a meeting between the four worlds, and made a combined command, which was to function as a single entity. Looking at their needs, educating them of the required actions, confronting problems and obstacles from all possible angles, finding the suitable solutions, observing the enemy, and most important of all to search for weak points in its gigantic, incredible and powerful body. "Remember, nothing in this world is perfect. There are weak points inherently present in everything; all we have to do is find them. Think of the worlds you belong to as different parts of the body and we, the council, are to act as its mind. Emron and the others were to establish a direct, democratic, and fast contact line, because that was to be their bloodstream, a lifeline. Their first step to open warfare had been taken. Whether they were to win or lose, was an unknown fact. Looking at the faces of his allies he didn't need to guess. The Genii were to provide the transportation facilities to Emron's army, the Subterraneans were to give them vital information about the movements of the troops, and point in the direction they were heading to.

"What about us?" asked King Kimertong.

"Please help others wherever needed. Your main task may come later!" Emron made it clear that the division of duties could change from day to day. They all were fighting a powerful enemy, which might require a daily change of strategy. They were to work untiringly day and night.

*   *   *

When the Genii, that were connected with Emron, looked at his few thousand men strong force, they were impressed by how well they handled their weapons. They all were in human form roaming about at ease. They showed a great interest in everything.

Emron had advised them to keep their identities hidden from his men. One of the Genii came to him, asking when they were supposed to transport the rest of his army. "What do you mean by rest of the army?" asked Emron.

"We are all gathered." The Genie looked confused, but when Emron explained him the same thing the second time, he rushed and brought another Genie.

"Tell them what you just have told me," requested the Genie. Emron smiled at his funny request and told them for the third time the same fact that there was no further transportation at the moment. He could see their opened mouths, standing and looking at him in disbelief. Suddenly they simultaneously fell into laughter, and laughed and laughed. Emron got irritated and asked them to go and laugh somewhere else. The Genii found the whole statement very funny and tragic at the same time. They had seen the mighty army of Dolec and had heard what they could accomplish, but not in their wildest fantasies could have believed that a force of a few thousand men or so could have the confidence of fighting and winning against them.

"Have you any clue of the army you are about to challenge?" one Genie asked.

"Yes, I have seen my enemy and am aware of his terrible might," answered Emron confidently and fearlessly.

"And these soldiers of yours?" the other Genie asked.

"No, they haven't," he said.

"I had supposed so," said the Genie and they all laughed. This time, Emron could feel that it was more a laughter of praise than of ridicule.

"Either this man is a complete idiot or a superior being," the Genii thought, and there could not be a third possibility.

10

They didn't have to wait for long. They got the message that a band of fifty or sixty horsemen were on the move. The direction and exit points were given to them and the approximate time of their arrival at the exit was calculated.

Emron took Aseem in his confidence and asked him to prepare his men for the encounter.

"And remember my warning. It's not an ordinary enemy we are about to face. It is going to be a test of courage and nerve. Don't be overwhelmed by their strength and might." Aseem smiled, ensuring him that his soldiers were brave and very good archers. The enemy was supposed to appear at the exit point at dawn, making it necessary for them to leave at once. They needed to study the area and find the best spot to ambush them. It was going to be their first encounter with the enemy, and the most important one. Everything depended on it and he had to make sure that nothing went wrong. If he was to take many of his men, it could be difficult to control and use a big force effectively. On the other hand, if it was too small a force, then it could be a seriously demoralising factor.

He had to decide quickly. He could not bring a large number of his men to fight against an enemy that was far superior, if not invincible. He decided at the last minute to take only Aseem, his cousin Saeef and four other tribesmen he knew, were their best archers. Without letting others know they had departed and came to the exit from where the war band was suppose to make an entrance.

It was a hilly area as they had expected it to be. It was dark but with the help from Volcanii, the visibility had been adjusted, making it possible for them to look around without much difficulty.

Emron wanted to attack the band of soldiers after they had come deep into the country. If they were to succeed, the attack had to be unexpected, abrupt, and with an unfaltering precision. They had to distract them before they attacked.

Emron chose a place, looked around, and discussed his plans with Aseem and Saeef, before quickly preparing the traps. They accomplished much with the help of the Genii and the Subterraneans. They dug a huge ditch and covered it properly. All of the archers except Emron hid themselves in the trees on both sides of the ditch. It was still dark when they saw the iron soldiers of Dolec approaching, unaware of any danger.

They were moving at slow and careful pace. When the party reached about a hundred yards from the ditch, the Genii made horrifying loud noises as they had been told. The heart piercing sounds were so close and so threatening that the horsemen galloped their horses merely thinking that there was some expected danger. The first riders must have noticed the ditch but it was too little too late. The pressure from other horses from behind pushed them headlong into the ditch. Many of them fell and the others looked to see what was going on. Emron waited for them on the other side of the ditch, invisible.

He aimed and shot in the eye of a rider, who fell dead. That was the sign the others had been waiting for. It started raining arrows from all directions.

There was shouting, screaming, and panic among iron men on the iron horses. Many of them were falling, hit by the arrows; others fell by the collision of the horses. There was general confusion until the horsemen retreated without even turning to look at their fallen companions.

There were many iron soldiers who were not hurt, but simply disoriented by the panic. Some were trying to come out of the crushing weight of other dead soldiers or iron horses. Their arrows put an end to the misery of those soldiers. There was a war cry from the four worlds but only Emron could hear all four of them, as none other was aligned to those worlds as he did. They had won the first real battle! They counted the dead. They had killed forty of the enemy's indestructible troops. Emron knew that the morale of those six men mattered very much. Now that they had accomplished their mission, nothing was impossible; they could convince their men that where there was a will anything is possible.

Emron greeted each and every one of his commanders. They had done an incredible task, and deserved praise. Emron could see that pride and disbelief were intermingling in the eyes of his commanders. The members of the other worlds would clean up the mess; the humans had a tough night, they were tired and they needed rest, but first they were to find a good place to do so. The Genii attached to Emron pointed towards a spot, so he decided to rest for a while there.

*   *   *

After a brief rest, they were on the move once again. They walked an hour or two and came to their camp. The news of their great victory was received with a deafening noise of jubilation. The whole camp was celebrating by singing, dancing and praising the bravery of those who had taken part in the combat. Many of those left behind regretted that they had missed a great opportunity to take part in such an important battle.

The commanders were telling their details to their men, boosting their morale, exciting their fantasies, and enthralling them. The soldiers' enthusiasm was kept by a promise that sooner or later they too were to get the opportunity to prove their talents, skills, and bravery. The Genii looked happy and impressed, but were still unconvinced that Emron's tiny army could prevail in the long run.

Each time they got the information of the iron men moving in a certain direction, Emron and his men would be waiting in ambush, using the only weak point those soldiers had; their vulnerable eyes, causing distress in the soldiers of the enemy. It was becoming more and more difficult to trap them; they were getting more alert, and began using some eye covers, making it almost impossible to detect and to hit them. Emron's initial successes were ebbing away, taking away the temporary enthusiasm from the three worlds; the fourth world remained unconscious, unaware of what was going on, except the tiny group of warriors at Emron's disposal.

Emron had already lost dozens of his men, and the situation looked desperate. A council of four worlds was not of any great help. His strategy to frustrate the enemy was failing, and if he wished to keep the fight on he had to find some new ways to deal with the enemy. His biggest problem remained unresolved; he was not receiving any intelligence reports. Many times he considered going himself to Atrostia to find out, but no one agreed to that risky task. There was a gloom and hopelessness among his allies, but then came the genius suggestion of King Kimertong.

The Volcanii were the master builders of the underworld, the experts of furnaces, unchallenged converters of the metals, and knew well their properties and qualities. By checking the samples of armour, they could tell how much heat those materials could absorb without being dangerous for the human body. If it were to exceed that barrier, then it would be impossible for soldiers to bear it. This information and knowledge urged Kimertong to present this idea.

If the Volcanii were to increase the temperature of the earth with only a few degrees it would be impossible for the soldiers to remain in their armour, forcing them to come out of their heated iron shields, giving the perfect chance to Emron and his men to kill them. They all agreed and were jubilant, but Khafil showed no excitement. No one took notice, except Kimertong.

"Don't you think it could work?" he asked Khafil.

"Maybe!" was his short answer.

"And what gives you doubt? Is it our capacity to heat up the earth that you doubt or our knowledge about the iron?"

asked Kimertong.

"None of these," said Khafil with a smile, "there is nothing wrong with your plan, except that you are forgetting something." And what's that? Kimertong asked curiously.

"That we are talking about human beings. If it would be burning heat, they would simply retreat to the cool passages of the underworld."

A silence followed with sighs of disappointment. All of the attendants looked deeply unhappy, as if they had been deprived of a great opportunity.

Emron also sat with bowed head, seeing a beautiful plan slipping out of their hands. Suddenly he jumped from his seat and made a big cry. Everybody looked at him with a surprise on their faces wondering what had gone into him. "Listen, I believe Kimertong's genius plan could work anyway," he shouted.

All looked in his direction anticipating some explanation. He expanded on the plan of Kimertong.

"The moment that the riders leave the tunnel and come out from the exit, the Genii and Subterraneans could seal the entrances with heavy stones. The retreating soldiers, dying of heat will find no cool place to turn to and then we will start our task," spoke Emron full of joy. They all cheered and greeted each other for finding a new way to deal with the enemy.

*   *   *

Their change of tactics worked beautifully. The summer was hot, but the hidden work of the Volcanii made it even hotter. The heat was getting unbearable for the enemy soldiers, who had gotten more and more confident. They were not being attacked anymore, giving them a false sense of security. They believed that they had been able to crush the little force that offered them resistance. They were once again the imperishable soldiers of the invincible army.

The size of their bands had increased to more than a

hundred, and so were their frequent arrivals and departures. It seemed as if each time a new team was sent to get used to and to get acquainted with the world they were about to invade when the time was ripe. These bands of soldiers were so confident that they were not finding it necessary to work in secrecy any longer. They were aware that their presence and designs had been revealed at least to some people of the primitive world, who were desperately trying to stop them. Now with their improved armours even their eyes were protected, so what more could be there to be frightened of, they convinced themselves.

There was a group of about a hundred and fifty soldiers who were riding on their iron horses. They emerged from the exit and started making their rounds in the nearest town, demonstrating spite for the local population, provoking anger among the warriors if there were any, exhibiting their power and superiority.

They kept moving but something was terribly wrong. They could feel it, but could not describe the feeling. The heat was becoming unbearable. It seemed as if the backs of their horses were on fire and transferring those flames to their armour.

They felt all sweaty, suffocated, and burning with a hellish fire. In pains they looked at their officer, who himself seemed to be very uncomfortable. He signed his men to return. They moved with such a great speed that just after a few seconds there wasn't any trace left of them. Riding like a storm they came near to the closed entrance and looked around, as if unsure of coming to the right place or not.

Emron and his men were hiding in the hills, waiting for their moment. Emron and his men were equally tortured by the raised temperature of the earth, but they were somewhat protected by strange outfits they had gotten from Volcanii. The rubberlike shoes were absorbing the heat without passing it on to the body, the light material cloths were both airy and heat dampening.

The soldiers on the other hand not only lacked these

protections but also were in the iron armour, which made them extra vulnerable. It appeared as if they could not take it anymore. They were panicked, confused, disoriented and most of all were suffering from the unbearable heat coming out of their iron horses and armours. Many of them jumped down from their horses but found no relief. The heat kept on tormenting them. They were now struggling to get out of their armour!

Emron and his men smiled, looking at each other, wiping the sweat from their faces they waited with patience. No sooner the soldiers had come out of their protective armour, gone was their indestructiblity and superiority. They were more vulnerable and exposed than others; because they stood in reach of the best archers of the primitive world they intended to take over.

They were getting out of the frying pan only to enter the fire! Hardly had they come out from the torturous armour and were trying to get some air, when it started raining arrows. Many of them didn't even get a chance to be on their feet; a few tried to run away but failed. It didn't take long before the enemy lay before their eyes, completely devastated, utterly defeated.

Their flawless victory was a turning point in the war. New bands of Dolec's army kept streaming in, only to be slaughtered and never return to report what happened to them. Emron received news that Dolec and his aides were furious and frustrated. They were ready to pay anything if someone could provide them with the information of what was going on in the primitive part of the world.

Despite the mysterious disappearance of his soldiers and horses, his determination to conquer the whole world and to be the unquestioned Emperor of the worlds remained strong. Dolec's problem was that unlike the Subterranean world, he had ignored the necessity to infiltrate the primitive part of the world; he wished to take it over and dominate it unquestionably.

But the realisation was too late. With the arising

problems, he had no chance of solving them if he didn't know what kind of problems he was facing.

One of his Subterranean collaborators gave him an idea to attach a few spies with the soldiers that would not accompany them, but would watch from a distance and report back what was happening in the world.

Dolec liked the idea and told his Subterranean friend that, "If it is your folks who are behind this, I swear I'll destroy you along with them." But he didn't have to. His spies came back and reported what they had seen.

Some mighty men had closed the exits with heavy rocks, blocking the way so that no one could go in or come out. They described the confusion of the returning soldiers when they couldn't find the entrance. They elaborated the scenes of his soldiers taking off their armour to get relief from the sizzling heat and how ultimately they were butchered by some strange-clothed men.

"If the entrance was blocked, how could you get in?" asked one of the Dolec's aides. "After accomplishing their task, they had opened the entrance once again," was the answer. How many were the attackers? What type of weapons they were using, and many such questions were asked, but they couldn't tell since they were so far away from the battleground and so distressed by the heat that only wish they had was to be away from there as quickly as possible. The only thing they could tell was that all warriors were praising their leader Emron, by shouting and hailing his name. "Emron, Emron our great leader!" Dolec smiled coldly and hissed, "Not for long!"

*   *   *

Emron was sick with fever when they heard the news that the enemy was approaching; there was only about two hundred of them. They seemed well equipped and moved rapidly. Emron started getting ready but Aseem pushed him back, saying, "We know you're very keen to destroy the enemy, but we can manage one day without you. Let Saeef be your commander today." Emron agreed only if Aseem was also to stay and continue training the others.

"He has the best archers with him, I'm sure that he will manage," said Emron. He was feeling dizzy, so he slept.

He was awakened by Aseem, who looked pale. He told Emron that he had very bad news for him. They had not only lost the battle but all of their companions as well.

Emron was shocked by the news and was trying hard to understand what had happened. The words of Aseem sounded as if he had spoken from the world of a dream. He wished it to be only a bad dream, but it was very real. There were no survivors; all of their friends had died fighting bravely. The picture of the happening was reported by the Genii, who had turned themselves into their original shapes and disappearing into thin air.

The enemy soldiers seemed to have gone to the side of the town, but that was only a manoeuvre. The enemy was aware of the presence of Emron's people hiding in the hills. They turned back without going to the town and encircled them from all sides, and before they knew that they were in danger, the attack came.

The enemy had weapons that destroyed everything they hit, taking all of their cover away. The large rocks were blown into pieces, the trees and bushes were burnt to the ground, making his men stand unprotected, unable to flee and powerless to harm the enemy. They all perished quickly, one by one. To lose such a significant number of his best men was nerve-breaking news for Emron. But to know that enemy was aware of him was news too. The soldiers of the enemy, completing their mission had screamed, "Emron, we have destroyed you!"

After the loss, the balances had tilted once again in favour of the enemy, which had taken the precaution of not sending the troops when it was too hot, but waiting for the evenings to roam about. They had started guarding the exits more vigorously.

There was little Emron and his men could do to stop them. All his allies had given up all hopes of stopping the march of Dolec. Most pessimistic of all were the Subterraneans. They were even getting irritated and impatient. Emron had to do something drastic if they were to give him continued support. They could not endanger their very existence; if Emron was to lose the ground, then it was better for them to distance themselves from him. It was obvious that they were planning to withdraw their support and that could occur any day now. "They're like that," confessed King Kimertong sadly. "They don't want to share the destiny of the loser."

Emron kept his men far away on safe ground. He couldn't afford to lose any more men, who despite a major blow, were in high spirits. They all desperately wanted to avenge the deaths of their friends, but found no way to do so. The enemy was overwhelming and increasing in number every day. Now their number had grown to many thousands. If there was any solution, it had to come quick or all of their efforts and hopes would be dashed to the ground.

Emron used the invisibility stone to infiltrate the enemy camp to discover if there was any possibility to stop them. He listened to them, surveyed them, and observed them from all angles, but it looked like there was nothing left for him to do. He decided to call a meeting. He intended to confess that his mission had badly failed.

He went to see King Kimertong, who was most intelligent of all of his allies, and to inform him of his decision to announce his defeat.

"It's too bad," said the King. "Even if we all have failed, we shall always remember your bravery and courage. No other being in no other world would have accepted such an impossible mission like you did. None of us had the means to fight such a monstrous force," said King Kimertong. While talking he was playing with something.

"What's this?" Emron asked.

"Oh, nothing," answered the king, looking at the empty

space.

"Please explain this to me, I find it a very interesting thing," insisted Emron.

"This is a piece of iron," the King said. "And this other piece is a magnet."

"What makes them attract each other?" asked Emron, still surprised.

King Kimertong explained how the two metals worked, as one of them got charged of energy. Emron did not understand anything the King was explaining, the negatives and the positives, the attraction and repulsion, the magnetic fields of the earth, the use of that force to control and stop the vehicles. The only thing that King Kimertong could notice was that Emron was looking at the objects of his hands with bewildered eyes and was not present in the conversation.

"What are you thinking Emron?" the King asked.

Emron told him excitedly what he was thinking. Kimertong listened with great care, and kept silent for a long time, and then he got up from his seat, went forward, and gave him an emotional hug. "What a genius idea! What a wonderful solution!" Kimertong praised him warmly.

"That's it!" he shouted triumphantly. He discussed the matter more closely and then asked Emron to leave the details of the plan of his and the Subterranean world to take care of. All the warriors were gathered to listen to Emron who intended to make a very important speech. He praised their courage to fight against such a monstrous enemy. He appreciated their bravery and the sacrifices that they made. He was proud that they remembered their friends and kin with love and warmth in their hearts, their dearest and nearest who had died honourable deaths fighting the evil. He told them that he too missed the great warriors who had vanished from their sight but lived in their hearts and minds.

He told them that their fallen friends were martyrs, who were to live forever and ever. He said that his heart also desired him to take revenge. The time for such a moment was approaching very fast; they were to face their enemy once again, to devastate its forces, to destroy its evil dreams to enslave their world. They were told to prepare themselves for great struggle and victory. His men looked as unafraid as they ever had been and were ready to die, but they didn't share his enthusiasm. Emron understood the reason for their dampened optimism, and could not boost their morals with empty words. Unfortunately that was all he could offer them at the time.

*   *   *

The resistance was non-existent, as Emron didn't want to lose his tiny force and that raised the morale of the enemy forces even higher. The moment the enemy forces detected any suspects they chased them and eliminated them at sight, without any questioning, without any accusation or a trial and without showing any mercy.

Often they were the armed strangers or hunters who were unaware of the situation in the area. They were the innocent victims of the turmoil. The local people feared the iron riders and were ready to do anything to please them. The iron soldiers were happy to deploy spies amongst them, they appreciated their information and rewarded them well and gave the guarantees of even greater reward once they had settled down. A few of the Genii were also working as double agents, posing as informers.

With the passing of each day, the soldiers of Dolec became more convinced that either the tiny force of Emron had been completely destroyed or dispersed, seeing the impossibility of engagement. "Everything was under control," was the message that Dolec's units were sending home. They had prepared the way for a full-scale attack, and the major transportation of the troops could easily be secured. Whenever the army chief saw fit, an attack could be initiated in the primitive world.

An informer had passed on the information to the iron

army that a very large numbers of armed men had been seen moving around in a certain area. The information was quickly passed on to the commander of Dolec's army in the area who decided to act immediately. He had the experience of many such hunts and knew that they had to act swiftly if they were to destroy those suspicious elements. Dolec's commander knew that he could easily destroy a very large army even with a small unit of his force, but decided not to take any risks, as his superiors had told him to do. He ordered his assistant commander to take a force of a thousand riders and ambush the enemy troops as usual.

Shortly after they arrived at their destination, Dolec's commander felt the increasing heat and looked to the sky. The sun was not as strong as he had anticipated. Perhaps he was suffering from fever; he was sweaty and the heat was increasing. The commander looked at his soldiers, who were also showing signs of unease. The realisation came like a thunderbolt that it was a trap. He looked at his soldiers and gave them an order to retreat. They must've been astonished by the change of order but decided to obey. They wanted to turn, but could not. They had been deprived of their movements. There must have been panic in their hearts, but they couldn't express it through their actions. Whatever they did they could not move their horses. The increasing heat was becoming unbearable, so many of them jumped to the ground to runaway. But what now? They couldn't even take a single step forward. They were glued to the earth, the heat penetrating into their bodies and burning them. They were desperately removing their armour.

The soldiers who had terrible weapons were shooting around in panic, hitting and destroying everything that came in their sight. Their indiscriminate shooting was relieving many of their own companions from the unending misery. When the sound of weapon silenced, the cries of distress continued from the soldiers. They heard the war cry of Emron's men, who came from all directions to take the revenge of their fallen friends, brothers, and relatives. The enemy was defeated once again, sending the shock waves all the way back to Atrostia. Emron the great leader was still alive, and capable of challenging and destroying the mighty army of Dolec.

Dolec was unable to understand what had happened, how a tiny force could destroy his most modern, most powerful, and most well equipped army. What astonished him even more was the simple question why no one saw a trace of his iron horses after the attacks. Dolec wanted to send a greater army to crush this Emron, whoever he was, but the others around him asked him to be cautious, and not do anything in haste. First they had to find out how this disaster had taken place.

*   *   *

There were great celebrations both in the Genii and the Volcanii worlds. The Subterraneans were to celebrate silently and secretly, as they were still afraid of Dolec, and didn't want him to know that they were happy about his setback. In the human world, celebrations were confined to just a handful people who, despite their small numbers, were doing miraculous work.

The heroic and selfless efforts of the combined forces at Emron's disposal were forcing their enemy to reassess its own strength and plans. Dolec was compelled to wonder if his estimates were realistic. Maybe the primitive world was not as backward as the evil prince had hoped and expected. The struggle of Emron's forces was to continue, but after such a great success they all deserved time with their families. Emron gave the soldiers and warriors all great praise and thanked them for their loyalty, their unquestioned faith and trust in him, and most of all for their courage and willingness to sacrifice. "I think that for the time being, evil will not dare to attack us, but surely they will not avert from seeking our world again. That day might be far ahead when the enemy shall confront us again, or it might be just around the corner.

I can't say for sure, but I sincerely hope that you'll come and fight by my side when the time comes."

11

Emron came home to Salisa and Amroush, and they were very happy to see him. Salisa was well informed of all the major happenings by Khafil. She was so relieved that the danger at least for the time being was over. She was proud of Emron's achievements, but he was modest. "No, it's not me, our success is due to combined efforts of all the four worlds. I just happened to be fighting as their head!"

Salisa loved his humble approach; there wasn't the slightest sign of arrogance in her husband's attitude. He told Salisa that none of their achievements could be possible had it not been for the wisdom of King Kimertong, the knowledge of Khafil and the hard work of so many who had been involved. Telling her about the details of their major encounter, he told her that after he had learnt about the magnetic power he had requested the Subterraneans to prepare new magnetic fields, which could be activated at need. That was not a difficult task for them, since they had been using these techniques for a long time. The combination of magnetic fields and furnaces prepared by the Volcanii were great tools, which made the miracle possible.

Salisa was amused to listen how a timely idea had saved them from a sure defeat and given them a temporary edge over their enemy. But Emron wanted to forget for a while that they were at war.

A month passed and nothing new happened. Dolec's had not stopped their activities but they had diminished their numbers drastically, making everyone hopeful. The units that moved from one point to another were small, and avoided daring movements. They had learned not to engage themselves with their opponents until they knew why so many of their soldiers had been killed. The clues were not many, and none had survived to tell the story. The war was not over, but it had taken a break. How long that intermission was to last? No one could say. It all depended on whether Dolec's army was to discover the cause of their unexpected defeat quickly or not.

If there was anyone who feared that the stalemate could not last for very long, it was Emron. He believed that they had little time to think and prepare for further battles which were to be much more difficult to win. Sooner or later, the enemy would discover the existence of the magnetic fields and find new ways to protect themselves from them. The Subterraneans and Volcanii shared the worry with Emron that once the cause of the disaster was discovered, there would be nothing left for them to do. They were all doomed then. They wanted to do something to prevent the forthcoming catastrophe, but the question was, how?

They resumed their daily meetings, but that brought them no closer to any new ideas or solutions. Emron was right in his assessment that humans had done everything that they could and if they were to stop Dolec it had to be something overwhelming, a last desperate attempt by all four worlds.

He asked the Subterraneans to describe the world they belonged to in full detail, with all of its weaknesses and strengths. The Subterraneans were astonished by the request, but did not say anything or protest. Instead he listened to the others carefully, putting forth questions, asking for explanations, sometimes amused by things that he didn't know before. He loved the passion with which they described their worlds and the wonders of each, and became a little sad that how little he knew about his own world.

The Genii and the Volcanii got silent after describing their worlds. The more secretive Subterraneans looked uncomfortable, most reluctant to say much about their world. They had an inherent tendency towards suspicion against the other worlds, and there was nothing anybody could do about it. But now they felt forced by the necessity to speak the unspeakable in front of people who had been considered adversaries till not so long ago.

Emron could understand their caution, but he had to learn about the world that he knew the least about. Finally, the Subterranean representative started speaking. He spoke slowly in the beginning, which made him difficult to understand. But slowly his fear gave away and his voice grew stronger and more confident. He was telling them about the planet Earth that housed all of its vastness, beauties, wonders, mysterious, its apparent qualities and its hidden potential. He eloquently described what they could see on the surface of the earth, with all its variations and wondrous multiple faces. But beyond all that visible face of the earth laid another wondrous beauty. In their underground world, flowed the rivers and streams of dark murky waters, and one could find the birth places of rare and valuable stones of all kinds. The outer world could never affect its inner beauty.

Emron could see the sarcastic smile on the faces of the Genii. Emron listened with great interest and fascination. The Subterranean was describing the inner world, about its different layers, about its crust, about its core, its inner beauty, its absorbed heat and the heat of its own, and the light of its own. About how the lands were made and what lay beneath the seabed. Far below them there was a massive plate, which was supposed to be impenetrable, but the Subterraneans were proud to be able to make ways even through that barrier.

"How could you do that?" asked one Volcanii, impressed.

"As a matter of fact it's not one single plate, but many plates that are connected in an unexplainable way. We exploited that knowledge," said the Subterranean proudly.

He went on talking about other things that happened down below the surface of the earth. What types of life could be found there, and how they had solved the problems of layers and such.

"What were these plates made of?" Emron asked.

"Your volcanic friends can answer it better," said the

Subterranean. "They are the master builders of those plates. They keep the metals and minerals used in its construction secret. Emron looked at Kimertong, who with a smile confirmed that it was true.

The brain of Emron was working with an incredible speed, he asked for an interval in the meeting and came out talking to Kimertong.

"So do you have a plan?" Kimertong asked with a smile. Just by looking at Emron he could tell that he was struggling with some great ideas. Emron told him what he was thinking. He listened carefully, but laughed when he finished. "That's a funny idea and very probable, but we are not dealing with Dolec alone. His Subterraneans friends shall never buy that," said King Kimertong, still amused by his plan.

"So you don't think there is any point in presenting it?" Emron asked.

"I didn't say that," answered Kimertong. "It's always beneficial to ask the opinions of the others."

When everyone had listened to the proposition they fell silent, struck by the mere possibility, but then came the objections that Kimertong had anticipated. There were too many ifs and many unanswered questions. They hadn't right away rejected his proposal, on the contrary it was decided that a combined committee of the three worlds were to deal with the question and find out if that could be feasible. They promised to act quickly and not waste any time in putting the findings of the committee before the council in shortest possible time. Within a week, the report was presented to them. The committee was of the opinion that Emron's proposition had potential and that it could be turned into a plan. There was a possibility that it would work, even though the chances were meagre.

The plan required not only the assistance and cooperation of all worlds but even circumstantial favourable winds and a great measure of luck. There were details and many problems, like Kimertong had underlined. There was little to discuss. If the plan had even the minimum chances of succeeding they had everything to win and nothing to lose from putting it into practice. They decided to implement and work on it immediately.

*   *   *

Reports from Atrostia were streaming in. All of the military activities there had been enhanced. More soldiers were being trained, more vehicles were produced, and the pressure on Subterraneans was increasing to respond positively to the requests of Dolec. It was now a most necessary step in the continuation of their good relations with the Subterranean world. It was promised that they were to be the benefactors of the deal. They offered the Subterraneans treaties, giving them guarantees that destructive weapons were not to be used in their underworld. It was getting harder for the Subterraneans to make further excuses.

Everything was pointing in the same direction. It seemed Dolec had made up his mind and was in the final stages of his full-scale attack. His advisers had convinced him that by looking at the unexpected resistance and growing opposition to his army from unknown quarters, it was not wise to delay any longer. It would just provide more time for the enemy to get more organised and more powerful. They didn't know the cause of their defeat, but could still count on the fact that no army in any part of the world stood a slightest chance against their full strength. Dolec was not very confident, especially after the recent setback, but agreed that they should prepare for the attack with or without the Subterranean support.

"We shall deal with them later. First, I want to crush the head of the snake Emron," said Dolec. Just the mentioning of that name made him furious. "I'll chase him to the ends of the earth!" Dolec was spiteful.

He was very impatient to lead his armies, to conquer the world, to be its first ruler and most of all to subdue the other worlds as well. "You beings of other worlds, listen and tremble. Soon I'll be on my way to make history. I'm bringing a present to you, a beautiful present of subjugation." Dolec boasted and laughed, his aides joined him. Despite all their efforts and preparations, it would take months, perhaps more than a year before he could sit on his iron horse to lead his mighty army. Somehow he felt deprived of the words indestructible and invincible, and some damn 'Emron' was to blame for that.

Emron didn't know that he had become a living nightmare for Dolec, whom he hated more than anything, even more than his fear of death. His scientists were busy researching why certain life forms could live much longer than the humans. They were searching for the answer in minerals, vegetation, animals, and other species of all kinds. They were to come with the answers very soon, and that would be a tribute to their patron, their protector, and financier. Whatever they were, it was all thanks to Dolec's appreciation and generous attitude towards them. They owed their high status, riches, power, and influences to him. Nowhere was Dolec so popular than in the army and among these despicably greedy scientists.

The general public in Atrostia was becoming more and more miserable every day that passed. The privileged elite, the army, and the other administrators consumed the country's vital resources. Ordinary people were forced to lead lives in terrible conditions. The state slowly withdrew all its benefits and privileges. All spending on developments were cut and opportunities to earn a living were drastically curtailed. There was only one profession open and that was the military.

There was unrest in the population against the Queen and her husband; there were feelings of dislike. There were spies everywhere, who would inform the authorities about the critics and the dissidents, who would be arrested under some pretext, never to be seen again. There was terror in the hearts of the people, but they could not speak of it. Their eyes witnessed all the evil, their ears heard all the lies, but their tongues were silent. They had lost all hope and lived with the sad knowledge that they were doomed forever. They were no longer free citizens of Atrostia; they were victims of their own stupidity. They made the monster Dolec strong by threatening and persecuting their fellow citizens who had recognized his evil long before them. They were prisoners of their own cowardice, but it was too late.

*   *   *

Khafil and Emron's other allies opposed his plan to visit Atrostia. It was too dangerous to walk into the lion's den. They all knew that Dolec hated Emron and his presence there in his own country would trigger a great provocation and an outrageous reaction, perhaps it could even lead to a premature attack on all of their worlds. The Subterraneans believed that Emron's arrival in Atrostia would be blamed on them, since they knew no other way to come in or out of Atrostia than their subterranean passages.

"That's not a problem," said Emron confidently. "I could have come as one of Dolec's soldiers, as they cross through your territory every day," the answer calmed them down.

The only person who didn't object was King Kimertong, who believed that it was Emron's responsibility to decide his own strategy. Kimertong was supremely confident in Emron's judgments. Khafil agreed that it was a good idea for Emron to go to Atrostia alone.

All the others could do was to take all the necessary precautions.

*   *   *

Emron and Khafil made the plans for his journey. An iron horse and armour belonging to a fallen Atrostian were placed outside the exit point in Atrostia, giving the enemy a clue that someone had entered their country by using their vehicle and disguise. When Khafil came to know about the real reason of his journey he smiled.

"You are incredible. Be careful, and I'll be waiting for your sign to come and transport you."

Khafil left him a distance away from Priva's house, his Atrostian friend. It was not difficult to find her home, but she wasn't there at that moment. He waited a long time, but still she didn't come. He was not sure what the best thing for him to do was to go on waiting or to proceed and visit Guliaki instead. At last he decided that there was no point in continuing to wait and started moving from there. He was leaving Priva's house when he saw her coming from the other direction. He kept invisible and followed her inside the house, remaining invisible.

"Hello, Priva! How are you?" Emron said. She looked frightened, surprised, and happy, all at the same time.

"You almost killed me," she said putting her trembling hand on her chest.

"I'm sorry, I couldn't make myself visible outside. You have been followed by two men" said Emron.

"Oh, really?" she asked getting scared. "Who were they?" Emron shrugged his shoulders.

"Shall I go and see if they are still there?" Emron asked and before she replied went out. After some time he returned and told her who they were and that they had gone now.

Priva told Emron that the situation in Atrostia had worsened. More and more of their liberties had been taken away from them. They were deprived of their basic rights and everything was done in the name of the collective good. It was said that the state was doing everything that to protect them from certain individuals who had been exploiting those rights and liberties and were trying to harm their perfect society. It was promised again and again that the withdrawal of the rights was only a temporary measure; it was just a necessary precaution.

People suffered from economic, social and political problems, but they had no one to turn to.

"What happened to your resistance?" Emron asked. She said that not much of the once powerful struggle was left.

Most of the people had deserted them or were rotting in dungeons.

"What about the army?" he asked. She couldn't tell him much because she hadn't been seeing much of her friend Hetzog, her only contact with the army. The army and civilians were consciously separated from each other, so that people wouldn't learn what was going on. She had not seen a single iron covered soldier or iron horse, as he had described to her last time. From time to time they heard of some terrible, uncivilised, cruel enemy, which threatened their whole civilisation, but people mostly considered that propaganda.

Emron told her about how Dolec's army had been able to make a breakthrough and penetrated into his part of the world. "But how?" Priva asked in disbelief. Emron told her about the Subterraneans' world, the passages connecting different parts of the world, and how the soldiers of her country had been tormenting his world. Priva felt very sorry for Emron's part of the world, and cried, begging for forgiveness on the behalf of Atrostia.

"None of you are to be blamed, you are victims!" Emron comforted her.

"But you would be happy to know that we are not sitting idle, we are giving them such hard time that they are deeply frustrated."

He gave her the details on how he and his men were fighting back with the help of their allies, omitting the details as to who they were, and which worlds they belonged to. He could not elaborate on such details, not because he didn't trust her, but because if she were to fall in the hands of authorities, they would have taken it out of her, and such risks he couldn't afford.

Priva kept silent, happy to know that Emron and his friends were not surrendering to the evil force of Dolec, but it ached her heart to know that her countrymen were sacrificed in the evil attempt to take over the world. She could not help feeling sorry then, even for the young countrymen who were blindly following the mad prince.

"Why did you risk coming here?" she asked. "For a single reason," he told her. He wanted to tell the people of Atrostia the truth, so they could see their prince for what he really was. She wondered what good that was to bring.

"Maybe nothing but it would be nice to incite anguish in the man," answered Emron, with a chuckle.

Priva told him that he could have the opportunity soon. After a few days, there was going to be a national liberty day. On this one day of the year, people were allowed to express their feelings in an unchecked and unhindered manner. They could say whatever they wished without any consequences.

"And this holiday is still respected by the authorities?" asked Emron in surprise.

"Yes," answered Priva. "But who would dare to express this freedom?" she added sadly. They went on talking about the liberty day, when and why it was initiated, what used to be the topics they discussed, how many people typically gathered at the Kilta to listen to the speakers.

Priva said that a lot of many people used to visit that place, Kilta, even knowing that their days of freedom were now gone. They would still come, if not for the freedom then to celebrate its beautiful memory.

"That would be a perfect place for me to talk to them. I'll renew this tradition once more for them," said Emron with a great smile on his face.

Priva tried to persuade him to give up the idea of speaking before a large gathering; partially because the whole place that day would be heavily guarded. But there was another reason to worry, how he was to explain his coming to their country? People would turn against him, seeing in this a confirmation that the enemy really was capable of reaching their land and harm them.

Emron said that he was aware of the risk, but had no other choice than to appeal to the common sense of people. Priva was to collect as many of their remaining dissident friends as was possible.

She was more afraid for his safety than any possible trouble for those who were to attend and celebrate the freedom day. She promised to invite everyone she knew, but asked him to be careful. While speaking his mind to the people he would have to be vigilant and take precautions when he received warnings from his friends.

"Don't tell anyone, not even to your closest friends, that you know me or that I am staying at your place," he requested of her. She asked him not to worry, but to come straight home after delivering the speech. No one knew about his presence in Atrostia but Priva, and soon the whole country would know that a stranger from the primitive part of the world was visiting.

*   *   *

The city of Pooba, with its incredible beauty looked as wonderful and breathtaking as he remembered. Its tall pillars and marvellous stone buildings and beautiful clean paths, its allies and all other details were exactly as he had remembered them, and were not the mirages that came out from the womb of night. The magic of the city was as powerful as ever before.

He looked at the crowd around him, who hardly took notice of him. He had decided to remain visible. Either no one had time to pay attention to his appearance or perhaps the Subterraneans among them had made them used to of different kinds of people. He kept walking a few yards behind Priva, who was leading him to the gigantic park, where the celebrations of the liberty day were to take place. Looking at the huge crowd, he was confused. How was he to communicate with these people? His voice would not be able to reach even a tiny fraction of them. Had he misunderstood everything that Priva had told him? He thought that it was a question of a few dozens or perhaps at the most a hundred or so people, but there were at least dozens of thousand people. Most of the people walked silently, hardly looking at each other. There were a few who talked in low sad voices. They all looked burdened, gloomy, and defeated, without any hope for the day or the distant future.

Priva led him to a place where a little stage was made. Speakers would talk about different subjects and went away, leaving the stage for others. Emron was surprised to see that despite the fact that it was a huge and open-air place, the sound of the speakers could be heard loud and clear.

Most of the people were expressing their feelings about day-to-day life, their personal problems, their social and cultural strengths, their social weaknesses, their economic difficulties, and their other worries. Some came to praise the Queen and her administration, admiring her prudence and will to change the country for the better. But Emron noticed that no one had dared to open the mouth against the government, Queen, or Dolec. There was no voice challenging the prevailing injustice in the society, misuse of power, and the theft of rights and liberties.

No one protested against the administration's nonchalant approach towards unemployment and other social ills. The crowd was large, consisting of both young and old, women and men, but they just listened without any glitter on their faces, or any shine in the eyes. That was because the more fortunate ones of the Atrostian used not to waste their free day listening to the depressing tales of people, or watching their sad, defeated faces. They had better ways to celebrate their liberty day.

They met each other, arranged glamorous parties, took part in the lively festivals that took place all around Pooba and in its suburbs. Life for them was not a miserable dragging from day to day, rather it was no less than a dance on rose petals. They were the elite, the privileged ones, enjoying the power and pomp, walking through the corridors of influence and abundance. So the only face of Atrostia that Emron could see was right before his eyes.

He went to the stage and kept silent for a long time, drawing the attention of the crowd, who wondered why he kept standing there if he had nothing to say.

He had been waiting for the right moment. He started speaking, praising the great country Atrostia, its long glorious history, noble traditions, long cultural heritage, and its citizens with their hard work in creating marvels like the city of Pooba. He praised their advancement in the science and other achievements that made life more comfortable. He went on speaking about different things without uttering a single word that could indicate whether he spoke for or against the system. People were curious to see where he wanted to lead them. "Stop fawning at us and get to the point!" Shouted some youngster.

No one laughed except Emron, who gave a broad smile. He turned directly to the crowd and said; "Look at you, what has become of the inhabitants of the liveliest city on the face of earth? You are too scared, too tired even to smile at a joke!" He provoked them a little by saying that they were less alive than dead. He could see an angry response growing on their faces. He was pleased that he had been successful in invoking anger in their otherwise dead hearts. He smiled, telling them that he liked them better when they showed their feelings.

"Have you never asked yourselves, what has gone wrong with you and your lives and the wonderful country which we all love, our Atrostia?"

He could see the anger on the faces, turning into astonishment. Who was he? What was he about to say? Would he dare to speak of the unspeakable? Was he about to criticize the government, to be gone forever into some rat hole?

"No, he wouldn't dare," said one old man to his wife.

"I bet he would! Not everybody is coward like you," she whispered back. And he did. He criticized the government for all their ills.

Their economic problems were due to too much spending on the military. The deteriorating situation of the people demanded an immediate attention, but who was to give that attention? Not their Queen, who was nothing but a puppet on a string, not the administrators, who were too greedy and selfish and could not see beyond their noses. Most of all, this attention and care could not come from a power hungry, cruel and heartless Dolec, who wanted to enslave Atrostia.

He looked at the crowd, which was listening to him tearfully. A few of the listeners of his speech rushed towards him. Emron knew that they could be no other than the most feared spies of Dolec, his notorious personal guards.

"Look at these rats!" He pointed to the advancing guards. "They believe that they can do whatever they please. But they can't imprison the freedom to think! You have to stand up against their terror or else you will be eternal victims. Do you want me to show you how you should deal with them?" Emron asked the public without showing any signs of fear of the approaching guards.

They all had drawn some kind of weapon but Emron expected them not to use them before so many witnesses. He let them come near, and arrest him without any resistance. The policemen got hold of him, and looked with spite at the crowd, who stood in utter silence and sadness. The audience felt for the young man who had dared to speak what they were thinking. They watched the royal guardsmen drag Emron away when suddenly something incredible happened.

Emron twisted his arm and stood free. He raised his hands in the air and smiled and turned to seven or eight of his captors, who were trying to get hold of him once again, but one by one were sent to lick the earth by the strong punches of Emron, not to get back to their feet again.

"That's the way we defend our rights!," cried Emron.

People looked amazed, but were still too afraid to show that he had charmed them with his bravery. He thanked them for listening with patience and understanding. He promised to come back to them at the time and places, when offered to him by chance and circumstances, to tell them more about the truths that they had been kept away from. He waved his hand to the shocked crowd and quickly disappeared into the multitude of the park.

He was the centre of all talks in the city. Many people discussed about him secretly and some dared to speak openly. Most of the people who had not listened to him in the park believed it to be some fabulous story, a rumour to spread unrest among already oppressed people of Atrostia. How was it possible to speak against the Queen, her administration and, most of all Dolec, and leave the park unscathed? There were as many versions of the event as were the people who had witnessed that unbelievable happening.

He was not only the talk of the citizens, but the elite and those closer to Dolec discussed him with similar interest. The only person who was not aware of what went on was Dolec himself. Nobody was ready to inform him, knowing that it involved the risk of becoming a target for all of his fury, especially when the perpetrator had got out of their hands, and was still at large. The more they hid the news of some stranger challenging his authority, the more difficult it got to inform Dolec by each passing day.

Emron was growing more and more daring. Out of nowhere he would appear before small gatherings of people, spread the message that he gave in the park, and then he would disappear. The royal guards were trying to hunt him down, but he was too quick for them. They would receive the news about his whereabouts, and would get there quickly only to find that he had already gone. All of Dolec's spies were now placed in Pooba, and strolled on each street watching every activity, but they could not find Emron. New rules were announced prohibiting large gatherings so he could not slip into a crowd. But the more they got active to stop him, the greater grew his contact with the people.

*　　*　　*

Emron abandoned Pooba and worked in the smaller towns where the conditions of the people were even worse, and people lived on the edge. It was from here that Dolec was getting most of the soldiers for his army. These people were angry because all their young ones were taken away from them. They were receiving meagre salaries, sent their sons and brothers, which were not enough to meet their day-to-day needs.

Emron exploited this situation. He was informing people how their innocent children were sacrificed for Dolec's insane desire to conquer the world. People who listened to him were shocked, and at first refused to believe that it could be possibly true. "Ask them to let you meet your sons, and they'll confirm the truth for you," Emron challenged..

It was not for long before the whole of Atrostia knew the name of Emron, a stranger among them who had risked his life to tell them the truth. He boldly faced the people who accused him to be the spokesman of the enemy.

"If some enemy has conspired against your land, where is that enemy?" "If we were to attack your highly developed civilisation, would I venture here alone, risking my life?" he would argue.

His growing support among citizens of Atrostia forced the aides of Dolec to face the unpleasant task of informing him of Emron's arrival amongst them. He looked stunned when the news was broken to him. He couldn't believe that it could be true.

"How long has he been here?" he finally asked. They had expected the question, but were not ready for the answer and tried to sneak out, but looking at the outrageous face of Dolec they dared not.

"Since the liberty day," one aide stammered.

"Hmm," said Dolec in a low voice, before exploding. "And I am being told now, almost a month later!" His outburst was very natural and expected, and they were doing all that they could to convince him that they did that of good intentions; that they had worked hard to arrest him, that they didn't want to bother him, and many other excuses.

Dolec was not going to accept any of that. He could see

that his greatest enemy had not only been able to come into his own stronghold, but also had the nerves to form a conspiracy against him, encouraging a revolt while he had not been even informed.

He ordered the arrest of all of aides and ministers for high treason, which was exactly what they had feared most. In this furious state he called for the army chief, and asked if he knew about the presence of the enemy.

He told Dolec that he was not aware of any such happening, except that he was informed that a missing horse and armour were found in the opening of a tunnel. Saying this, army chief had solved the mystery regarding how Emron had entered their world. Dolec told the army chief that his civil administration had failed completely. He didn't trust their abilities to protect him from the enemy or from the angry revolt of the people if they were to rise against him. "Bring a large number of the army who shall track down this enemy of mine, and show the people that there is no point to even try to resist."

The army chief tried to persuade him that such drastic actions were not required, but Dolec was determined to catch Emron and demonstrate his tremendous might to his citizens. "Make sure that you deliver this perpetrator to me alive."

The Atrostian army searched every inch of their country, entering into the homes of people, searching thoroughly, blocking each and every street corner, harassing and arresting all the suspects. This tactic worked, making people afraid to go out. Their staying at home made the hunt easier, but there was still not a sign of him anywhere. The road leading to the Subterranean tunnel was watched day and night, so there wasn't any possibility left for him to escape. Dolec was ready to give anything to get hold of Emron. He was losing his patience. While this hectic search was going on in Atrostia, Emron sat among his council members informing them about all that he had accomplished. They were pleased to hear that he had been able to frustrate Dolec and was successful in hitting directly at his heart.

"I'm sure that the man will never recover from this blow," said Emron, and they all agreed.

"You've succeeded in hurting his ego," said Khafil with a smile. "His ego, which is nothing less than his driving force!"

"I have been more pessimistic I must confess, but I believe Emron's plan could work," said Forsa, looking embarrassed. They told Emron that all the preparations had been made by all three worlds. The Subterraneans had prepared the way, the Genii were ready with their misty smoke and other preparations and so were the Volcanii. Now all they hoped was that the human world through Emron would succeed in its task to draw Dolec and his army to the Subterranean passages. They all looked optimistic but tense. They still believed that their plan stood a fair chance of succeeding, but no one could guarantee its success, not even its mastermind.

*   *   *

Emron found not only the city of Pooba, but all of Atrostia in the grip of terror. All the roads were blocked and everyone passing through was thoroughly checked by soldiers, who were not ironclad but wore ordinary uniforms. Unlike their leader, they looked more at ease. They did not share the anxiety and fear of their prince.

The knowledge that all was about searching apparently one single unarmed individual could not excite them very much. They knew that somehow it was very vital to catch the dangerous person along with all his collaborators, but that was all. They were not very worried about the growing antagonism, they saw it only as an act of frustration, which was to die away after a realistic evaluation of their power. They were confident that no one would dare rise against their powerful army. This knowledge made them relax and perform their duties well, without becoming hysterical.

Emron roamed about without any concern. He observed the young soldiers, the frightened faces of the passers-by, and even noticed people who found the whole search an exciting thing. Who showed their curiosity by asking different questions from the soldiers? These were some inferior units of the army, who were not aware of anything. Most probably they were trained for some other purposes than to fight an enemy.

Emron was right. That force was prepared to crush the indigenous insurgency, if it was to ever rise against Dolec and his rule. These were the soldiers who had no interest in making a friendly approach to the general public. Emron walked through the streets, unnoticed and unhindered, and came to Priva's house.

She looked scared and nervous. Many of her friends had been arrested and she waited for her own turn and believed that it was just around the corner. The soldiers had already searched her house twice and could come even for the third time. He asked her not to worry, because they could not find him even they came a hundred times. He had clearly failed to grasp that Priva was worried about herself, as there could be horrible consequences if it was disclosed that she had anything to do with Emron. "Your invisibility would not have helped you, had he known that you have such a shield."

"Maybe not, but now he doesn't know. Good luck for me." Emron laughed. He asked her if Dolec was using ironclad soldiers in the massive search, and she said that they had not seen any of them yet.

Emron told her that the final hour had arrived. They were about to make a last encounter with Dolec and his forces. He couldn't tell her if they were to prevail or die fighting that evil force, but promised to fight like a man of honour and dignity.

"If we succeed, not only shall the other worlds be saved from the tyranny of Dolec, but your country too will get rid of the evil prince. But if we fail, then we can expect Dolec's victory to usher in a Dark Age," said Emron in a sombre tone.

She was one of the few Atrostians that he could confide

in. She didn't understand how he could possibly engage Dolec and his mighty army in a decisive battle so far away from his own world, without any powerful weapons, without any army, and expect a complete success? Only one thing made her calm, and that was his shield of invisibility, a defence that Dolec with all his might couldn't break at the moment, simply because of one reason alone, he was not aware of it.

*　*　*

After dinner when Priva prepared his bed, he smilingly told her that he had no intention to sleep as he was about to be out and wouldn't be coming back until later that night. What he could possibly accomplish that late, he didn't answer. Priva was worried but didn't bother him with her questions; she had learned to trust Emron's judgement.

The night was dark and all the street of Pooba deserted, even the artificial lights were dimmed. The only people still on duty were the soldiers who watched the streets and buildings of the city. Even the soldiers on duty sat and dozed, not seeing any movement on the streets.

Emron calmly passed all of the checkpoints and came to the royal palace, which was heavily guarded by ironclad soldiers. They kept the watch on all entrances, making it impossible for him to enter the palace. He waited with patience and finally got his chance when a high ranking army officer distracted some of the guards with a useless errand, giving him the opportunity to slip in. Silently he walked through the corridors and took the stairs to second storey. It was not difficult to guess where he could find Dolec. There were at least two dozen soldiers guarding the door. He passed them by and came to another small corridor, which was guarded by a few guards who were sitting and talking to each other.

*　*　*

Emron silently crossed the corridor and came to the open window, guarded by a single guard who was sleeping on his watch. A strong blow sent him into unconsciousness. Emron looked inside and smiled. A man lay on the bed sleeping. He entered through the window, became visible, and awoke the sleeping person by holding a hand on his mouth and a large dagger on his throat. It was Dolec. The fright in his eyes was indescribable.

"A tiny sound from your mouth and I will send you to hell!" Emron warned Dolec in a whisper. Dolec signalled that he had gotten the message.

"Who are you?" Dolec asked with a trembling voice.

"I'm your death, EMRON."

"Please don't kill me," said Dolec still feeling the pressure of Emron's sharp dagger. "It's up to you. If you don't want to die, then do as I ask you to." Emron said in a cold voice. "I'm not a coward like you, so I will give you a chance to fight. I'll be leaving for my world tomorrow; you gather all your army and can try to stop me if you can. Beyond the tunnel on the other side you'll find me and my friends waiting to give you the gift of complete defeat and utter destruction. See you, little devil, if you dare," said Emron; in a whisper and knocked the man unconscious with the hilt of his dagger. Emron safely retreated from the palace the same way that he came in. The guards were busy talking to each other, unaware of what had happened to their king.

When Dolec regained consciousness, he was terrified, hardly even able to utter a sound, but slowly he came into his senses. Outrage replaced his fear. He had completely gone mad. He took his iron soldiers and left to the army headquarters, waking up all of the commanders and ordered them to get ready to march.

They tried to explain that it was neither wise nor recommendable to attack in such a hurry. They needed preparations, and time to plan. But Dolec wouldn't listen to anything. How many horsemen they had at their disposal, he asked and was told that they could count on about forty thousand.

"And still we need more preparations," he screamed. The soldiers and their officers were awakened, and were asked to prepare in a hurry. They were to attack and destroy the whole damn world, but first of all they had to capture a single rider, who had dared to challenge his authority and force. They tried to reason with him that such a big force was not needed to arrest one single individual, but Dolec would feel safer if all of his soldiers were with him. So he insisted that each and every one was to follow their great leader on a manhunt and later to conquer the world. Looking at the instant preparation Emron signalled Khafil, who came with Rino. He wished Emron good luck, and left to inform others that the final moment was at hand.

*   *   *

Dolec's army moved towards the subterranean passages. He was sitting on an iron horse, all ironclad, leading his incredible force of great numbers. He sat erect with an arrogant smile on his lips. Each time he turned to look at his army, his ego swelled with pride, and he could hear his heart beating like a drum. He was about to capture and destroy Emron and then write his name in history as a first emperor of the world, his first step to the ultimate goal of conquering all of the worlds.

They seemed not to haste, only moving with measured pace. He wanted to enjoy the moment, very much confident that they would catch up with Emron within no time. When they all had entered the passage, Dolec could see someone moving very far ahead of them. He was sure that it was Emron. A very dark, cruel smile spread on his lips and he accelerated the speed of his horse. The others followed, and soon the whole army was moving with a speed of a storm. Dolec's head was just filled with a single thing: Emron.

Strangely enough he was not coming nearer to his object.

Despite his full speed, the distance between him and Emron was hardly any different than at the beginning when he had first gotten sight of him. Dolec felt so obsessed by his desperate wish to get hold of Emron that he took no heed of the request of his commanders, who saw no reason to rush in that fashion. They felt the change of the air, which had grown a little cloudy and smoky, but they kept pressing ahead, refusing to stop. Those in the lead pressed on because they had to follow their revered prince. Those in the middle wanted to know what the mist was, but could not stop for the fear of being trampled by those who were behind them, coming at full speed. The Subterraneans were worried but the stress of the movement was so great that they also stopped caring and moved fearlessly like their companions. Khafil was right in his conclusion that the smell of different essences and the mist of deception had taken hold of the senses of Subterranean warriors. It didn't take long before the mist engulfed them completely.

Those cunning warriors were disoriented and confused but calm. Dolec could see through the curtain of thin mist that Emron was struggling on his horse to keep the lead, but he was losing ground. Slowly but steadily Dolec was closing the distance. Soon he would kill his greatest enemy. He kept the pace in order not to lose sight of him. The mist was getting thicker and thicker, but Dolec did not stop or diminish his speed. He could still see Emron and his horse at a distance, and as long as he did so he was hopeful. Suddenly he felt that Emron was trying desperately to make a last attempt to brush him off.

"No way, you dead man!" Dolec growled to himself. The distance between him and Emron was again increasing, inch by inch. He looked back and was pleased to see that his army was following their prince with the same dedication and loyalty as he had expected.

All of a sudden he lost Emron; there was no sign of him any more. But then it could be the fog that was obstructing his sight. He kept his chase up and carried on, without knowing that they had been fooled by the combined efforts of all the four worlds. They were unaware that they had left the Subterranean world far behind and had just crossed the gigantic hole made by Volcanii and subterranean in the plates on which everything stood. They were not aware that from that pit it was impossible to escape, even for his Subterranean friends, who would be the first ones to realise that they had been tricked into underground hells, when the toxic effects of the Genii prepared smoke of deception was to give way.

*   *   *

Emron watched the last iron horsemen crossing the great hole, and then signaled for the Volcanii and Subterraneans to fill the opening with molten metals, which hardened very quickly, sealing Dolec and his dreaded mighty warriors deep beneath the earth. The enemies must have realised their gigantic mistake before the work of the Volcanii and Subterraneans were done. There were triumphant cries and uncontrolled scenes of joy. The sighs of relief could be heard and sounds of greeting were pronounced, the new allies embracing, dancing, and singing in unison. They all had succeeded in achieving an impossible task and saved many worlds from slavery.

A victory siren was sounded in all of the worlds, pronouncing that the danger had been dealt with, if not permanently then at least for a long time to come. All the worlds paid tribute to the great services of Emron, who remained humble, giving equal credit to them all. The Atrostians dethroned their incompetent Queen and set up a council of citizens who was to rule and solve the country's problems. They offered Emron help and knowledge to make his part of the world modern and scientific, but he graciously refused. He was happy with his own primitive world, and didn't want to exchange it for anything else. He went to visit Khafil and returned his freedom of movement. He didn't need it any more.

"Just give Rino back to me and I'll be happy," he joked.

"Keep the freedom, you've earned it for life!" Khafil tried to persuade him.

"I can come to you if I need any quick transportation," Emron said smilingly.

"You know you're always welcome in the three worlds," assured Khafil.

Emron gave the white magic stone to King Kimertong and said; "Now you can at last get back your lost stone. It is your legacy, your treasure. Take good care of it and don't lose it next time." Kimertong thanked Emron for his generosity and tried to give him other precious stones, but he refused and promised that he would not hesitate to ask if he needed them in the future.

"We're ready to offer you all the riches we have." Kimertong was emotional, a rare happening in the volcanic world. After visiting all of his allies in the three worlds he visited his friends in the human world, who greeted him with love, respect, and warmth.

The great news of complete victory made them joyous and they expressed this joy through dance, songs, and laughter. These festivities went on for days and refused to come to an end, but he was forced to take his leave.

He wanted to return to his family who had been so understanding, helpful, and supportive in his otherwise unattainable mission. The reception, admiration, and appreciation for his great deed back home was far more rewarding and uplifting than he could ever receive from any other quarters. He was the unfaltering hero of both Salisa and Amroush, who would never grow tired of his narration of the thrilling events, and begged him to tell again and again the story of his strife.

Emron had all that he ever desired, a loving family, a peaceful home, and a calm, happy life. He never took anything for granted and appreciated all the good that came his way, remembering that how close they had been in losing the things that he held dear. He and Salisa lived happily ever after.

THE END

Epilogue

"We are told that he had had other labours, and other impossible tasks to perform but we don't know the details about them. If we find some new material, which may enable us to narrate some of his other labours, we promise not to withhold it!

Not much is known about the demise of Dolec and his army. There are legends that tell of their frustration after finding out that they had been tricked into the bottomless pit. They were outraged and swore never to give up their struggle to come out of there and seek revenge. The Subterraneans among them told their companions that it was impossible to escape. However, if they could find the places where these plates were cemented together, they could try to escape by breaking the connecting material and then push the plate upward, making enough space for them to escape. We've learned that their struggle goes on still today.

Whenever the world shakes, and a tremor is felt, it is believed that those warriors are trying to escape from their bottomless pit. The worlds' shake and tremble by the mere prospect of the nearing of these warriors. We don't know if it is true or false, but it's widely believed that very strong earthquakes are the indication that a certain amount of these warriors have succeeded in making an escape.

After coming back to their human world they would join some new armies and continue seeking the dream of the world dominance and conquest. That explains the unending upheavals and turbulence in the world by certain power-hungry individuals and the nations seduced by them."

.

i